RITUAL OF BLOOD

Leeanah reached for the cup, dumping the waxen dolls onto the surface of the altar. Synn continued his downward curve, the dagger slicing through the air until it hovered over the images' heads. After a second of hesitation, he plunged the point into one.

Raising his arms, he repeated the gesture with the second wax head. Moving them until they were side by side, Synn placed the sharp edge of the blade over the necks of the dolls and cried out, *"Now!"*

The heads, sliced cleanly from the bodies, rolled a few inches away. Not a sound could be heard in the room. Riley saw each person's attention riveted on the decapitated waxen figures.

A trickle of blood dribbled from the stump of each neck....

Also by John Tigges:

UNTO THE ALTAR
KISS NOT THE CHILD
GARDEN OF THE INCUBUS
EVIL DREAMS
THE LEGEND OF JEAN MARIE CARDINAL

THE IMMORTAL

JOHN TIGGES

LEISURE BOOKS   **NEW YORK CITY**

For Tim, who is *not* Tine.

A LEISURE BOOK

Published by

Dorchester Publishing Co., Inc.
6 East 39th Street
New York, NY 10016

Copyright © 1986 by John Tigges

All rights reserved. No part of this book may be reproduced or transmitted in any form or by any electronic or mechanical means, including photocopying, recording, or by any information storage and retrieval system, without the written permission of the Publisher, except where permitted by law.

Printed in the United States of America

THE IMMORTAL

PROLOGUE

Scheveningen, Holland, 1760

The hollow rattle of hoofbeats echoing through the night accentuated the dismal quietude hanging over the small town outside 'S Gravenhage, which lay to the south and east. Two men, their mounts walking, looked from side to side as if waiting for someone or something to leap upon them from the inky shadows all around. In the distance, as if drawing them like a magnet, a dim light from the window of an inn beckoned. Perhaps there they would find their quarry who had slipped away from them four days earlier.

Claude Paget glanced at his fellow rider, head motioning toward the speck of light and said, "I hope that is it, Paul. I am tired and if he is not there, I suggest we take rooms and rest for the night."

Paul Tibot nodded. "Oui. My back is paining me. Eighteen and twenty hours a day in the saddle is madness. Not even for the Duc will I sacrifice my health. Besides, he will never know we stopped to rest for an entire night. Not unless you tell him, Claude."

"There is little if any likelihood of that happening. We will search this place for the Comte. If he is not here, we sleep. Agreed?"

"Agreed."

Both men spurred their tired animals forward and the slow, steady clopping of hooves incresed in tempo to a quick tattoo. At the inn, reining their horses to a halt, they dismounted before hitching them to the rail in front. Striding up the steps despite their fatigue, they pounded on the door hoping to rouse someone from a sound sleep, to have their questions answered and perhaps to sleep themselves for the rest of the night.

After waiting several minutes, they slammed their fists against the unyielding wood again but stopped when the door swung partway open.

"Yes?" a soft voice asked.

"We are emissaries of the Duc de Choiseul, Foreign Minister to the King of France," Claude said, removing his tricorn. "We must speak to the master of this inn."

The door swung wide, permitting the pair to enter. Hats in hand, they passed the woman who held a candle high to better light the way, noticing her red eyes, her disheveled blonde hair.

"My—my husband is already retired for the night. Perhaps I can help," she offered, her voice cracking as if she had been weeping.

"Madame?" Claude said, peering at her. He found her attractive, young and certainly not what he had expected. "Are you all right? You sound—"

"I am fine, Mein Heer. What is it you must know? If you want rooms, we have accomodations." She looked away from his penetrating stare.

"We are searching for a man," he said, changing subjects. "A Comte de Saint-Germain. We have followed him for the last week but lost track of him four days ago. We have reason to believe he might have been headed in this direction. Since that time we have been stopping at every inn, even going off the roadway that leads to 'S Gravenhage, his ultimate destination. Have you given him a room for the night?"

She shook her head, tears forming in her eyes. "We—we have but—but one guest this night. A count but not the one you seek. His name is Rakoczi and he is—"

Paul placed a hand on Claude's arm. "It is he!" he hissed. "It is a name he uses from time to time."

"Oui! Show us his room. Is he in now? It is certainly late enough that he should be retired for the night." Claude leaned expectantly toward her.

"He has been here for three days. And I—" She could no longer contain herself, erupting into tears, sobs racking her body.

The men looked at each other, puzzled by the young woman's strange behavior.

"Madame? What is it?" Claude stepped forward, lifting her tear streaked face upward. Her finely molded features, marred, but in a strange way also enhanced by the tears, held him for several minutes.

She opened her eyes, staring up at him in a defiant way despite sobbing between breaths.

"It is nothing. It is of no concern to you. Please allow me to show you to the Count's room." The last words barely escaped her lips when the crying began anew.

"We go nowhere until you tell us what is paining you so that you weep unabashedly in front of strangers. Speak." Claude looked to his friend who stepped nearer to hear the explanation, thoughts of apprehending the Comte de Saint-Germain relegated to the back of their minds for the time being.

She dabbed at her eyes. "You will think me foolish."

"Nothing could be further from the truth. Tell us, ah—what is your name?"

"Katerina. Katerina Van Meer. My husband—my husband and I—I own this inn. I fear—I'm afraid that—my husband has found another woman."

Claude smiled covertly and caught the same expression on his companion's face. "Is that so bad, Madame? After all, a man must think of himself whenever opportunities present themselves."

"You are of—no help," she snapped, sobbing at the same time. "He neglects me. Terribly. We haven't slept together for the last three days or nights. He is too exhausted, he says. Hah!" Her voice grew stronger as her anger rose to the surface, pushing aside her injured feelings.

Claude held his arms open and she stepped forward, just as quickly pulling away before he could encompass her in his embrace.

"Mein Heeren. Please. Follow me. We forget why you are here. This way."

Claude shrugged in a futile gesture to Paul and both smiled broadly. It was their French instinct which prompted them to pursue a wronged woman to the indulgence both felt they needed but were too tired to think about. Following the lithesome young woman up the steps to the second floor, they watched her hips swing back and forth in a natural, seductive dance. Before either could form a mental image of Katerina without clothing, she stopped before a door and stepped aside, not knowing what to do next. She gestured toward it and opened her mouth to speak. Before a word could escape, Paul clamped a hand over her full lips. Claude held a finger to his own mouth, cautioning her to be quiet.

She nodded her understanding and was released.

Claude placed an ear to the door, trying to determine if the man they sought might still be awake. When he could hear nothing, he motioned for Paul to listen. Both shrugged and Paul reached for the latch, forcing it down in a slow, deliberate motion to keep it from making a noise. Nothing happened. It was locked, secured from within.

"We have no choice," Paul said softly both to his partner and to the woman. "We must break it in. Now."

Claude nodded, clamping his tricorne on his head. Katerina looked aghast. Before she could say anything both men threw their shoulders against the door, breaking into the darkened room to the sound of splintering wood as the lock tore from its mooring.

"A light. Bring a light," Paul shouted.

Katerina handed the candle to Claude who stepped inside. The bed was empty. Their quarry had somehow escaped or had not been in the room as the woman thought.

"Mon Dieu! He is gone," Paul gasped.

"I can see that," Claude snarled. Their search, their work was still unfinished. Saint-Germain had managed to elude them once more. Moving to a small table, Claude lit several candles before handing the smaller one back to the hostess of the inn.

"What—what is this?" Paul asked, pointing to two bottles of clear liquid standing behind the candles.

Claude stepped closer, examining them.

Finally shaking his head, he turned to find the other man holding a sword belt. He leapt to the tall wardrobe, throwing open the doors. It too was empty.

"Did he have luggage with him?" he snapped.

Frightened by their attitude now that they had forgotten about her problems, she merely shrugged but said nothing, unable to remember if the Count Rakoczi had brought anything with him to the room.

"What do you suppose is in the bottles?" Paul asked.

"Who knows? But you can rest assured it is something evil. Something of the devil himself."

Katerina stepped foward. "Of—of the devil?"

Claude nodded brusquely.

"In my inn? The devil? Here?"

"Not the devil, Madame, but one who is surely in league with him. The Comte de Saint-Germain claims many things. Things that no one else would even think of much less attempt."

"Such as?" she asked, a curiosity holding her fine features, her own problems forgotten.

"He is an alchemist and claims he can produce gold from lead. And make fine gems from ordinary pebbles and rocks. Why, there is even a rumor in Paris these days that he is supposed to be over two thousand years old.

That he knew the Queen of Sheba and Solomon himself."

"Tell her what he said when asked about Jesus Christ, Claude." Paul snickered under his breath, a smirk wrinkling his tired face.

"When asked if he knew Christ, he had the temerity to say that he was a family friend and always knew the youngster would come to no good."

"Blasphemous!" Katerina said softly, crossing herself.

"What should we do with the bottles, Claude?"

"Best we take them with us. We wouldn't want to upset Madame Van Meer any more than she already is." He smiled, reaching out to pet her on the cheek. "Perhaps your husband is merely ill, my dear. I wouldn't worry. With someone as beautuful as you around, I cannot see a man seeking out another."

She smiled demurely, dropping her gaze from his as she blushed.

"Is your husband here now?"

She nodded. "He is asleep."

"I think it might be best if you called him. We should speak to him yet tonight before we retire. I have a few questions to ask of him."

"I will fetch him," she said, leaving the room.

"Look," Paul cried excitedly. "Look at this." He pointed to the only window in the room.

The Immortal

"What?" Claude asked.

"*It* is locked. *The door* was locked. See, the key is still in the latch on this side. How could he have gotten out?"

Claude's face drained of color. "Perhaps he is in—" His eyes focused on the two bottles.

"That is impossible. Who would have put the stoppers in? See they are both closed."

A scream pierced the quiet before either man could offer any more speculative ideas about the disappearance of the Comte de Saint-Germain. Startled into action, they hurried to the hall, seeing an open lighted doorway. Running toward it, they burst in, not knowing what to expect.

Katerina stood next to the bed, pointing to her husband who appeared to be asleep.

The two Frenchmen stared wide-eyed at what had been one arm of the man. A pile of dust at the end of the nightshirt sleeve was all either could see. Claude stepped forward, Paul crowding in from behind to look over his shoulder.

"What is it? What is wrong, Madame?"

She tried to speak, her jaw waggling up and down, but no sound issued from her. Instead, she shook her husband's body, which began disintegrating into dust.

Both men stared at the unbelievable sight, then at each other, horror and revulsion tearing at their hearts.

PART ONE

THE BENEFACTOR

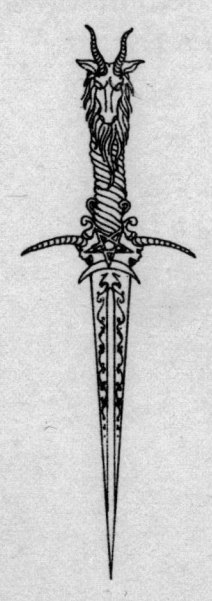

*Be not emulous of evildoers;
nor envy them that work iniquity.
Psalm 36: V.1*

CHAPTER 1

Friday, October 31, 11:45 P.M.

Clouds appearing to be heavy with rain blotted out the light of stars and the cold moon from the late October sky. An errant breeze vainly tried to blow along Lily Cache Lane but gave up, waiting for a better moment to stir the dried grass in preparation for an unexpected chilled soaking. Whatever night birds had been flying about, gathering insects to satisfy their hunger, had long since sought refuge amid the evergreen trees lining one side of the narrow road. Along with the wind's occasional whisper, only one other sound violated the late night's quietude: the scraping of footsteps along the graveled road.

Riley Larson carried his six-foot frame in an erect, forthright way, energetically striding along the verge of the lane, breathing deeply, enjoying his usual walk with his dog, Grendel. He anticipated a good night's sleep following this last purposeful expenditure of energy. His habit was to go to the turn in the road almost three quarters of a mile ahead and then retrace his steps home.

Fingering the silver dog whistle hanging from around his neck, he watched his black Labrador retriever rove into the ditches that paralled each side of the lane, seeking out and identifying the different animals' spoors intersecting his own. The strongest would be followed for a while and then, the trail exhausted or tiresome, the huge dog would check back with his master, staying near him for several minutes until another olfactory message beckoned to be investigated.

In a way, Riley lived for the moment, yet now anticipated the next day when he would put the finishing touches on his article concerning the new school structure, which would increase everyone's taxes by a considerable amount. The irony of his steady, part-time job as a sometimes janitor, sometimes handyman at the Hawthorne High School, while turning out an article for the Hawthorne Village News, was a source of amusement to him. Most of the time, whenever the editor called he wanted Riley to write something about politicians or taxes or elections in general. Although Riley made no secret of his affiliation with the school, he thought it hiliarious that a janitor was analyzing the local politicians' intents and purposes where the community's tax dollars were concerned. He had no quarrel with his own position in life. In face, he rather enjoyed it, since it gave him the freedom he needed to cope with the world in which he found himself. There were times when he even wondered if there might not be a kind of conflict of interest in writing about increased taxes for the school while being an employee of that very system. Until someone actually complained, however, he'd merely take the money and run.

He needed every cent he could lay his hands on to satisfy the court order resulting from his divorce. Vicki, his former wife, wanted to be treated fairly, but knew Riley didn't have much to begin with. She realized that a huge monthly assessment would be ridiculous considering his income, which was sporadic at best over and above the amount for essentials. Since there were no children involved, Riley had approved the idea of paying her living expenses while she finished her college education. At the time, he had said it seemed to be the only fair way out for everyone. After all, she had supported him all the while he was earning his degree at the University of Michigan.

Vicki's main gripe was that he had done nothing with his education. Granted, he wrote, but preferred the uncertain income offered by freelancing as opposed to a regular job. The cottage and small acreage that lay between Lily Cache Creek and Lily Cache Lane, which he had inherited from his uncle, Griggs Larson, seemed to remove any ambition he might have had. All he had to do was earn enough to buy necessaries and pay the taxes on the property, beyond which he didn't worry about competing with the other "rats" in the race. When he thought of the fact that in less than two years he would be free of having to earn that extra nine hundred dollars each month to give Vicki, he could begin to relax. Then he'd plan his novel and begin writing. But for now he had to maintain some semblance of an orderly, productive life.

Grendel charged up to his side, leaping to give him a sloppy kiss before turning and bolting away at right angles to the road. The animal passed through the barbed wire fence bordering the ditch and raced up a gentle incline toward the dark horizon.

Riley turned, watching him disappear into the gloom, wondering what had attracted him. Then he saw. A glow—a dim glow flickered unsteadily on the horizon, barely lighting the rim of the hill.

"What the hell is that?" he asked aloud, stopping. It seemed to be a fire of some sort. But from what? Or where? As far as he knew there were no houses along this side of the road and very few on the other. In fact, his was the last one before reaching the Golden Country Club property that bordered most everything farther down the road. Where could a fire be coming from?

Then he realized that Grendel was nowhere to be seen. Placing the whistle in his mouth, he blew, the passage of air the only sound noticeable. Grendel, as black as the night, materialized from the dark and faced his master seventy-five feet away. Huge tongue lolling from one side of his grinning mouth, the dog's stance and appearance seemed to invite Riley into the field to play.

Without a word, he crossed the ditch and clambered through the barbed wire fence. The dog ran to meet him and he half-heartedly swung an affectionate blow at the animal's head. Grendel took off again but Riley continued walking toward the horizon and the dim light. Something *was* probably on fire and he had better damn well check it out. Even though clouds hung overhead he knew rain was not in the forecast. The grass was tinder dry and one thing he couldn't afford was a brush fire sweeping through the countryside, devouring his meager property. Insurance covering the house was a luxury he'd have to wait to enjoy until Vicki got her sheepskin.

When he neared the top of the hill he stopped, a cold chill running down his back. Voices? Voices out here in the middle of a pasture around a bonfire of some sort? Maybe there was a house or something over the hill that he didn't know about. But he had driven along Lily Cache Road, toward which he walked, as well as the lane behind him many times, and each was in view of the other for most of the distance. If there was a house or barn or something, he surely would have seen it from one vantage point or the other.

Slowing more by instinct than anything else, Riley stopped before dropping to his hands and knees. If there were someone close by, he didn't want to be taken for an eavesdropper, though he knew that was exactly what he was at this point. He'd check out the situation and then decide if his presence should be made known or concealed. If the former, he'd choose at the time how to introduce himself.

Inching forward, he smelled wood burning, definitely a fire. But the voices he heard weren't excited, not as though a dwelling were alight or someone's belongings and property were going up in smoke. Instead, he thought he heard a distinct rhythm to the sound—like singing—no, more like chanting. *Chanting?* Definitely. And what the hell would that mean?

Intuitively dropping to his stomach when he reached the top, where any more height would have given his location away, he wriggled forward.

He could see the fire and what appeared to be ten or twelve people moving around the blaze. Then his eyes widened even more when he realized the scene he was looking at was contained within the ruins of an old building. Why had he never seen it before now? Peering beyond, he could see that the building was located in a tiny valley, which was probably why he'd never noticed it from either the road or the lane.

Refocusing his eyes, he could make out people who seemed to be dancing about the blaze dressed in long, black, hooded robes. Then they stopped and moved to either side. For the first time Riley saw the figure of a man who appeared to be tied hand and foot, lying on a slab of rock. One of the dancers stepped forward, throwing back the robe that covered her. Large, bare breasts jiggled alluringly as she moved closer to the bound man.

Riley stared wide-eyed. What the hell was this? Then he thought of the fact that it was Hallowe'en and dropped his head, laughing. Someone was having a party—a weird party—but a party, nevertheless. Lifting his head to continue watching, he saw the woman standing next to and over the man on the altar. Something glinted in the light and Riley found himself narrowing his eyes, trying to determine what the woman grasped in her hands. She stood posed for what seemed an eternity before the flames were reflected from a shiny surface and for an instant he could see the long, thin-bladed knife she held. The chanting stopped and a timid wind wiped the top of the hill, whining about Riley. No other sound. Nothing.

Then, he heard something from behind him. Footsteps. Running footsteps. Pressing himself to the ground, he hoped that whoever it was would not see him and pass into the valley to join the partygoers. The steps stopped. He held his breath.

Riley almost cursed when Grendel licked him on the ear and barked. The animal wanted to play. After another bark, he looked into the valley, seeing the firelight dancing in the dark, and whined. Not an ordinary whine but one that made Riley's skin crawl. Grendel had never before made such a sound.

Riley shushed the dog. Christ! How could he have forgotten about him? Grendel lay down next to his master, his tail wagging, thumping against the ground, panting hard enough, Riley thought, to call attention to their location from just about anyplace on earth. He tried flattening out even more when he realized the chanting had stopped and a single voice cried out.

"Who's there?"

Riley figured that where he was lying had to be out of the aura of the fire and that he couldn't be seen by those within it. Lifting his head, he again trained his eyes on the scene below. The woman still stood poised above the supine form of the man, who had raised himself to one elbow. It was obviously

The Immortal

he who had called out.

"Who's there? Come forward!" he ordered.

"There's no one there," the woman said, lowering her arms. "It's probably an animal or something."

The voices carried clearly to where Riley lay hidden. Then he heard the man say, "Get on with it. We'll have to hurry and get out of here."

Riley strained his eyes. Get on with what? He watched intently as the woman raised her arms again. The other people merely stood there. In fact, now that he thought about it, none of them had even turned around when the man called out.

He could hear the woman mumble something before she made a slashing stab at the man lying on the altar-like rock. The others began milling about and Riley could not see any more of the man as the circle of people closed in about him.

Riley dropped his head to the earth. What had he just witnessed? A murder? His stomach heaved, jerking spasmodically. "Good God!" he breathed. Murder was what it appeared to be from where he saw it. Why didn't the other people react in a way that would be more normal? What *was* normal? Certainly dressing up in hooded robes, dancing around a fire in the ruins of an old building on Hallowe'en could hardly be construed as commonplace. What the hell *was* going on? Maybe it was a ritual or an initiation of some kind. That had to be it. The last thing in the world he wanted or needed was to be present at a homicide.

He had to get out of there. Even if it were a strange ritual of some sort, how would those people take to having someone spy on them? Inching his way backward, he moved away from the crest of the low hill until he felt it was safe enough to stand. When he did, he motioned for Grendel to heel as the animal started nervously dancing about in circles. The dog had definitely been uneasy at the scent of something from the little valley. What could the plaintive whine have meant which came from that deep chest?

The dog followed submissively until they reached the gutter, then ran ahead of the road waiting for Riley to climb through the fence and renegotiate the ditch. When his master stood on the road, Grendel fell obediently in behind and followed him toward "Worthless Acres."

Now, if anyone asked Riley, he had been on the road all the time. Never left it once. Hadn't seen a thing out of the ordinary. Nothing.

Then his curiosity bounded back. What did he see? What was going on back there? Had a man actually been murdered? Not likely. If that were the case, the fellow was certainly eager to have it over with so *"they could get out of there."* Hadn't he said something like that? More questions formed as

The Immortal

Riley walked, fueling his inquisitiveness. The one thing he decided before the lights of his home came into view was to go back the next day and investigate. Besides, he was curious about the building, something he hadn't even known existed in his six-plus years of living on Lily Cache Lane. More than likely the whole thing had a reasonable explanation, but he had to know—to satisfy himself. He didn't care what act he had seen, as long as he understood. Aware, he could decide on a plan of action, if one were needed. Still, that would only be necessary if he felt his own security were threatened. Which was silly. Why should his safety be jeopardized?

No one had seen him at the top of the hill. No one knew he'd been near there. And still his inherent nosiness, his reportorial instincts were fighting with his common sense. If indeed a murder had been committed, it was up to him as a journalist, as a citizen, to convey the fact to the authorities.

A laugh formed somewhere deep inside his chest, erupting through his larnyx. *Journalist?* Did he actually think of himself as a journalist? For the Hawthorne Village News? Why not uncover this sordid mess and gain some notoriety—waltz right into the Chicago Tribune or the Sun-Times and demand a huge salary and private office? That would be the last thing in the world he'd want. Regularity in his hours. A symmetry to his life. The respectability of an ordinary job. That was why Vicki had left. She needed the security rendered by a steady job and a regular paycheck. He felt he could neither sell his soul, if he had one, nor his integrity, which he thought he had, and certainly not his ability to communicate by means of the written word to anyone on demand. Riley Larson was not for sale.

But a man had been killed. Riley saw it happen. At least he thought he'd watched a woman with jug-like breasts ram a long knife into a guy someplace between the groin and the neck. He was almost certain.

Vicki bobbed into his mind again. She would be the pragmatic one in a situation like this. She'd simply say it probably was something else and not what he thought he'd seen. Then, she'd merely forget it.

Riley couldn't do that. Not in a million years. Nor could Melanie.

Melanie. Melanie Brandt formed in his mind as he walked. She was night to Vicki's daytime practicality. Where Vicki was petite, almost fragile in appearance, Melanie had a statuesque figure that demanded attention. Whenever she entered a room, her presence commanded respectful admiration. Some air, some manner in which she moved, warned predatory males to stay at a distance. Not that she wasn't sensual or interested in the more earthy things. Riley knew that for a fact. But her overall situation told strangers to keep their distance until she gave them permission to approach. Perhaps it was her hair, red, coarse, worn in a slipshod manner—which reminded Riley at times of a lion's mane—that kept some of if not most people at bay. It might be her eyes — emerald green, seldom blinking, fixing on the person to whom she spoke—that held more confident men or women in an invisible bond until she released them. And whenever she spoke, her statements were usually peppered with a dash of expletives, which was totally out of touch with the real woman.

Although their relationship had been purely physical at first, Riley soon discovered the true person hiding within that fabulous body, beneath the wild hair and behind the strong eyes. They met at a writers' conference and it had been his ability with the written word that attracted her to him. At first, he was flattered by her attention at the meeting and almost disbelieved his ears when she called, asking him to have coffee. Within a month she moved in with him, and Riley learned that the magnetic animalism she exuded was not phony, nor were her interests in writing, sculpting and painting, although the first two had suffered somewhat because of her concentration on painting at the time.

Then suddenly something happened. Not between them as friends, but as lovers who thought they were on the right track. They decided, quite mutually, that their individual personalities needed freedom. Freedom that marriage, or an arrangement such as the one toward which they were heading, would almost surely suffocate. They agreed to have sex, to live together, to go their own ways whenever they wanted, to share expenses and to respect each other's choice of friends —whether they be temporary or permanent. And they agreed to love one another as friends and confidants. For most people it would not have been a tenable situation, but for Riley and Melanie it worked perfectly.

Overhead, the clouds continued moving in an easterly direction, toward Chicago, but the air smelled dry, reaffirming the weather forecast that there would be no rain until the next day. In the distance he could see light beaming from his living room window into the black night, acting not unlike a beacon on which the wayward wanderer set his sights. Grendel sensed they were nearing the house and yelped excitedly before dashing into the ditch on the left side of the road, then into the field that bordered Riley's three acres.

Riley felt his cheeks tighten as a smile crossed his lips. Vicki had called the small plot of ground and the two-bedroom bungalow "worthless" when she saw it for the first time, just before they moved in. It had been then that Riley assumed his, according to Vicki, aimless life style—not worrying about rent payments because he didn't have any, and managing to earn just enough to pay taxes, utilities, and buy food. His old Toyota, rusty and looking like a reprobate from a junkyard, ran well enough to get him around, and he could think of no reason to bust his balls to buy a more presentable car and be saddled with unnecessary payments.

The last straw to break the back of his marriage to Vicki was the sign he fashioned for the front fence that paralled the road. "Worthless Acres" painted in bright yellow letters against an equally bright red background launched an argument that was never resolved and their next meeting had been before the judge's desk. He'd meant it as a joke and she'd read it as a sign of their future. No matter, the sign still hung from the wire fence and in many ways Riley was proud of "Worthless Acres."

Wiping his shoes free of the road dust on the rug in front of the door, he turned the knob and stepped inside. Melanie half sat, half lay on the couch, her eyes closed but facing the television set that mutely reported the last minute news during a commercial break. Riley turned off the set and gently shook Melanie by the shoulder.

She opened her eyes, remaining rigid, and looked at him in an uncomprehending way. Then, little by little, a line fell into place here and an eye focused there to eventually make her understand that Riley had returned.

"You back already? What the fuck time is it?" She stretched and threw her shoulders back.

He winced but said nothing about her language. Because *he* tended not to use foul words or gutter talk, as he put it, did not mean he would impose his beliefs on anyone else. "It's just about midnight. Ready for bed?"

She nodded, fighting a delicious yawn, before fixing her gaze on him. "What's wrong?" she asked simply.

He spun about to face her. "Wrong? Why, nothing."

"Come on. I've lived with you for almost eighteen months. I know when something's bothering you." She stood, crossing over to him. "Come on, tell me all about it."

Riley studied her for a moment. Perhaps Melanie could talk like a stevedore but her gentle nature belied any roughness the casual observer might detect. She was wide awake and had already picked up on his uneasiness—his sense of indecisiveness. It had to be obvious. But then, witnessing a murder was not an everyday occurrence.

"Have you ever seen an old building across the road—maybe half a mile away from here?" he asked hesitantly.

"Half a mile in which direction?"

"Toward the Country Club."

Pursing her lips for a moment, she thought

The Immortal

and then said, "Not that I can remember. Why?"

"Any coffee left?" He strode toward the stove in the small kitchen.

"Want me to make some fresh?"

"I will," he offered, and quickly set about emptying the grounds from the pot.

"So, why? Why, already?" she asked impatiently.

"Huh? Oh, I saw something. Something sorta weird."

Melanie took two mugs from beneath the shelf where they hung and sat down at the small kitchen table. "Weird, huh? Like you're going to tell me a Hallowe'en story? So, what is this, 'Hallowe'en Number Ninety-Seven'?"

"I thought about the fact that it was Hallowe'en, but what I saw wasn't a bunch of kids or anything like that. At least I don't think it was."

"Will you tell me or are you going to make me guess?" She shook a finger at him. "I know what you saw. You saw a bunch of witches dancing *widdershins* around a bonfire. Right?"

He dropped the can of coffee and spun around to face her. "Wh-what did you say?"

"You're as white as a sheet, Riley." Her tone was soft. "What's the matter?"

"What you just said. How did you know?"

"Know? Know what? You mean about witches and dancing? I was kidding. I didn't— Wait a minute. What *did* you see?"

"I don't know what you meant by *'widow's shins'* but I saw a fire and people. I think they might have been dancing. And I saw—"

"It's *'widdershins'* not 'widow's shins.' Where? Where did you see this? Around here?" She leaned forward.

Riley didn't answer right away. He suddenly questioned his own ability to observe. Had he actually seen the man stabbed? Not that he would be willing to swear it in a court of law. He wasn't anywhere near that positive. It merely appeared that the woman with the big breasts had stabbed the man. If he told Melanie about the fire and dancers or whatever they were, he had better not mention anything about an alleged murder.

He put the coffeepot on the stove and turned to face her.

"Riley? Answer me. Was it around here?"

"Yeah. Like I said, about a half mile toward the Club property and then over the first hill."

"Oh, Christ, that's exciting," Melanie gushed, motioning for him to sit down at the table. "Tell me all about it. Geez. On Hallowe'en, too!"

"Normally, I stay on the road but tonight I saw this glow and thought of the fact that it might be a fire and as such, it could come toward the house here and burn everything

I—we've got. So I decided to investigate. When I reached the top of the hill, I heard voices and went forward on my belly. That's when I saw the ruins of an old building of some sort. A big fire was burning inside and I could see people moving around the blaze."

"How come the building didn't burn?"

"I guess it was probably made out of rock or stone or something that wouldn't burn. The roof is gone and some of the walls are caved in."

"What do you think you saw? Witches? A pagan rite of some sort? A cult? A coven? What? Come on, tell me. You saw it. Tell me."

Riley turned away, inhaling the aroma of coffee. He decided it would be best not to mention the murder if that was in reality what he had witnessed. "Actually, that's about it. It was probably nothing."

Melanie slumped back in her chair. "That's sorta disappointing. I was hoping they'd dance in the nude and have an orgy and get all worked up. You're sure that was it, huh?"

Riley nodded and stood to turn down the burner under the coffee.

"What are you going to do?" she asked.

"Do? About what?"

"What you saw."

"What does one do about something like that? Report it to the police? What would I say? I saw some weirdos dancing—what did you call it?"

"*Widdershins.*"

"What the hell is '*widdershins?*' "

"Dancing counter-clockwise and backwards around a fire. Witches in the Dark Ages were supposed to do that whenever they went to their sabbats or meetings."

Riley cocked an eyebrow. "Just how the hell do you know that?"

She giggled, her laughter sounding not unlike a wind chime. "That was from my occult period. Back in the tenth grade in high school, I think. But that's what they did way back when there wasn't radio or TV to entertain the folks." She laughed again.

He nodded. "I don't think I can go to the police. If I owned the land, I guess I could file a complaint. But if they were trespassing, so was I. I guess I'd have to turn myself in along with them."

"That sounds logical." Melanie rose and went to the stove. After filling each of the mugs, she resumed her place. "I'm going to drink this and then hit the hay. I've got to work at Doctor Cushing's office tomorrow for his receptionist. She called while you were out walking Grendel. She's got the flu or something."

"Do you think I should go back tomorrow and investigate in the cold, hard light of day?" he asked, ignoring her statement about having to work the next day.

"Why? You said it was probably nothing."

"I know. But maybe there's a feature story in it. I could get pictures and write a post-Hallowe'en spook story. I could use the dough. The story about the new taxes will only bring what the paper owes me up to seventy-five bucks and I still need a hundred fifty to make up Vicki's allowance for November."

"You know what you saw. If you think there might be a story in it, go for it, Riley. For heaven's sake don't be indecisive."

When she finished her coffee, she left the kitchen and went to her bedroom. He rinsed the cups and turned out the light before going to his. He could hear her humming a nameless tune as she undressed. He might not have to contend with her in bed, not that he didn't enjoy the nights they did spend together. It was just that he felt he needed some thinking time before going to sleep. The question as to what he had seen in the pasture still hammered at him. Had the big-breasted woman actually stabbed the guy?

He quickly stripped and crawled between the sheets. After turning out the table lamp next to his bed, he heard something and turned it back on. Melanie stood in the doorway.

"Want a bed partner?" she inquired, leaning against the doorjamb.

He threw back the covers and she stepped into the circle of light. Shrugging off her light robe, she stood nude before him. She squared her shoulders, thrusting her breasts out as they rose and fell with her breath. Her nipples, perpetually hard and erect, seemed to stare pleadingly at Riley. He held his arms out and she slipped into bed next to him. Separate rooms had their advantages but then so did having a bed partner.

Melanie's long, graceful fingers traced their way toward his lower body, caressing him as they moved, only to find his penis flaccid. "Not interested?" she asked huskily.

"I'm really sorta tired."

"You don't have a headache, do you?" Her voice teased, but bordered on the sardonic.

"Actually, no. But you have to get up early and so do I—but don't wake me when you get up. You know you could sleep an extra hour if you'd let me take you into town."

"Then I wouldn't get my daily exercise." She reached across him to turn out the light. "What are you going to do?"

"I think I can get a good story out of this. Ah, you do take rainchecks on what you were proposing, don't you?"

"Oh, I've been known to do that. But only with certain people."

Propping himself up on one elbow, he turned to face her. Bending down, he kissed her full lips, their tongues greeting each other as they met at the brink of their mouths.

In minutes, they both dropped off to sleep.

The Immortal

Not to dream awful things but to hover in that half comatose state where everything becomes horrendous, shapes and sounds distorted, frightening.

Melanie and Riley heard the noise at the same time, sitting bolt upright in bed.

"What was that?" she whispered hoarsely.

He shrugged but said nothing, peering through the half open door of the bedroom into the dark living room. They could hear the rustle of steps as someone or something came closer. The door swung open.

Suddenly, the black shape of a huge body formed in midair over their bed and crashed on top of them.

"What the—?" Riley snapped.

"I told you, no *menage-a-trois*, Riley. I'm not into that sort of thing," Melanie said, stifling an embarrassed laugh when she realized along with him that it was Grendel.

"Come on, boy," Riley ordered. "Off the bed. You know better than that. Come on. Down. Down on the floor."

Grendel reluctantly moved to the edge and dropped to the rug that lay next to Riley's side of the bed.

"That's the boy. Good Grendel." He patted the large head and turned to Melanie. " 'Night again."

"G'night. Sleep tight and keep the dog on the floor," she said through a yawn.

He closed his eyes and kept them closed even when Grendel stood again to lower his head nearer his master. Riley laid his arm across the dog's neck wondering why Grendel, who always slept in the kitchen or living room, suddenly decided he needed companions with whom to share the night.

CHAPTER 2

Saturday, November 1, 6:30 A.M.

Melanie was gone to work by the time Riley woke up and got out of bed. Grendel followed him from the bedroom to the bath, bringing to his mind the animal's uncharacteristic behavior of the night before. Once he had shaved and showered, Riley felt more like taking on the world. Before going to the school that morning, he wanted to check out the scene of the—how should he refer to it? Orgy? Black Mass? What had Melanie called their dancing? *Widdershins?* Whatever he decided it was would have to be relatively accurate if he were to write an article about it. A sneering half smile widened his mouth while he drank his coffee. In order to believe in witches and ghosts, demons and evil spirits and things that go bump in the night, didn't one have to believe in God and religion? Wasn't an acceptance of all those things necessary for salvation? That's what the TV preachers in their smart-ass, know-it-all wisdom offered, but only for generous dollops of money.

Riley lit a cigarette. At least he was whipping that habit, if only because Melanie threatened to move out if he continued. He had promised to quit by the end of the year and intended to taper off until he smoked only one a day. Then he would be able to stop completely. So far he'd kept his desire under control and had gone from two-plus packs to less than ten cigarettes a day. He sucked the acrid smoke into his lungs. It bit and he coughed. Maybe he'd quit before the new year, especially if smoking was going to cease being pleasurable and start hurting.

After finishing his coffee, Riley rinsed the cup and left the kitchen to go to his office off the living room, next to Melanie's combination bedroom/studio. The large picture window offered northern light and seemed perfect for her. She had squealed delightedly when she first saw it after the idea of her moving in with Riley was broached. Peeking into her room, he smiled when he saw the bed dressed neatly. That had been one reason for her wanting to bunk with him last night. She could sleep a few minutes more and not have to worry about making her bed if it hadn't been slept in. Not that that had been the only reason, of course. They enjoyed each other physically as well as mentally and Riley never once thought he was being used by the vivacious Melanie Brandt.

The Immortal

Closing the door to her room, he went to his small office, passing through it to the closet-turned-darkroom where he had several prints hanging from yesterday's developing session. He could take them along when he went into Hawthorne and drop them off at the paper's office. Printing their photos might only be a mere twenty dollars to someone else, but to him it was a necessary piece of the overall income he needed each month.

Grendel bounded to his side when he walked to the front door, anticipating his own morning romp through the countryside. Riley turned toward the Country Club and marched down the road. The dog marked his territory in different places after reading the signs of those animals who had passed through during the night.

Watching Grendel go from one side of the road to the other, nose to the ground, tail wagging happily, Riley wondered what had made the dog spend the night in his bedroom. That had happened only once before—the night Vicky left. He recalled wondering at the time if the dog's offer was to be a prediction of things to come in Riley Larson's love life, left only with canine companionship. Then he had met Melanie and wondered no longer. Even though she was eight years younger, he found something very mature in her, never once thinking of the fact that she was less than twenty-four.

His thoughts zigzagged back to the

previous night. Why *had* Grendel spent the night in the bedroom? Did he sense something unusual in that pasture? Riley quickly replayed the scenario, trying to place Grendel relative to his own location. As far as he could recall, the dog had bounded about primarily behind him, and had only come to the crest of the hill once, when Riley had been startled by his sudden appearance. The breeze, when it blew—if he remembered correctly—had come from the west and south, toward the fire and the ruined building. Therefore it was highly doubtful that Grendel had even been aware of the dancers' presence. Still, he had whined in such a strange way. More than likely the dog had picked up on Riley's own apprehension, reflecting his master's concern with worry of his own.

When Riley reached the spot where he thought he had passed through the ditch to enter the pasture, he turned, descending below road level into the trench, and clambered up the far side of the fence. Grendel, who had raced on ahead, retraced his steps, followed Riley's scent and jumped between the bottom and middle strands of barbed wire.

Overhead, clouds poised menacingly, threatening to drop their load of rain any minute. A chilly breeze wrapped around Riley and he shuddered, pulling the thin jacket he wore closer about his body. Before going to school, he'd have to get his heavier coat out. Today's weather would not be clement.

When he reached the top of the hill, he stopped short. Below him, trees pointed their leafless branches to the leaden skies, standing guard on either side of a dry creek bed. Lily Cache Creek flowed on the other side of the lane and this was the upper part of a small tributary that at one time fed into the larger stream a mile or so west of Riley's property. But there was no building of any type. None. He looked to his left. Had he imagined the whole thing? Was this what cutting out cigarettes would do? Make him hallucinate? He turned the other way, quickly breathing a sigh of relief. He had left the road too soon. There, a hundred yards or so to his right, the ruins of what appeared to be a schoolhouse or small church cringed ashamedly between two low hills, hidden from the roads that paralleled the field.

Angling down the hill toward the old building, he watched Grendel charge on ahead, nose to the ground as he half trotted, half walked. As Riley approached the ruins, he decided they must once have been a church. The Gothic shape of the two windows on either side of the pointed arched entrance were still intact and he wasn't surprised at finding the back wall to be curved. Definitely a church, though the steeple, assuming there had been one, had long since crumbled to nothing. Raising his camera after readying it, he took several shots of the building.

When he stood in front of the doorway, Riley stopped. What denomination had built it? What kind of people had attended services here in a little valley in the middle of nowhere? When had it been built? He glanced to either side, looking for a cornerstone with a date, and frowned when he found it to his left, smashed. Its interior was empty to any contents that might have been helpful to future historians. His curiosity completely piqued, he made a mental note to stop at the courthouse and look up some records to help solve this little mystery.

Tentatively checking the weathered steps before putting his full one hundred seventy-five pounds on the old boards, he found them to be sturdy, and mounted each one in a slow, deliberate manner. The door half hung by one hinge, blocking most of the inside of the building from his view. Lifting it, he found it moved easily, as if it had not been left in that position for a long period of time. But then, how would the dancers of last night have gotten in if not through the door? There might be another way, but this was easy and safe, since the steps seemed as strong as the small porchlike landing outside the Gothic arch.

After leaning the door against the wall, he stepped inside. For the first time he noticed the stench of an old fire. Undoubtedly that of last night, though it could also be the stink of the building's death which clung tenaciously to the fieldstone walls. An odor of decay laced its way through the funky smoke. The corruption could be that of decomposing vegetation which had dropped into the roofless building from nearby trees. Or the smell of damp wood being devoured by termites or simply rotting away sliver by sliver as the years rolled by.

Maintaining the thought of rotten wood uppermost in his mind, Riley walked forward slowly, carefully, making certain that each spot he placed a foot on would be sufficiently strong to hold him. He never even encountered a squeak or sway. The floor seemed to be as strong as any he'd ever trodden.

When he saw the huge cauldronlike pot that sat between the middle of the room and the apse, he slowly approached it. The smell of smoke thickened as he got closer. Peering inside, he caught his breath. Amid the charred embers of a spent fire, bones, small bones lay at random. They didn't look like human bones. At least none that he'd ever seen. But then, he wasn't a doctor. He had, however, eaten enough chicken to recognize a legbone here, a thighbone there, and the ends of a ribcage sticking out from beneath a half-burned piece of wood.

To further confirm his deduction, he found chicken feathers stained with blood lying near the pot. That's why the church floor hadn't burned. They built the fire within this large kettle and danced about it.

Replaying the previous night's activities in his mind, he absently stuck one of the feathers in his jacket pocket and turned, looking for the altar. He had walked right past when he had seen the cauldron and now moved back toward it. It was only a piece of flat rock resting on what appeared to be two small barrels, which were centered in a washed-out, chalky circle with divergent lines contained within it, drawn on the floor in the middle of the room. Riley stared at the dark stains creating a puddle effect on the surface of the rock. Blood? The blood of the man he saw murdered last night?

Turning away, he fought a gagging retch but lost. He threw up his morning coffee and pulled out a cigarette to rid himself of the acidic taste of bile. In control once more, he turned back. The dark blots were brown—almost black. But were they dried blood? And if they were, was it human? Quite possibly the stains were from a sacrificed chicken. Spinning about, he confronted the evidence that at least one chicken had died here at some time, probably—hopefully—last night before or after he arrived.

But then, the stains were large. Could a chicken have enough blood to make that much of a pattern? Inching nearer the rock altar, he bent down to look more closely, examining the blotches. Varying shades of

The Immortal

brown overlapped, which could mean there were other sacrifices over the years and a lot of chickens died there. How could he bring himself to believe that people would murder someone in the way he thought he'd seen last night? And in the name of some weird religion? He didn't know that for a fact, but why else would otherwise normal people gather on a cloudy night in the ruins of an old church and stab some poor son of a gun to death? No, he couldn't say that with any degree of certainty. But even the idea of parodying a murder sent shivers up his back. What if the gal with the big breasts didn't like the guy on the altar? He shuddered.

Looking about, he found nothing more of interest and checked his camera's lens. He took pictures of the cauldron, the feathers, the blurred circle of lines, the altar, the interior of the building, all from different angles and several shots of each. Deciding he had absorbed enough of the strange atmosphere into his system, he felt he now had sufficient material to do a spook story which would satisfy some editor's jaded ideas, and started for the door.

He stopped, frozen in his tracks. Framed in the doorway, underneath a tree that stood opposite the entrance, Grendel sat on his haunches, staring at him. He had forgotten completely about the dog. Where had he been? Why hadn't he come into the building with him? Normally, he'd follow Riley anywhere.

"Come, Grendel? Come, boy. Come!" he called, holding his free hand out to the black Labrador.

A deep-throated doleful whine, pleading, crossed the distance between them.

That was not like Grendel. He was nosy. In fact, he had almost been dubbed "Nosy" because of his incessant sniffing and poking about the house when Riley first brought him home. But, when Vicki had screamed at him for some silly reason, calling him an evil beast, what came to Riley's mind was the man-eating monster who lived in a cave beneath a lake and haunted the lonely moorland until he was slain by Beowulf. And the black Labrador became Grendel. Now he was acting like Caspar Milquetoast.

"Grendel! Come!" Riley ordered sharply.

The dog lay down, head on his front paws, eyes fixed on the doorway and his master, the same sad, mournful whine filling the air.

Shaking his head, Riley started to leave the building. Grendel leaped to his feet, turning circles before starting up the hill. When he reached the door, Riley stopped, his attention caught by something in the corner to his right. He turned, stepping toward it. A book, half burned, lay propped against the wall at a right angle.

He stooped and picked it up, almost dropping it when he recognized what he held. A Bible. Someone had half burned a Bible and thrown it in the corner. Wasn't there something about burning or destroying one that was supposed to bring bad luck to the perpetrator? He couldn't recall. But for some reason, despite his own lack of belief in organized religion, he felt someone was asking for consequences they might not enjoy.

He blinked his eyes, trying to focus on something on the floor next to the wall. Then he saw it. A knife, its long blade trying to reflect the early morning light, lay in the shadows where the book had leaned against the wall. Bending down to retrieve it, Riley stopped short of picking it up. Instead, he placed the burned book on the rock altar and focused his camera, taking a picture of the dagger. Satisfied, he picked it up and, turning it over and over, examined it carefully.

The handle seemed too awkward for the slim blade extending from it and he concluded it must be made of a heavy metal. When he looked at it more closely, he gasped. *Gold.* Or so it appeared. Stepping away from the wall into the center of the room, he hoped to have more light by which to study it. Lines, barely discernible, graced both sides of the handle. He squinted, trying to make out the design. Dropping it into his camera bag, he spun about at a noise outside.

Grendel barking from the top of the hill brought Riley out of his contemplation, and he left the building carrying the Bible in one hand, fingering the shoulder strap of his bag with the other.

Neither of them noticed the figure standing on the opposite hill as Riley turned to walk toward Grendel, who fell in behind him, obediently heeling all the way to the road. Once he had made it through the fence, the retriever followed but remained close to his side.

He wondered if the animal might be sick. It certainly wasn't like him to be subdued and mild. As they walked along the lane, Riley glanced at the charred book in his hands.

"Idiot!" he exclaimed. How could he have been so stupid? Fingerprints! Had he destroyed any evidence of whoever handled the book before he did? He could picture it now. The cops would be most cooperative in investigating his suggestions that perhaps a murder had taken place, then arrest *him* because the clearest fingerprints they could find would be his! That was dumb. He hadn't even come to the conclusion that he should report what he saw last night. And if he did, who said he had to tell them about the Bible? But wouldn't that constitute a crime as well? Destroying evidence or tampering with evidence—something like that? Hell, he was no attorney.

Arriving home, he was about to look at the Bible more closely, but realized he would have to get to school if he didn't want to lose his part-time employment there. When he walked into the small living room, Grendel trotted to the corner where his sleeping blanket lay rumpled, then circled once before lying down. A deep sigh escaped his great chest as he lowered his head to his paws and closed his eyes.

"Are you sick, boy?" Riley put his camera on a table along with the book. Squatting next to the animal, he picked up his big head and looked deeply into his eyes. Clear, sharp, steady. Not seeming the least bit ill. No dullness whatsoever. Nose cold and moist. "I guess I could take you to the vet's, couldn't I?"

He almost wished the dog were human, able to jump to his feet and exclaim, *"Hey boss, I'm fine. Really. I am. Just a bit under the weather on a dreary day. That's all."*

Well, if Grendel wasn't up to par by the time he returned home that afternoon, he would take him to the doctor. Something had to be wrong.

Hanging his light jacket on a peg, he took his heavier one down, slipping into it. When he got home this afternoon, he'd start the article and hopefully get the pictures developed before Melanie got home. She might be able to tell him something about what he'd photographed and help him with the article. Anyone who knew about *widdershins* would be invaluable as an expert. He grinned. Had he been sleeping with a witch all this time? Melanie was earthy, yes. But a witch? He hardly thought so, considering she'd said something about an interest in the occult while still in high school. Normal. Normal teenage curiosity. That was all there was to it.

He left the house and walked to his Toyota, which, despite its anemic appearance and terminal rust, turned over easily. He backed out of the driveway. Melanie, the health nut, had walked into Hawthorne to the doctor's office. Being a member of the part-time secretary pool headquartered in Chicago did not afford her many opportunities to work this far from the Loop. But she preferred it that way. The money she made was sufficient to help him with expenses and did not detract that much from time at the easel in her room.

Riley, on the other hand, found it necessary to indulge in creature comforts, as simple as those needs were. He preferred riding to walking. Though the Toyota appeared on its last legs, it was his, paid for, didn't gulp much gas money, and that suited him just fine. In addition, he rather enjoyed owning "Worthless Acres" simply because the property was completely paid for and the taxes low enough to cover without much effort. Beyond that, his camera equipment and darkroom were fun as well as work, paying for themselves by occasional sales of photos to newspapers and magazines along with his articles. If Riley Larson's philosophy were to be summed up in a few words, it would be as much luxury as possible with the least amount of work.

As he drove along the narrow lane toward the highway that led to Hawthorne, he began composing his opening paragraph.

By the time Riley finished his Saturday cleaning at the high school, he had managed to survive an attack of conscience but had nevertheless called the sheriff's office. He arranged for a deputy to meet him at his home after one that afternoon. When he approached "Worthless Acres" he frowned at the sight of a department car already parked in front. He had overreacted. That was all. What could he tell anyone from the sheriff's office without sounding like a fool? *"See, I went walking with my dog and saw this strange rite taking place and a guy slit open or something. My dog got upset and I guess I was a little uneasy about it, too. Could you make it go away?"*

Pulling into the driveway, he braked to a stop and grinned at the foolish monologue running through his head. When he stood next to his car, the deputy got out and strode toward him.

"Riley Larson?" he asked gruffly.

Riley half expected him to say something about being under arrest and having his rights read to him. "Yeah. I'm Larson. I called the office about—"

"I know about it," he said, interrupting him. "Where's the site?"

"I'll show you. We'd better drive. It's about a half mile or so."

"You ride with me."

Riley shrugged, following the deputy whose name he hadn't caught on the tag pinned to his jacket.

Once inside the car, Riley repeated his name in a friendly tone and offered his hand.

"Stu James," said the deputy, taking Riley's hand and shaking it firmly. He turned the motor over and eased away from the shoulder of the road.

Riley held up a hand after several minutes. "You'd better stop here, Stu. We'll have to walk up the hill over there and down the other side."

Deputy James slowed to a stop and radioed to the sheriff's office that he would be out of the car for a while and would report back shortly. They got out and immediately looked skyward as rain began falling.

"That figures." Riley pulled his collar up and around his neck.

"It's been threatening all day and naturally it would have to start now." The officer hauled a slicker from the back seat of the car.

Riley hated such efficiency. Why couldn't Stu get soaking wet the way he was going to

The Immortal

be? Rain wasn't falling hard yet, but dark clouds overhead which made early afternoon seem more like dusk on a winter day, promised a steady downpour in time.

Slogging through the ditch, Riley wiped all thoughts from his mind of what it would be like at home. After crawling between the strands of barbed wire, they half ran, half walked up the hill. Neither stopped at the crest, both continuing down the other side toward the ruins of the church.

Leading the way, Riley ran up the steps knowing they would bear his weight. Deputy James followed hesitantly, showing his concern for the state of the building. Riley lifted the door out of position and entered the roofless ruins, half expecting the rain to subside when he passed through.

He waited for James to join him and then gestured. "There it is." He waited for a reaction.

The lawman didn't speak immediately. "There's what?"

Riley spun on a heel and looked, amazement crossing his face. "What the—?"

The altar was gone. The floor was cleaned of any chalked lines. The cauldron was gone. Everything he had reported as evidence in the possible commission of a murder had been taken away. For all practical purposes, he and Deputy Stu James were standing in the ruins of an old church and nothing more.

"Tell me again what you said you saw."

"I—well that is—I—Damn it! I saw a man stabbed here last night. There were people milling around like they were dancing. A woman with big tits gutted some poor guy who was trussed up like I don't know what, lying on an altar. Right here. Here." Riley stepped to where the rock slab had been and pointed. The thought of the knife in his camera bag at home suddenly filled his mind. Should he tell the deputy about it? For the moment, he decided not to.

"There's nothing here now, is there?" Stu James broke into his thoughts.

Riley looked at him, at first thinking he detected a note of derision in his voice, the knife momentarily forgotten. Then he decided that Deputy James was no more happy about standing in the middle of the roofless ruins, getting soaked, than he was. But someone or something certainly had made him look the fool. Where was his evidence? Where had everything gone? He looked heavenward, letting the cold rain wash his face. Why? Why did it have to be him?

"I think maybe you thought you saw what you reported. Don't let it bother you. There's lots of people who report strange things that turn out to be something else when we look into it. Right now, let's get back to the car." The officer started through the doorway.

Riley turned to follow but stopped. *The door.* He had lifted it out of the way when he entered that morning. When he and Stu arrived, Riley had lifted it out of the way again but hadn't touched it when he left earlier. Someone had been here. Someone who had cleaned the floor, gotten rid of the altar and taken the fire pot. Maybe that someone was looking for the burned Bible and the knife. Both of those items should convince the lawman that Riley wasn't imagining things. "Hey, wait a minute!"

James stopped and turned. "Yeah? What now?" His voice was edged with sarcasm.

Riley didn't like his attitude. He sounded patronizing. Why tell him about the door? Or the knife? Or any other details? He'd only make crap out of it anyway. "Wait for me. I sure don't want to walk all the way home." He ran to catch up with the deputy.

Neither man spoke as they plowed through the muddy pasture. Riley lost himself in thought. Something here didn't add up. Not that he could blame the officer for his reaction. Riley himself would have been damn mad if someone pulled something like this on him. But that was the strange part. He hadn't pulled anything. Whoever didn't want to run the risk of having the altar, the lines on the floor and the pot found had gone to some lengths to get rid of all evidence of last night's festivities. Riley wanted to know and he didn't want to know. If someone wanted to keep such things secret, he had no idea what consequences he might suffer if the fact of his snooping became known.

Right now, his coattails were clean. He had the knife and Bible, true. But no one knew that. If he wrote an article, he could camouflage the locale and events, still making it all seem real enough that no one other than those who had partaken in the rite—or whatever it was—would know the difference. Maybe, to be on the safe side, he would scrap the idea of an article and keep his nose totally clean. Then, too, if someone were aware of his having looked at the scene earlier, he didn't want to know any more than he did right now. Why jeopardize himself and possibly Melanie if he didn't have to? On the other hand, how safe would his neighborhood be if strangers could come in and slice people open any time they chose? At least he hoped it had been strangers and none of his neighbors.

When the deputy dropped him off in front of his house, Riley said, "Thanks. I'm sorry about this. I know I saw something but obviously it wasn't much or there would have been something there for you to see."

"No problem, Mr. Larson. It happens more often than you think. Don't worry about it. If you see anything else and you feel something might be wrong, don't hesitate to call. That's one of the functions of our department."

Riley closed the car door before he was lectured on how to report something like this. James wasn't being smart or condescending. At least that was a plus but Riley still felt like a fool.

He ran to the front door and let himself in. Grendel greeted him, playfully jumping up to have his head rubbed.

"I'm glad to see you're feeling better, boy." He jumped, startled when the phone rang, and picked up the receiver. "Hello?"

"Riley? This is Vicki. Have you got the money yet? I need it. I really do. I wouldn't—"

"I—I guess I don't have it here in my hand. But I'm starting an article. It should get me some bread from one of the papers. Can you wait?"

"How long?"

Riley wasn't even certain if he wanted to write the article. He had the pictures. He had his openings. And he needed the money. Money to give to Vicki. What a waste of effort on his part. Earn some good dough and then have to give it away immediately.

"More than likely by the end of next week," he said, hoping she wouldn't pin him down to a specific time. Payday from the school board wasn't until the middle of November and Vicki wanted her money now. He had no choice. He had to write the article since nothing else was going for him. Melanie was virtually broke and also wouldn't be paid by Secretaries Unlimited until the middle of the month. "Yeah, I'll have your money by then."

He'd have to rely on his friendship with Andy McLain for purchase of and payment on delivery for the article. He wished he could afford the luxury of going to the Trib or the Sun-Times, but to do so at best would be a calculated gamble on his part. He had no solid friendships or contacts on either paper. The situation called for an ally who would sympathize with him and buy the story about strange rites. Andy McLain would fit that role especially well since Riley had done more than a few favors for him at college and later while he was climbing the ladder of success. Andy could buy the article and run it in the Sunday Supplement for which he worked. That would mean additional exposure for Riley as well, because the tabloid ran in many newspapers each week. If he asked properly, Andy might pay him right away for the piece so he could satisfy his obligation to Vicki.

"I guess I can wait until then," she said. "Shall I stop by and pick it up?"

"How about if I bring it to you? Save you the trip out here and all. Why blow my money on gas to have you come pick up my money so you can live while—"

"Funny, Riley. Real funny. I'd better have it by next Saturday."

"What? No 'or else'?"

"No," she said softly.

He knew she still held feelings for him but wasn't quite certain if the feelings were of love, or compassion for his slovenly ways, or outright pity for the waste she claimed he was making of his life. He didn't dislike her. He just didn't want any trouble with anyone right now—especially Vicki.

"You'll have it. I promise. Right now I've got an article to write. 'Bye." He hung up before she could say anything more and walked to his office. The line he would use as a lead sentence burned in his mind:

Is it possible that a coven of witches is at work somewhere in the vicinity of Chicago?

Saturday, November 1, 7:30 P.M.

For the remainder of the afternoon, while Riley wrote about what he had witnessed the previous night, dark ominous clouds continued building below the slate sky of the last few days. Brief spurts of rain seemed to indicate what would happen before the day ended, yet when Melanie, clutching a bag of groceries in one arm, had walked into the house shortly before four o'clock, the expected onslaught had not yet arrived. It was after she finished preparing their simple evening meal that she called Riley from his office to the accompaniment of a crashing thunderclap.

"Wow!" he said, entering the kitchen. "That's quite a drumroll for the last call to dinner. What the hell are you having that merits such an introduction?"

She smiled. "Would you believe bologna sandwiches and tomato soup?"

He turned, leaving the room, saying over his shoulder, "Let me show you what I found today when I went out to investigate." He returned carrying the Bible and knife.

"Won't that wait? The soup will be cold."

"The soup'll be cold. The soup'll be cold. Come on Mel, we can look and slurp at the same time. Look at this." He deposited the charred book on the table.

"What's that?" she asked before recognizing it. "So somebody got pissed off and did a Bible in. Big deal."

"What do you make of this, my cynical friend?" He laid the gold-handled knife in front of her.

"Now that's really beautiful." She picked it up to look at more closely. "Where'd you get it?"

"I found both of them at the ruins of this old church. That's where the rite or whatever it was was held last night." He went on to tell her about everything he'd found, his conclusion of having witnessed a murder, the pictures he'd taken, and what had been there when he and the deputy sheriff returned earlier that afternoon.

"Nothing? Nothing there?" she exclaimed when he finished.

"The place was as clean as Grendel's teeth. Spick-and-span. Spotless."

"What did the deputy say about the pictures?"

Riley bit into his sandwich and chewed it before answering. "I didn't show them to him."

"Why not, for heaven's sake?"

"I shouldn't have called him in the first place. Good Godfrey, Mel. Think about it. I was the one eavesdropping on them. For all I know the *widdershinners* own the land that Grendel and I trespassed on. I'm the one who could get his buns in a sling over this."

"I assume, then, that you didn't show him the burned Bible or the knife either?"

He shook his head. "Hey, I'll write my article, make a couple of hundred or so and satisfy my 'Vicki obligation.' Cut and run. What's wrong with that?"

Melanie finished her soup, dabbing at her lips with a napkin. "Nothing, I guess. It's just that you were so curious about it last night."

"I changed in the light of day—such as it was. Listen to that rain."

The steady beating of raindrops on the cottage roof seemed to increase in volume and tempo as Riley mentioned it.

Melanie picked up the knife. "This really is beautiful, you know?" She turned the slim weapon over in her long-fingered hands. "It sure is worn down, like it's very old and has been handled a lot."

The hilt, polished almost smooth, barely showed the intricate design that had been etched years before. The triangular knob at the end contained two teardrop shaped emeralds that bulged to either side. Fine lines flowed away from the jewels until they were lost forever in the solidity of the gold itself.

Turning it over, she looked closer. "Hey? Is this a goat's head?" She offered it to Riley.

"Yeah," he agreed after a few minutes. "I think you're right. I didn't really stop to examine it closely after taking the photos. Did you notice the lettering?"

"Lettering?" She stood, came around to his side of the table, and bending down looked over his shoulder. "I didn't notice that. *A.M.D.G.*"

"I think that's an '*S*' not a '*D*'. Here, look at it yourself." He handed the blade back.

"I remember," she said peering at it intently, "when I went to Catholic grade school how the nuns made us write that at the top of each page we ever turned in. *A.M.D.G.* I think it means 'to the greater glory of God.'"

"You get all of that out of *A.M.D.G.?*"

"The letters were abbreviations of Latin words. But I think you're right. That is an '*S*' and not a '*D*.'" She squinted before nodding her head.

She shrugged. "Notice how the letters are

The Immortal

contained within intersecting triangles that surround the head of the goat. Weird."

"You've got me intrigued, Mel. Do you know anyone you could call and find out what it means when it's '*S*' and not '*D*?' "

"What do you suppose," she asked, choosing to ignore his question for the time being, "the significance of the triangles might be? Look here. On the back inside. Two little red triangles touching at the points. I wonder what makes them glisten like that?"

She wiggled the knife back and forth under the light hanging over the table. Thread-like shafts of blood-red light reflected in different directions. Handing it to Riley, she watched him do the same maneuver.

"It reflects like a jewel would. Let me get my magnifying glass." Standing, he went to his darkroom, returning in seconds. "You know what I think?" He scrutinized the highly magnified shaft.

"What?" she asked laconically, gazing over his shoulder at the red shapes.

"I think they're jewels, too. I'm just guessing but they look like tiny, tiny jewels. Maybe rubies or something like that." He turned the handle over, focusing his attention on the two green jewels. "If those are emeralds, and I think they are, them I'm willing to bet the red ones are rubies. What do you think?" He handed the knife and glass to her.

After several minutes she spoke. "Just being logical, I'd have to agree with you. Why would someone stick bits of colored glass into what is obviously a gold handle? That wouldn't make much sense." She turned it slowly under the glass. "God, it sure is beautiful. What are you going to do with it?"

"I decided not to mention it or the book in my article. I've got more than enough junk in it already. In fact, I'm almost finished with the first draft and it reads pretty good. I don't need the knife and book. Besides, the way I've written it gives no clues as to the location of the church or where I was when I saw it or anything like that. If I mentioned the dagger and the Bible and what they looked like, whoever was there would know immediately that I'd been spying."

"So what are you going to do with the knife?" she repeated, placing it on the table.

"If nothing comes of the article and no one advertises for the knife, I'll pawn it. It should bring me a pretty good piece of change."

"Advertise for it?" Her tone was sardonic. "I can see it now. 'Lost: one sacrificial dagger used to conjure up the devil and his flock, for use in Black Masses. Contact Ima Weird.' " She laughed.

"Yeah. I guess you're right. No one would actually advertise for it. So, I guess I'll just hock it after a while."

"Was the deputy pissed when you found the place empty this afternoon?"

"A bit long-suffering. If I ever want to report something again, I'd better be damned sure I know what I'm talking about."

"Why do you say that?"

"Because I was ready to swear last night that I thought I witnessed a murder. Right? Well, that blade is as clean as a whistle, and I don't envision anyone taking the time to wipe it that spotless and then just throw it away. What I think I saw was a symbolic ritual of some sort. At least that's what I've come to believe. Can you imagine how embarrassing it would have been to pursue the idea of a homicide and then find there wasn't anything to it? I'd have come off looking like a demented old maid spying on my neighbors."

Melanie stood, crossing to the telephone, and pulled the book from beneath it.

"What are you going to do?"

Flipping through the pages, she stopped, running a well-manicured finger down the list. "I'm going to call a priest and ask him about *A.M.D.G.*"

"Oh. I'll do the dishes while you play detective." He gathered the soup bowls and plates. By the time they were finished, she'd hung up.

"*A.M.D.G.*" she began, "stands for *Ad majorem Dei gloriam*, which translated means 'to the greater glory of God.' "

"So what does *A.M.S.G.* mean?"

"He didn't know for sure but ventured a guess. 'To the greater glory of *Satan.*' "

Riley sat down heavily. "I suppose I could have guessed. But I think way down deep, I was hoping that what I saw was a college fraternity or sorority initiation, or something like that. Did the priest ask anything else about it?"

"Not really. All he offered was the fact that *A. M. D. G.* is the motto for the Jesuit Order and that a lot of religious groups have adopted it for their own use."

"Well, why not devil worshippers then?" Shrugging his shoulders, he stood and looked at Melanie. "At least there's a record of my having reported the incident to the sheriff's office. If something should hap—"

"Hey? What could possibly happen? You said yourself that your tail is protected by the way you wrote the article. You got nothing to worry about."

By the time they retired, she had convinced Riley he had written a good article and that no one would care about it or come looking for him. After she dropped off to sleep, he lay on his back staring at the dark ceiling listening to the low rumble of thunder, as another storm moved into the area and the rain picked up its tapping rhythm on the roof.

The Immortal

Shortly after Riley's eyes closed, Grendel padded into the room and lay down on his master's side of the bed, his own eyes darting from side to side, a minuscule whine threading its way from deep within his chest.

CHAPTER 3

Saturday, November 8, 1:00 P.M.

"I hope you didn't have to rob a bank to get this, Riley," Vicki said, a note of humor hidden within the words.

He knew she disliked having to hound him for money but the conditions of the divorce were quite plain and simple. He had to support her until she finished with college or dropped out for some reason or other. Once she graduated, he was free of any further obligations, his debt to her fully paid.

"Believe it or not, I worked for it. I wrote for it. I did not break the law for it, so you don't have to worry about losing your free ride through life." He stared at her, and she turned away.

"You know what I mean. Have you developed any good work habits since I saw you last?" She waited for an answer, wondering what he would say.

He shook his head. "When everything else is changing so darned fast in the world, I would think you'd find it refreshing to have one thing, one person, who remained solid and rock fast in his dedication to not changing. But no! Here we are, two people, one paying the other to learn how to teach, which is the only thing tying them together, and she still wants to tell him what to do. The marriage is over, Vicki."

"I know that. Don't you think I wake up at night sometimes, trying to figure out what went wrong?"

"I know what went wrong. You decided my way of looking at life didn't please you any more and you wanted to get out and build *security* for yourself. Well, a change of clothing will get you buried when you die and all the security in the world isn't going to change that little fact."

"Let's not argue, Riley." She folded the money he had handed her, placing it in her handbag. "How are things out at 'Worthless Acres?' "

"Fine, I guess," he muttered, quieting the storm he had felt building within him.

"Still living alone?"

He shrugged. Why should he tell her about Melanie? Why run the risk of having her make snide remarks? That was the reason he had told her he'd bring the money to her rather than have her come out from the city. "It's easier that way. No commitments, no problems. Just me and Grendel taking on the world." He glanced at her, relieved to see her smiling. She was the total opposite of Melanie, tiny, petite, blonde, very dainty in appearance.

Her brown eyes crinkled at his mention of the dog. She hadn't been overly fond of Grendel, who had been less than two years old when she left. Yet more than once she had laughed at the ungainly rawboned pup galloping across the livingroom, sliding on a rug, bumping into furniture. She had taken that sort of foolishness in stride. When Riley insisted on doing nothing more than writing and living on the tiny acreage he owned, she began easing away from him spiritually, mentally, and finally physically, until they both blew up and she moved out.

Stepping closer to him, she turned her round face up to his. "I've got to get cracking on my homework. No play and all work. That's me." She slipped her arms around his neck and kissed him lightly on the mouth. " 'Bye. See you."

"Yeah," he said softly. "Next month. With more bread. Right?"

She didn't answer, and he stepped through the door of her apartment into the hall. The door closed with a quiet, dignified click. She turned, hurrying to the table where her books waited. For several seconds she fought the tears, and then, having forced them back into nothingness, opened the history text.

* * *

Riley strode along the hallway to the stairwell, taking the steps two at a time, running away from his past. He needed fresh air. Not that Vicki affected him in a bad way. He just didn't want to be inundated with memories about something that didn't work out. They were good memories for the most part, but the bad ones seemed to overwhelm and suffocate the others whenever he reflected.

Once in the street, he slipped behind the Toyota's steering wheel and laid his head against it. Now the whole awful routine began again. He'd have to start building another nine hundred bucks for Vicki's rent and food and whatever else she needed. In some ways he resented the extra strain it put on him, but knew in his heart if he could make that much extra for Vicki, he could do the same for himself once she graduated. But that wasn't exactly what he wanted out of life. She was hung up on security. He wanted freedom. Would chaining himself to the ritual of making that much additional money to enjoy a few extra creature comforts be worth sacrificing his unstructured existence?

He turned the key and the motor roared to life, its pistons whirring dependably to the rhythm of a fast foxtrot. Patting his shirt pocket inside his jacket, he felt the thin, stiff hundred-dollar bill left over from the check Andy McLain had given him. It would either buy the few necessities he felt he needed or start next month's "Vicki Fund."

A smile twitched his mouth when he thought of asking the bank teller who had cashed the check to give him three one-hundred-dollar bills, just to make it necessary for Vicki to go to the bank and break them into small ones. It wasn't nice because he knew she was busy, but then he was busy too, and it was an awful inconvenience to have to earn extra money each and every month for four long years. Well, another eighteen months and that, too, would become history, just like his marriage to Vicki.

Putting the car in gear, he checked the rearview mirror and pulled away from the curb when traffic allowed. He wondered how many more articles he might be able to sell Andy McLain. The reason he had never thought of approaching him before surfaced in his memory.

Andy had been a year behind him at Michigan. Although Riley had never quite maintained the average grade that Andy did, he managed to sell short stories to English majors who hadn't allocated enough time for a particular assignment. And Andy had been among his customers. Their relationship grew over the years, during which Riley always made a point of not doing business with close friends unless he happened to be faced with an emergency, when he needed money and didn't care if the piece was bought for quality or as a favor.

He had found Andy the previous Monday, frowning and yelling into his telephone, motioning Riley to sit down opposite him, listening intently to the speaker on the other end.

"If you don't have that article in here by three this afternoon you can cross me off your list of sucker-editors! Do you hear me?" His normally quiet voice boomed out the words. Just as quickly as he had spoken, he paled and hung up.

Riley shook his head. "You'll have ulcers by the time you're thirty-five—if you haven't got them already."

"That—that—rotten sonofabitch! He told me to go get fucked! What the hell is the world coming to when freelance writers talk to editors like that? I'll never buy from that bastard again—even if he wins the Pulitzer." He pulled out a handkerchief and blew his nose.

Riley lit a cigarette but said nothing.

Andy looked up, wrinkling his face. "You still smoking those things? I thought you were quitting?"

"I am. I am. The first of the year. What's the problem here, Andy? Can ol' Riley help out?"

"That—whatever you want to call him, just pooped out on an assignment I had given him out of the goodness of my heart. Now he tells me he won't be able to finish it.

That he hasn't even *started* it yet and the deadline I gave him is three this afternoon. Now what the hell am I supposed to do?"

Riley winked at him. "I've got something here that might be of interest to you."

Andy ignored him. "Christ! The feature lead, too! I wonder what I've got in my files that can be put together on short notice?"

"Hey!" Riley said loudly. "Listen to me. Watch my mouth. I'm speaking to you. I've got something you might be able to use." He threw the manila envelope on the desk as Andy's head snapped up.

Grabbing the package, he opened it, spilling the contents onto his desk. He picked up the pictures, examining each one in turn, and then eyed Riley. "Without reading it, let me guess. It's an article on sloppy housekeeping, right?"

"Don't be smart! Read the lead sentence." Riley looked about for an ashtray and when he couldn't find one, flicked the ashes into the cuff he rolled on one pant leg.

Andy read the first page, his eyes scanning the lines in a practiced, hurried way. When he continued to the second page, Riley felt he had him hooked.

Five minutes later, Andy looked up. "You're kidding?"

"No way. It's exactly as I told it and you've got the pictures there. Can you use it?"

"Too bad you didn't show up two or three

weeks ago. It would have been a dandy Hallowe'en story."

"Kid stuff," Riley snapped. "You're too good an editor to treat a story like this lightly. Besides, the only reference to Hallowe'en is the fact that that was the night I saw it happen."

Andy nodded his head, slowly, deliberately as his mind obviously raced through the story again, his eyes scanning the photos once more. "I'll tell you what I'll do. I'll run it as the feature story only because I need one and don't have the time to write one myself."

"You always were a poor time manager, Andy. Ah, about the money. I need some to satisfy Vicki. She's developed the damnedest habits. Eating and wearing clothes and living in an apartment where she has to pay rent. I could use a couple o'hundred, at least."

"You'll get half now and half a week after publication, just like always and everyone else. I show no favoritism. You know that."

"How much? I've never had you buy one of mine as a feature before."

"Three fifty now and three fifty then. Fair enough?"

Riley had nodded, wondering what he would do with the extra money he'd have left once he paid Vicki.

The Immortal

Monday, November 10, 8:00 P.M.

The day after the story appeared, he got a telephone call. At first he wondered how the person had gotten his number; the caller wanted to talk about the article. Riley had maintained an unlisted number since Vicki moved out, not quite knowing why or what he had expected to happen on the phone. When their separation and ultimate divorce proved to be amicable, he had never gotten around to putting it back in the directory. A lot of people knew it and he alway included it in any correspondence with editors.

"Just out of curiosity," he said before getting into the conversation, "how did you get my number?"

"I called the editorial offices of *Sunday* and they gave it to me. Why?"

"No reason. What can I do for you?"

Riley couldn't place the voice, distinctive in its hoarse scratchy sound. He felt as if he should cough for the man, but decided it must be his normal speaking voice after he continued.

"I read your article and wondered if you might be intereted in more information—maybe witness a—a rite."

Riley didn't answer immediately. He felt his palms dampen. Could he be in trouble? It might be a put-on of some sort. A rip-off. He'd have to play it tight to the vest, hoping the man would offer some information that would confirm in Riley's mind that his caller was involved with the same group he'd seen. Maybe it was just another cult or coven. He smiled at the way he made it seem so commonplace, sarcastically thinking to himself that things like this simply didn't happen. He envisioned a clearing house for devil worshippers where they could exchange names for potential members.

He coughed, clearing his throat, more out of the man's need to do so than any reason he could think of. "And where would this—this rite or whatever it's called, take place?"

"My apartment—on the near North side."

Waiting to see if he had more to add, after several seconds Riley said, "What do you really want?"

"Hey, man. This is serious. You interested or not? I can call other newspaper guys. This is good stuff. You ain't never seen nothin' like it."

Riley felt convinced that it was a rip-off of some kind. The man sounded like he spent a lot of time on the streets. Certainly he didn't sound like a person interested in the dark side of things concerning life, nature, religion.

"If I agree to come," Riley went on, raising the level of his voice several decibels in an attempt to attract Melanie's attention, "I'll tell you right now, there will be people apprised of my whereabouts." He waited, playing the cat-and-mouse game.

The Immortal

"Hey, that's fine. Crazy. No problem. You tell whoever you want to tell. We don't care. You'll be safe as if you were sitting in your own home."

Riley narrowed his eyes. That didn't make sense. If there was no reason to suspect something wrong and his safety would be virtually guaranteed, what was the real purpose? Didn't cults and covens and people who dealt in things mystical or out-of-the-ordinary where religion was concerned, try to keep a low profile? Why would this character want to get publicity out of it? It had to be a scam.

"What's the catch?"

"No catch. This is all legit."

"What about—" He paused. There had to be some reason. Some motive. A dim light dawned. "What's this cost?"

"A C-note, that's all."

"A hundred bucks? What do I get for that?"

"You get to witness the rite—like I said."

He looked across the livingroom into Melanie's bedroom. "Can I bring a friend?"

"Sure. Sure. You can bring the Pope if you want. But it'll cost another hundred—for each of you."

Riley furrowed his brow. He had the hundred left from the first payment from Andy, but couldn't bring himself to ask Melanie if she had that much just to go to some far-out religious service. "Where and when?" He preferred to worry about the second hundred when the time came. Maybe he'd get the other half for the article in *Sunday* before he met with the man on the other end.

"Tomorrow night?"

"You asking me or telling me?" he snapped, wondering just what the man would say next.

"Telling you."

"And where do I go?"

"You know Eckhart Park—just off Chicago?"

Riley pictured the approximate area of Chicago Avenue and thought he knew the park the man referred to. "I'll find it. How'll I know you?"

"I'll find you. What kind of car you drive?"

"Toyota. A red Toyota."

"Okay. You park along the north side of Eckhart and wait. Will you have someone with you?"

"I might."

"Man or woman?"

"Woman."

"Okay. I'll walk past your car three times before I say anything to you. I'll ask if you've been to church yet. Okay?"

Riley shook his head fighting the urge to laugh. "That's fine. What time am I going to church?"

"Make it around eleven. These things

work better at midnight. Hell, you should know that."

Riley wanted to ask him now he, a janitor-cum-reporter, would know about the best time to do anything dealing with the occult but thought better of it. Although he doubted the man and his offer, the possibility existed that this could be legitimate and he'd get another story out of it.

Melanie wasn't against the idea of going with him, but wondered about the common sense of blowing two hundred dollars on something that at best had to be a questionable situation. When he suggested approaching Andy for the extra hundred as expense money to followup on the first article, she agreed to go only if that were arranged. As it happened, Andy's office had been overwhelmed by the response to Riley's article. He quickly agreed that a follow-up might be in order, and handed over the money in addition to the balance Riley had coming.

Tuesday, November 11, 10:38 P.M.

The next night, Riley and Melanie sat in the Toyota, waiting for their gravel-voiced host. After thirty minutes had passed, he turned to her. "You about ready to chuck it in?"

"It sure looks like we're going to be stood up. God, that hasn't happened to me since eighth grade. This one boy wanted to take me out in the woods for a picnic and play with my tits. Anyway—"

"Hold it, Mel. You can confess to me later. I think that's our man. It's the second time he's walked past."

They both watched a thin, slovenly dressed man turn and walk back toward the car. When he reached the front, he stepped into the gutter and came around to the driver's side.

Riley rolled the window down part way and waited.

"You been to church yet?" His voice was harsh and rough. It was their man.

"Yeah." Riley suddenly felt foolish. He thought of himself as being a spy or something and this was the big moment in the book or movie.

"I'm glad you brought company. Sometimes these things get outta hand." He laughed nervously and continued, "Go down into the next block and park wherever you can find a space. The address is here on this slip of paper. I'll be there right after you. When you see me go in, follow. Understand?"

Riley took the paper, handing it to Melanie. "Gotcha." He turned the Toyota's motor over and pulled away from the curb, driving slowly, keeping his eye on the mirror, watching the man walk in the same direction.

After several minutes, Melanie pointed. "There's a spot—on the other side."

He snapped his attention away from the inside rearview mirror, focusing his eyes on the outside one to see if any traffic was coming. As there were no other cars within several blocks, he spun the wheel, the car did a tight U-turn and he quickly parked. They got out and crossed the street to wait for the man.

When he walked up, he ignored them, turning into the next doorway, hurrying down a flight of steps to a basement apartment. He opened the screen door and entered, leaving both it and the inside one ajar so they could follow.

Riley took Melanie's hand and they stepped inside, wary of the bluish darkness in which they found themselves. Soft strains of organ music seeped from a small, portable turntable.

"D'you take precautions like you said you would?" the voice rasped from the dark.

"You bet. I wasn't born yesterday," Riley tried to sound confident. "If my friend and I don't come out within the hour, this place will be crawling with—"

"Don't worry. Most of the time these things take half, maybe three-quarters of an hour. You got the money?"

Riley pulled two bills from his pocket and handed them to the spectral shape that formed in front of him as the man stepped closer to take the money, motioning the two of them to follow. A single blue light bulb did little to illuminate the room.

"Be careful you don't fall," he said, slipping the bills into his shirt pocket. "We'll go down this hall to another room. That's where you'll see the rite take place. Watch your step." He turned away to lead them.

Melanie stepped in front of Riley when he indicated her to do so and walked after the man. She had barely taken three steps when she tripped over a fold in the rug and sprawled forward, tackling him around his shoulders.

"Oh, God, I'm sorry." Flustered, she stood up straight, smoothing her clothes of imaginary wrinkles.

"That's all right," the rough voice said, "just be careful."

After groping their way some ten feet down the hall, they stepped into another room as he held a curtain back. Melanie went first into the dull light of two red bulbs vainly trying to illuminate the room in shades of crimson. Riley followed and they sat down on two chairs behind a third, which the man took.

He clapped his hands and curtains parted at the far end of the room. Two nude women entered. One appeared to be in her late teens, her supple body not quite mature, straight blonde hair hanging down below her shoulders. The other had seen her best days at some moment in the distant past, though evidence of a striking figure was still noticeable.

The younger of the two lay down on a table covered with a black cloth, spreading her legs. The other woman raised both hands to the low ceiling and chanted something.

"Louder, we can't hear you," the man said, nervously wiggling in his chair.

"I said, 'Oh, mighty Satan, ruler of the black world—ah—help us here tonight when —ah—when we pray to you." She bent down and made loud sucking noises when she neared the blonde's pubic area.

Melanie tapped Riley on the arm, head motioning toward the curtained doorway. She stood, tiptoeing toward it, he right behind her. The man sitting in front of them was completely enthralled with the sex act being carried on for his benefit and that of his guests.

Riley stepped around Melanie, leading the way down the hall toward the front room and the outside entrance. Hurrying up the steps, they ran across the street to the Toyota and got in.

"Have you ever?" she began and burst into a gale of laughter.

Once the car was out of the parking place and racing down the street, he joined in. "Judas Priest. What a rip-off. And to think I talked Andy out of a hundred bucks for that. I'd better pick your brains and write an article that sounds factual or he'll scalp me."

"You can do that if you want but don't worry about the money." She laughed once more.

"What the hell's so funny, Mel?" He pushed the car to the legal limit on Ashland, which would pick up Interstate 55 and get them home in a hurry.

She held out her clenched hand. "This is for you."

He looked at her and then back at the street before holding his hand out, palm up. Something light and crisp fell into it. Slowing the car, he looked and gasped. Two crumpled hundred-dollar bills bounced around on his fingers.

"What the—? Where in hell—?"

"I decided the whole thing was a scam of some sort when I saw where the little creep was taking us. Once inside, I knew it for sure. Remember when I fell—supposedly?"

He nodded—a wide grin creased his lower face until his eyes wrinkled as his cheeks moved upward—but said nothing.

"I picked his pocket—just like he had picked yours, my gullible friend."

"Don't rub it in, Mel." He wiped his eyes, trying to hide the embarrassment he felt forming on his face. "Anybody could have been taken like that. How come you didn't fall for it?"

"He had no toys."

"Toys?"

The Immortal

"You know—no sacrificial knife like the one you found. That's very important in cabalistic rites. He also had no clothing with esoteric symbols on it. The women were probably his whores and the three of them thought they could make a couple of extra bucks putting you on. Don't feel bad. You suspected right from the beginning. I simply had the opportunity to get you a refund. But learn from it. The next time you'll know better."

He turned to look at her and cocked an eyebrow. "Are you patronizing me?"

"Me? Little ol' me? Why, perish the thought, sir." She winked broadly at him.

An hour later, they pulled into "Worthless Acres" and he parked the car. As they approached the house, he heard bells. "Hey, the phone's ringing. Come on." He hurried ahead of Melanie and unlocked the door.

Grabbing the phone, he picked it up and said breathlessly, "Hello?"

"Smart ass!"

"Who is this?" He recognized the rough, scratchy voice.

"You'll get yours, smart ass! I got connections and you—"

"Listen, jerk-off!" Riley growled. "Don't mess with the press. I've got you dead to rights on a con game—a real stupid scam that no one would stand for. Hear? Be happy if my paper doesn't prosecute you. Remember, I've got a witness and I know where you live."

Nothing but dead silence spilled from the phone.

"You didn't know about the tape recorder my friend had in her purse either, did you?"

The only response was a quiet click as the man hung up.

Melanie looked at Riley. "What tape recorder?" He laughed again and she crossed the room, pressing her body against his as she stood next to him. "I'm glad you had suspicions from the beginning but you need some expertise. I think you'd better let me be your adviser on anything to do with ghosties and monsters, Riley." She spoke softly, her breath aimed directly into his ear. "In fact, I'll tell you what I think is in order. Let me show you a *rite* that'll be *right—all right?*"

That brought a smile to his lips and he tipped her head back. "You've got a deal."

Arm in arm they walked to his bedroom where they quickly undressed and embraced. Her breasts barely flattened in contact with his chest even though he crushed them against it. Their tongues met in a slippery duel for dominance before each relinquished the role of aggressor and settled into mutual, caressing lovemaking. Without separating, they made their way to the bed, slowly lowering themselves on it. Melanie eased her way to one side, Riley to the other, and while their tongues continued exploring, their hands sought out those secret areas which would enhance each other's sensations of eager anticipation and longed-for fulfillment. She spread her legs, offering herself invitingly. He raised then lowered himself toward her, penetrating her lower body. She sucked in her breath at the tingle coursing through her. Their pelvises met in a gentle bump, then another and another as their animal passion built to a savage climax. Spent, they lay coupled together for a long while before either moved or spoke for fear of destroying the magical moment they had created.

In the living room, Grendel lay in the middle of the floor, staring at the front door. His eyes bore through the gloom toward the center panel as if anticipating someone's arrival or sensing a near presence. A minuscule whine wove its way through the quiet, interrupted only by the dampered, gradual slackening of Riley's and Melanie's breathing coming through the closed door as they unwound back to normalcy. Lowering his head to rest on his outstretched front paws, his eyes remained fixed on the same spot.

The distinctive Rolls-Royce outline floated down Lily Cache Lane, barely making a sound as its quiet engine pulled that luxurious body through the night. Without pausing in front of "Worthless Acres," it continued toward the curve three-quarters of a mile distant, where the road wound out of sight. When it reached the bend in the lane, it stopped, one of its back doors opening to disgorge the shadowy figure of a well-dressed man.

He stepped to the back of the car, raising binoculars to his eyes. Moving the focus wheel, he brought into sharp definition the blurred light seeping from beneath a drawn shade in Riley's bedroom. He could read, when he moved slightly to his right, the yellow letters against the red background, then swung back to his left for an instant before lowering the eyepiece.

He returned to the car which ghostlike, quietly, continued down Lily Cache Lane.

CHAPTER 4

Wednesday, November 12, 10:30 P.M.

The next night, Melanie entered Riley's office, crossing to the closed door in the far wall. "Riley?" She tapped on the darkroom entrance.

"Yeah, Mel?" he called, swishing the eight-by-ten around in the final solution.

"You about finished? You've got company."

"What?" He stared at his watch in the red light. Ten thirty at night and he had company. "Who? Who is it?"

"You'd better come see for yourself. If I told you, you wouldn't believe me."

"I'll be a few minutes yet. Entertain whoever's out there. Okay?"

"Hurry up."

He wondered what kind of game she might be playing. They didn't have that many acquaintances who felt comfortable enough to drop in anytime much less ten thirty at night, and even fewer friends who felt that welcome. He clipped the photo of the knife to the line and wiped his hands dry. Flicking the switch, he plunged the room into utter blackness and opened the door. Melanie was standing there waiting for him.

"I thought I told you to entertain."

She nodded. "Wait until you see who's here—you devil, you. And to think I thought I had a monopoly on you. Oh, I know we said we could do whatever we wanted with whoever we wanted but my God, Riley, I would think you'd want to brag about this one."

Her eyes sparkled and he stared at her, uncomprehending. "What the hell are you talking about?"

"Come on." She took him by the hand, led him to the livingroom and said before he entered, "Here he is, Miss Thorndyke. Riley Larson in the flesh."

She stepped aside, making a sweeping motion with one arm, as if introducing a famous personage onstage to an eager audience.

When Riley stepped into the room, he fought the urge to gasp and felt the color rush to his face. Standing near the door, a woman a bit shorter than Melanie's five feet nine inches turned to face him. The black cloak she wore, hood thrown back, floated out like a wing before settling down again. Raven hair spilled about her face, cascading shoulder-length, where it bobbed from the

The Immortal

sudden motion before quieting.

"Mr. Larson?" she asked, stepping forward. "Mr. Riley Larson?"

"Ye-yeah. I'm Riley Larson. Miss—ah—" His voice sounded peculiar, dry, out of order, barely usable.

"My name is Leeanah Thorndyke. How do you do?"

He glanced at Melanie, a wide grin on her face, enjoying his discomfort at being confronted with the beautiful woman who came toward him and stopped less than two feet away. He inhaled; an exotic scent washed his nostrils until he thought he would get lightheaded.

"Ah, what—what can I do for you, Miss Thorndyke?"

"May I sit down?" She looked from Riley to Melanie and back again before taking in the furniture of the room with a glance.

"Of course. Please, sit down, Miss Thorndyke." He gestured toward the only easy chair.

Melanie stepped forward. "Would you like something? A drink perhaps or a cup of coffee?" She stared at Riley, merriment dancing in her eyes.

Before Riley could say anything, his visitor said, "No. Thank you, but I must say no. I seldom drink either alcoholic beverages or coffee. Perhaps a glass of water?"

Melanie nodded and turned, leaving the room.

Riley studied Leeanah Thorndyke. Her black hair accentuated a face which seemed more pallid than it probably would have under normal lighting conditions. When he stopped to look at her mouth, he decided she was actually quite tanned despite the contrast of hair with complexion. But her eyes held him. Pale blue that bordered on white, they stared at him unflinchingly until he diverted his gaze downward where it locked onto her breasts. Even though her dress came to the neck, it clung tenaciously to each curve, each tiny indentation, as if it were a part of her rather than a complimentary piece of clothing. Her chest rose and fell in a slow even tempo which seemed to indicate no effort on her part to move the large breasts. She folded her hands in her lap but said nothing, apparently enjoying the perusal of her host.

Riley looked away. He had never seen such a breathtaking woman in his life. Melanie was beautiful, but in an animal, earthy fashion that also stopped people's breath. Yet, for some reason, he felt she suffered by comparison to this woman who, although exuding a sensuality that fairly screamed for attention, seemed almost fragile in her dark beauty.

"What can I do for you?" Riley asked again. What did she want? Did it have something to do with—? The article! Had she read it? Was she here to chastise him for trespassing?

Melanie entered carrying a glass of water, several ice cubes tinkling against the walls of the tumbler.

"Thank you, Melanie." She took the proffered glass regally.

Melanie blanched but said nothing.

Turning to Riley, she sipped, looking at him over rim of the glass before she lowered it. "I believe you have something that belongs to a friend of mine."

Riley shot a quick look at Melanie whose color had returned to normal. "I—I don't know if I understand you." He spoke quietly, wondering if she would sue him for trespassing or swear out a warrant for having stolen the knife or Bible.

"I think you know what I'm talking about, Mr. Larson. May I call you Riley?"

A quick shock of energy worked its strange effect on Riley's back at the manner in which she had said his name. He nodded for fear his voice wouldn't respond in the right way.

"Very well, then. You may call me Leeanah. You see, I thought I saw someone on the hillside the other night when we were —ah—"

"Just what the hell were you doing?" Riley was suddenly in command of his voice and the situation. Why beat around the bush?

She knew he had been there. Why lie? Better to find out everything about it.

"What you witnessed was a symbolic rite that is representative of the continuation of life."

Riley nodded as he slid onto a straight chair opposite the woman. Melanie took another and pulled it next to Riley's. Both looked expectant, waiting for her to continue.

"Your article, incidentally, was quite well written although not very informative. You left out the part about finding the knife and Bible. Why?"

He thought he might be blushing, but answered, "I didn't want whoever owned it to know that I'd been snooping around. Actually, the whole thing wasn't by design."

"I hope not." Her voice was throaty, yet serious.

He told her about walking Grendel and following him into the field.

"Then it really was quite by accident?" Her beautiful dark brows lifted.

"Of course. I don't normally go around eavesdropping or spying on people."

"You said, Miss Thorndyke," Melanie interjected before either could speak again, "that Riley's article was not too informative."

"It seemed to hedge around the real issue."

"I don't understand." His writer's ego was about to be offended.

She stood, looming over them. "You didn't know what you were talking about."

He nodded silently. How could he have known exactly what was going on? He never once hinted in the article at the purpose of the ritual he saw that night. How could he? He had no idea what they'd been doing. In fact, the article zeroed in more on the condition of the ruins the next morning. That much he had seen close up and had photographed.

"You said," Melanie put in, leaning back in her chair, "that what Riley saw was part of a 'continuation of life' ceremony. Just what is that?"

"I'm not at liberty to tell you."

He glanced at Melanie, hinting with his facial expression that she shouldn't ask any more questions at the moment. Instead, he stood, walking to the table. "How would one go about getting such information?"

"What would you do with it if you did obtain it, Riley?"

A chill ran down his back again when she said his name. He hoped his discomfort didn't show, since he felt he had long since passed the age of being thrilled by a beautiful woman just by looking at her or talking to her. He shrugged. "I'm not sure. What could be done with it?"

"I guess I meant something about your profession. Would you write about it? For newspapers? In a sensational way?"

Riley pondered for a moment. He might. He couldn't really say no since he did have a reporter's nose for a story, with the ability to sift chaff from fact and present a good, readable piece.

He turned, looking at her. Those icy blue eyes seemed to drill into him, penetrating his very body, coursing through his blood, seeking out the seat of his soul, attempting to analyze his honor, his integrity, his life, his future.

At length, he cleared his throat. "What are you suggesting? I can—we—Melanie and I can keep our mouths shut if that's what you're asking. If I were told not to say anything to anyone, you could sleep peacefully with the knowledge that no one would find out. At least not from us."

"I see. That was the conclusion we drew after we checked both of you out."

Melanie gasped, turning to gape at Riley. He returned her look and they both confronted Leeanah Thorndyke.

"You investigated us?" he asked softly.

"Yes. When Sebastian and I decided someone had actually seen our rite, we decided to try to find out who had been spying—or if you will, covertly watching us."

"Who's Sebastian?" Riley asked, feeling Melanie's attention fixed on him as well as on their uninvited guest.

"Sebastian was on the altar that night. He is very wealthy and had the means to find out who might have been near us at the time. The next morning, we decided to remove all evidence of our having been there. When we arrived, he went on ahead of me, saw you leaving the ruins with your dog and followed you at a distance. When we learned where you lived, the rest was easy." She smiled demurely and waited for a response from Riley.

"What did you find out?" he finally ventured.

"Not all that much. We learned that you do janitorial work at the high school and are a writer. Melanie is an artist and works part time for a doctor in town. No one seems to know that much about you—really. But considering the article you wrote, Sebastian and I felt perhaps you both might be interested in learning more about our—our group."

Melanie stepped nearer Riley and took his hand. Before he could speak, she said, "I know I'd be interested in learning. Just what does your group do?"

"It's not so much a question of what we do, but what can be done with the power we possess for those we choose to help."

"You used the word 'group.' Don't you mean 'coven' or 'cult'?" Riley was curious.

"No, I don't. A coven is made up of witches. A cult is made up of devoted followers who blindly obey their leader. Ours is a group, dedicated to furthering the careers and positions of its members. Sebastian is the prime example. Someday he may tell you about himself. I do not feel at liberty to discuss him and his background."

"What about yourself?" Melanie asked.

"I am merely Sebastian's assistant, for lack of a better word. When the ceremonies are performed, he acts the part of the sacrifice and I the priestess offering to our lord and master that which is rightfully his."

"Your lord and master?" he repeated questionly as Melanie mouthed the words.

Leenanah looked first at Riley, then at his lover, before returning her level gaze to him. "Satan," she said simply.

A death-like stillness filled the room. He seemed to feel the air crushing in on him. Granted, he didn't believe too strongly in a God to whom everyone wanted to give credit for everything, yet seemed equally at ease in calling on Him to damn anyone and everything. Conversely, he didn't give too much countenance to the opposite end of the spectrum either. Without God, he didn't worry too much about the nether world of demons and other attendant phantasms. Now, this beautiful woman standing in the middle of his living room was saying that she belonged to Satan, that Satan was her lord and master. And she didn't even bat an eye while claiming it.

The Immortal

"You actually worship Satan?" Melanie ventured, the words dry and void of feeling despite the awe they carried.

"Of course."

Melanie shook her head.

"Forgive me—if we seem slightly taken aback," he came to the rescue. "It's not every day one meets a genuine devil worshipper."

"Please, Riley. Satan is a fallen angel—not a devil, as you put it. He has great power. Power to help anyone attain whatever they want here on earth."

"What's the price?" His cynicism was aroused just a bit.

"Of course there's a price. One must be willing to lay down one's life for Satan. There are not too many so-called Christians today who would be willing to lay their lives down for their God as they did in the past. They are so close to worshipping Satan that it is frightening. I—"

"Frightening?" he interrupted, looking quickly at Melanie who seemed equally caught up in the dialogue.

"Christianity as it is 'sold' today, is so close to our beliefs, that the similarities are endless. Those who preach on television are the closest. Their motive is greed: worldly pleasures for themselves under the guise of helping people's immortal souls gain salvation. They build edifices and monuments to themselves in the name of God, bilking people out of money. It is quite shameless."

"And how does your organization differ?" Melanie wanted to know.

"We ask nothing but undying devotion to Satan and belief in our way. We don't ask for money like the preachers on television. Instead, we reward those who are faithful. Worldy gains, riches, success are for the asking, if one obeys. But our followers should not expect them to come in so many pieces of gold, so to speak. One will gain success in one's chosen field and from that will arise prestige and wealth." Her eyes blazed in a fury of zeal and enthusiasm.

"No free handouts, then?" Riley deliberately tried to lower her intensity.

"Not as such. No," she said quietly.

"Why couldn't whatever happens to someone in his chosen profession merely be coincidental if success comes along?" He frowned at his own question. It seemed too pat, too simple.

"Because it will happen in such a way that even the most thickheaded person would not be able to draw any but the correct conclusion."

Melanie nudged him. "I'd like to know more—maybe even join."

He looked at her. Why not? He'd had enough hard knocks. Why deprive himself of luxuries if they could be acquired without changing his life style. True, he hadn't worked at writing as assiduously as he should have, but that didn't mean he couldn't succeed if he tried. On the other hand, this might be the way to shortcut through a lot of waiting and gain the necessary fame needed to demand the biggest money. "I think I would, too," he finally agreed.

"Very well. We hoped you would at least want to look into it further. There will be a meeting tomorrow night. We will expect you to attend."

Riley wondered what would happen if he said he had another commitment, but decided he'd better play it straight. There might be another article in it, assuming they would give him permission to do one. He recalled what Leeanah had said earlier about sensationalism and wondered if they would object. "Where is this meeting to be held? At the old church?" He felt stupid asking—facetious—but as far as he knew that's where they met.

"No," Leeanah said, smiling. "I'll have someone pick the two of you up. If you are sincere in your desire to learn more about us, you can demonstrate your willingness by bringing with you tomorrow night the items you found and took from the church. Then you may return them to Sebastian yourselves."

His skin reacted to the way in which she said the name Sebastian. "If you want I can give them to you right now," he said, half turning away.

"No." Her tone was sharp, bringing him to a quick stop. "That isn't necessary. Tomorrow night, as I suggested. The car will be here at ten o'clock. Until then—" The words hung as she turned, her cloak flaring outward. She flipped the hood into place and opened the door for herself.

Chill November night air flowed into the room, snapping Riley and Melanie out of their trance. They watched her hurry, effortlessly striding down the path to the gate, where the Rolls-Royce waited beyond. Its rear door opened from within and she all but floated into the large automobile. Without a sound, it eased from the side of the road and drove away.

CHAPTER 5

Thursday, November 13, 10:58 P.M.

The Rolls-Royce purred along Interstate 55 toward Chicago, maintaining the legal speed limit, headlights slashing through the night. Riley and Melanie sat in the back seat, not speaking, soaking up the luxurious atmosphere of the interior. The rich smell of leather filled the passenger compartment, the soft comfortable hide-covered seats yielding to their body weight but nevertheless firm.

The chauffeur had knocked at their door precisely at ten o'clock, an hour after Melanie began a vigil at the front window for sight of the magnificent vehicle which would take them to the meeting where they would be guests of honor. At first Riley chided her good-naturedly about acting like a child, but then stopped his verbal barrage to set about checking the tiny camera he had loaded with extra-fast film.

"Why are you taking a camera, Riley?"

she had wondered aloud, seeing him fiddle with it shortly before the Rolls arrived.

"I guess I'm just going prepared. God knows what we'll run into or see tonight. I don't want to be caught with my pants down."

She chortled at the idea of Riley's pants falling around his ankles, hobbling him into virtual immobility. Though excited about the prospect of meeting more people who believed in worshipping the devil as opposed to a more conventional Judeo-Christian approach, she still wondered if perhaps they had acted too hastily. "I hope we're doing the right thing, Riley."

"This is a hell of a time to wonder, Mel."

"It's just that last night I think we were both caught up by the mystery Leeanah exuded."

"I didn't read your reaction like that when I came out of the darkroom. You were enjoying my fumbling, weren't you?"

"I can't deny that. But once she got talking about why she'd come and who she was and what she believed in, I really got interested. Didn't you?"

"Of course I did. She's a beautiful woman and her manner of speech makes her sound highly intelligent."

"What do you base that on?"

"Her choice of words, for one thing. Then, too, she seldom repeated anything, yet expressed herself in a way that made the

The Immortal

listener remember and understand."

"That makes her intelligent? You're sure it wasn't her big boobs?"

He smiled. "No. It wasn't her big boobs. Hers aren't any bigger than yours. Besides, I'm not necessarily a breast man. You know that."

"You don't think we accepted too quickly, do you?"

"What makes you say that?"

"You've got to admit it all sounded pretty far out—some of the things she said. Worshipping the devil and all."

"What about the stuff she said about TV preachers? You've said a lot of the same sort of thing yourself, Mel."

"Granted. But anybody with half a brain is going to see through those phony bastards."

"Incidentally," his tone told her a change of subject was about to take place—"what is this Sebastian's last name?"

She puckered her lips in thought. "I don't think Leeanah ever said, did she?"

Then he paused and finally nodded. "I agree. She didn't. Oh, well, we'll be introduced soon. Any sign of the car yet?"

"Uh-uh! It's as dark as my navy blue skirt out there. Wait a minute. I see headlights coming." She'd bounced off the couch and quickly closed the drapes. "I don't think we should appear too eager. Do you, Riley?"

"Considering the fact you've been waiting

by the window for over an hour I think you're probably right. Don't act too eager, Mel." He laughed, watching her run into the bathroom for a last minute check of her appearance.

She smoothed her slacks and blouse, making certain they'd not suddenly become wrinkled or unkempt. Turning the light on over the medicine cabinet mirror, she'd touched up her pale lipstick and smiled open mouthed to make sure her teeth bore no traces of excess cosmetic. Despite her red hair she had very few freckles, and those were pale and almost invisible. Her complexion, soft and creamy, both complimented and offset the impressive mane of coarse hair surrounding her triangular face.

"You coming, Mel?" he called from the living room. "Somebody's already at the front door."

"Christ Almighty, I'll be there right away," she cried loudly. "Give me a fucking minute. I don't want to go looking like a bag lady. Jesus!"

"Knock off the street language, Mel. We're going into high society tonight—I think."

She knew and understood his aversion to obscenities and cursing. Still, she didn't try to make him use her kind of vocabulary and she felt he was wrong to ask her to change in that respect. For some reason she never quite understood, she truly enjoyed yelling "fuck" as loud as she could whenever frustration seemed to be winning the battle against reason. Not that she would have done such a thing at the doctor's office or wherever she might have been assigned by Secretaries Unlimited. But it gave her a trump card to play if Riley started getting on her nerves with his "superclean" language.

"You think? This had better be a mansion or something we're going to tonight or I'm going to go after the captain of the fucking football team." She entered the living room just as the doorbell had sounded.

Riley was there to open the door for a short man decked out in a chauffeur's uniform who told him he'd been hired to take the two of them to Mr. Synn's residence.

Melanie had smiled broadly at the name and before she could comment, Riley shushed her, helped her into her coat, took her arm, and ushered her out of the living room into the November night. He carried the burnt Bible and knife in a brown paper bag, thankful he had prepared them that way once he saw the car. Both of them had at first been speechless when they got into it, its rich smells overwhelming them. They'd felt like royalty when the driver closed the sliding glass partition separating the passenger compartment from the front seat.

As they rode along the broad expanse of the Interstate, Melanie thought back to the previous night when Leeanah arrived unannounced. At first, she felt a sensation quite foreign to her: jealousy. She had actually experienced it only once or twice in her life, and when it happened, she had difficulty handling the emotion. But then, deciding to tease Riley, she quickly regained control of her feelings, which is the way she preferred that aspect of her life to remain.

It was always difficult for her to work at a full-time job because she would soon start looking for ways to improve the overall operation. Whenever there was more than one woman—herself—working in the office, trouble usually erupted because Melanie would embark on her improvements and the others would draw the conclusion that she was out to run everything—including them. But though she'd lost many jobs, she seldom had trouble finding work. Then, after meeting Riley, she decided to give all her energies over to art and signed on with Secretaries Unlimited, knowing she would be able to accept work when she wanted to and not when she had to because of someone else's whims or ideas. Ever since she moved in with Riley, she had felt totally independent and enjoyed every minute of it.

Now she tried to anticipate what their host for the evening would be like, mentally tearing off sketch sheets with crumpled up ideas of different faces and images. Glancing covertly at Riley, she saw him check the pocket of his jacket to make certain the

The Immortal

camera was ready. A little smile crossed her lips; she liked him but wasn't quite certain if she loved him. She'd been to bed with quite a few lovers since her high school days, always attracting men older than she. He was certainly no different in that department. And he was good in bed. She enjoyed everything he did to her body, reveling in the delight he created. But then, too, she was aware of being no slouch herself when it came to making love. Men had more than once commented that she'd done things to them with her mouth which few other women could ever master. And she liked those compliments—as much as she did when someone had something nice to say about her work as an artist.

A sudden thought concerning their safety bombarded her and she turned to Riley. "Do you think we'll be all right tonight?"

Grabbing her hand, he squeezed hard. "Sh-h-h-h," he admonished, nodding toward the driver.

"The glass is up," she said in a normal voice, pulling away from him.

"I know that," he whispered, "but there are intercoms in cars like this, I should think. He might be listening to everything we say."

"Well, that hasn't been much." She started slipping back into her reverie. "Besides, he said he'd been hired to bring us to this Synn guy."

"I don't think we have anything to worry

about." He patted the hand he'd squeezed.

She didn't answer, instead watching the streetlights pass by, wondering when they had gotten off the Interstate and into a residential neighborhood. Residential? She looked again. Lights from houses showed through the dark, but seemed to be half a block or farther from the street itself. When they zipped through a pool of light from an overhead road lamp, she could see wrought-iron fences standing protective guard around different estates.

"Where in Christ's name are we?" she blurted.

"Lake Forest. At least that was the exit we took. Sh-h-h."

Riley was going to be a pain in the ass, she decided, if all he was going to do was give his imitation of a leaky radiator all night.

The car slowed, and gates of intricate wrought-iron filigree swept past the windows on either sides as the Rolls-Royce turned in, advancing between stone columns that moored the gates' hinges. The automobile wound its way through tight curves up a gentle hill. When it made a full one-hundred-eighty-degree turn, they saw the mansion, poised aloofly on a small point overlooking Lake Michigan.

Melanie sucked in her breath and Riley echoed the sentiment. Lights blazed from every window. When the car stopped in the circular drive beneath a two-story portico, they prepared to get out. The chauffeur had already debarked with alacrity, gone to the back of the car and opened the door with a flourish. Riley stepped out, brown bag under his arm, offering his free hand to Melanie who took it.

She thrilled at the situation in which she found herself, pretending for a fleeting millisecond that the house was hers, the chauffeur and car were hers, and Riley was hers in a way she knew she could never possess him. They walked abreast up the few steps to the entrance and stopped. When the door opened, the striking figure of Leeanah Thorndyke, wrapped in a floor-length, white toga, stood framed in the doorway.

"Welcome. Welcome, my friends. Come in. Please, come in. Sebastian will join us in a few moments." She stepped back, gesturing without moving, for them to enter.

Melanie moved past her, smelling the expensive cologne. She sensed Riley following, but more slowly, and pictured him stopping beside the beautiful woman to inhale deeply.

"Come," Leeanah said graciously, leading the way out of the foyer toward a large double door. Overhead, a chandelier, its thousands of glass droplets reflecting the light of only a few bulbs on the interior, illuminated the entranceway. Leeanah effortlessly pushed the double doors open and stepped into a dimly lit library. "If you will be seated in here," she purred, "I'll find Sebastian and hurry him along. Make yourselves comfortable."

Turning, she left the room, which noticeably dimmed as she withdrew and the brightness of her dress was gone.

"I know I said I've investigated the occult and other scary stuff, but I'm not sure if we were all that swift in the head department coming here like this, Riley." Melanie turned to find him fiddling with the camera, the brown bag on a large reading table in the center of the room.

"I want to get some pictures. This is fantastic." He ignored her sudden concern. His eyes swept the dark paneled library that reminded him of the type of room Hollywood would have created for a murder scene in a Sherlock Holmes movie. Huge pieces of furniture, appearing to weigh hundreds of pounds, were arranged into little sitting areas where three or four people could converse quietly. Other than the large table, an oversized desk dominated the back of the room, over which the walls, lined with shelves full of books, closed in on the entire scene. A lamp on the desk created only shadows, its beam of light directed down, while a floor lamp to one side of the couch, in front of a wall of books, spilled a golden glow through its stained glass shade.

He moved near one of the walls, looking up at a panel that separated two sections of shelves. An antiquated coat of arms hung at his eye level and he quickly snapped the camera's shutter. Stepping back, he took another, advancing the film.

"Riley? Will you listen to me?" she begged in a whisper. "I think we should just apologize and get the fuck outta here. Tell him you're sorry for having spied on him and you'll never do it again. All right?"

"Uh-uh." Riley focused on the wall of bookshelves opposite the coat of arms. "We've come this far. I don't see why we should be worried at this point. They've done nothing to upset anyone. In fact, Leeanah is rather nice and friendly."

"Leave it to a male to think a black widow is really a poor misunderstood little bug," she said sarcastically.

"I hear someone coming." He thrust the camera into his pocket.

The doors swung open and Leeanah stepped in, followed by a man.

"Riley Larson and Melanie Brandt, I'd like you to meet Sebastian Synn." Quiet dignity and respect coated each word.

Riley tore his eyes from her and fixed them on their host. Melanie had begun observing him, ignoring Leeanah, the instant the doors opened.

"How do you do, my dear friends?" Synn gushed. He took both Riley's hands in his, gently shaking them, then turned to face Melanie. Repeating the gesture with her, he motioned them to be seated. They perched stiffly erect on a leather couch until their hosts sat down as well.

"I suppose I owe you an apology, Mr. Synn," Riley began. "But I had no idea as to what I should do when I found the dagger behind the Bible. You see—"

"Please, Riley, if I may call you by your first name. There is no reason for you to apologize. I will have it back and that is all that matters. It is most precious and I would surely hate to think of it being gone forever from me. I'm not sure I could live without it."

Melanie wondered about his last statement. Was he the type who always exaggerated? She hoped not. That was something she could take precious little of in the course of an acquaintance.

"I was struck by the knife's beauty," continued Riley.

"Yes. Yes, it is that, isn't it? Most beautiful," Synn murmured.

Leeanah stood and crossed the room, returning in a few minutes with a tray and four small glasses filled with an amber liquid. She offered one to each of them, took one herself, disposed of the tray and resumed her seat.

"Please, relax," urged Synn. "Leeanah has told me all about the two of you and the charming conversation you had last night. She tells me you're interested in joining my—ah—little group. Is that correct?"

After sipping his drink, Riley began speaking, referring to things spoken of the previous evening. Melanie nodded in agreement but studied the man sitting across from them in more minute detail. She tasted the drink, finding it sweet and strong, then downed half the glass and wondered about Synn's voice. It was well modulated, but throaty as if it might still be changing. Yet the impeccably groomed white hair left no doubt as to his age. She estimated him to be in his sixties, or maybe early seventies. In the half-light of the room she found it difficult to get a good look at his face, other than the profile, which appeared delicate. A fine nose complimented a slightly rounded forehead, separating his eyebrows from a peaked hairline. She could not tell what color his eyes were or if his complexion was sallow or tanned. In time she would see him in a different light, and smiled inwardly at the silly little pun she had made.

Leeanah retrieved the bottle and filled the glasses again.

On occasion, Synn diverted his gaze from Riley, who was still speaking to Melanie; she felt compelled to drop her eyes whenever that happened. But each time his look was fleeting and always redirected to Riley.

"And how do you feel about this, Melanie?" He suddenly broke into her thoughts.

At first she was flustered and wanted to scream her favorite release word, but quickly pulled herself under control. "I—well, I was interested in things concerning the occult at one time. A long time ago. But I think everyone probably has a certain curiosity to explore the opposite viewpoint of their own upbringing."

"Very well put, my dear," Synn said quietly. "All I can say, Riley, and yes, you too, my dear, is that should you join us, you will begin receiving rewards that are beyond your wildest imaginings."

Melanie looked away. She recalled hearing something like that once in college when she answered an ad that in reality was trying to get people to sell household products. The pyramid idea of getting others to do the selling for someone who was a distributor or "captain," as the man who conducted the interview referred to the position, seemed totally unrealistic. When Melanie had asked who the consumers would be, once everyone in the world was selling his product, he ended the interview and she told him to go fuck himself. That man, too, had promised income beyond her most extravagant expectations.

Riley nodded; she felt him nudge her in the ribs and quickly bobbed her head in agreement.

"Very well, then. If you are prepared to receive your first indoctrination, I am pre-

The Immortal

pared to administer it." Synn stood, as did Leeanah. Riley then jumped to his feet and Melanie followed, trying her best to maintain dignity getting off the couch. "Leeanah will show you to your room where you can change." Synn turned to leave.

Riley glanced at Melanie who returned his perplexed look. Change? What did that mean? Had she heard right or was she drunk on two small glasses of wine? Before she could say anything, Leeanah stepped forward. "You will wear robes to this first meeting. However, you are not allowed to wear anything underneath."

"Why is that?" asked Melanie before Riley could stop her.

"I really don't know," Leeanah responded, quickly adding, "Yes, I do. But you'll find out as the ceremony progresses. Fair enough?"

"Sounds good to me." Riley's voice was a bit too cheerful.

Melanie shrugged doubtfully. What would the ceremony require?

Leeanah led them, gliding up the wide staircase in the entryway that curved around to the second floor. Melanie felt relief that she wasn't drunk. When they reached a door, their hostess stopped and opened it. "In here," she said quietly. "There are two robes on the bed. You'll find hangers in the closet for what you're wearing. Please, take everything off. Wear just the robes. I'll meet you downstairs in the foyer when you're ready. I'll be changing too." Without another word, she left, closing the door with a dignified click.

"Well, there you are." Riley moved to the bed.

"Where?"

"We gotta change clothes." He picked up a robe. "No pockets, either. I guess that precludes my taking any pictures of the operation."

"I think you were a little batty to even think of bringing a camera in the first place."

He shrugged.

"What do you think your new friend would say if he knew you had that with you?"

He shrugged again as he undressed.

She opened her blouse, exposing her breasts. "Do you think he's queer?"

His eyes shot up to fix on her. "Queer? What do you mean?"

"Shit! Do I have to explain *that* to you? Didn't your folks ever tell you about anything to do with having sex with other guys?"

"That's not what I mean and you know it. What's the matter with you, anyway? You've been acting like you're really mad at me. Are you?"

Melanie slipped from her bikini panties and stood completely naked. "No. No, I'm not. I guess. I think I'm upset with this whole thing."

The Immortal

"But you're the one who was so gung ho last night. What the heck happened to make you change your mind?"

"Just the whole thing. How come they've got two robes laid out for us as if they knew we'd go along with everything? Last night when she insisted we bring the knife and book back ourselves made me wonder, too. It was like she was trying to implicate you and didn't want to let you off the hook because of your snooping."

He frowned.

"Did you notice," she continued, slipping into the smaller black robe which was trimmed in red, "how he virtually ignored me and paid all of his attention to you?"

Riley looked up. "No. No, I didn't. Did he?"

"You bet he did. It was almost as if he were tolerating my presence against his better judgment."

"Well, maybe it's because of Leeanah. She might be the superjealous type. You never know."

He shook out the robe and put it on, pulling it around him, tying the sash at the front.

"Does mine have something on the back of it?" she asked.

"Why? Does mine?"

"Yeah. Turn around." She stepped nearer Riley and looked closely at the red figure of two triangles, their points touching, and the same triangular shape that was at the butt end of the dagger's handle.

He turned and looked behind Melanie to find hers decorated with a goat's head surrounded by interlocking triangles and the letters *A. M. S. G.* in the middle of each.

After they hung their own clothing in the closet, they left the room and hurried down the wide stairway. At the bottom stood Leeanah, dressed in a robe, watching them approach. When they reached her side, she moved away, gesturing for them to follow.

The small entourage made its way along a hall opposite the library and stopped at an inconspicuous door. Leeanah opened it, holding it wide as they stepped through. Closing it behind her, she stepped around them and continued leading the way down a long flight of narrow, carpeted steps. At the bottom, they stood in a large egg-shaped room lit by black candles held in sconces positioned at regular intervals around the walls.

Adjusting her eyes to the semi-gloom, Melanie noted the three-color scheme of black, red and white. The black tiled floor was marked with a white pentagram surrounded by a double circle of white, expertly worked into the pattern to produce no sharp corners at the edges of the different colored pieces. The white walls were decorated with double triangles and knob-like triangles identical to those on the handle of the

The Immortal

dagger. She puzzled over the significance of the strange symbols. Overhead, a huge goat's head was painted in varying shades of brown, reds and whites on the arched ceiling, as if watching everyone who entered and everything that happened in the strange room.

She turned and looked behind her. On the wall was painted a goat copulating with a naked woman, while assorted demons leered at the spectcle.

"This way," Leeanah whispered.

When they stood in the center of the room, she stopped, indicating them to wait there. Across from them, opposite the stairs which they had descended, a door opened and a column of people entered, filing toward them. A small altar stood between the new arrivals and Riley and Melanie. Slowly forming a semicircle on each side, the group stopped shuffling when the initiates were completely surrounded.

Leeanah, throwing her hood back after having put it in place for a scant moment, moved around to the rear of the table-like altar. Mounting steps, she bowed deeply and picked up what looked to be the sacrificial knife Riley had returned. Opening her robe, she freed her arms, the material falling down her backside as she raised the knife over her head.

"Oh, mighty Satan! Open the folds of your wings! Accept these two poor mortal beings as your children and slaves. Make them successful in attaining their goals and give them the riches necessary to lead a *good* life. By Baphomet and Asmodeus, and all the others who fall subject to your evil will, may this be done."

The sound of a lamb or goat bleating somewhere in the shadows brought Riley's head up. Melanie's eyes searched the dark recesses of the room. They could see nothing. The same plaintive cry sounded again. Then silence fell.

Synn stepped forward from the ranks surrounding them, throwing the hood back from his head, his arms sticking through slits in the robe, the sash tied loosely across his middle. When he confronted Melanie, he reached out, untying the sash at her waist, and opened her robe.

She didn't react. For some reason, she felt completely subordinate to him, as if she had given him permission to do anything he wanted with her. And yet, in the deepest corners of her mind, she felt like rebelling when he extended a hand to stroke her breasts. His fingertips were soft, completely free of calluses, and expertly fondled Melanie's erect nipples. His other hand snaked out and down until it cupped her pubic area. She felt a gentle tingle as he touched her vulva. The sensation coursed through her body and she felt relaxed. What had he done to her? She felt as if something more than just a touch had passed between them. Perhaps there was something to Satanism after all. She had never experienced anything like this in all the years she had gone to church. But then, the priest had never felt her up during Mass, either. She fought the urge to grin.

Synn moved to Riley and opened his robe. While one hand deftly touched his chest muscles and played with his nipples, the other worked its way downward toward his penis and scrotum.

Melanie strained her eyes to the side, trying to see without turning her head. She had no idea if it was permissible for her to watch overtly or not. Still, she wanted to see if she could detect anything in Synn's hand, something that would give off a little shock of some type. She could follow the man's hand going for Riley's crotch and the thought of what she'd said earlier in the bedroom came back to haunt her. Perhaps, Synn was nothing but a homosexual looking for quick thrills.

His fingers closed on Riley's penis, holding it up and away from his lower abdomen. She saw Riley lurch when he must have felt the same shocking sensation that she had.

Then Synn stepped back and away from them.

Leeanah stared at Melanie, then at Riley. "Are you willing to give your all, your bodies, your souls, to the Lord of

Darkness?"

Synn whispered, "Answer 'yes.'"

Both hesitated for just a second. Melanie wondered just how binding this would be if in the future they decided they'd had enough of the dark side of life. Then, she chorused with Riley, "Yes."

"In the coming weeks, you will be taught how to pray to Satan, how to pay homage to Satan, how to pacify Satan, how to love Satan and all his evil works. Until then, my devout initiates," Leeanah said strongly, "you will begin to receive the benefits of your new affiliation."

Benefits? Melanie wondered if she might be referring to a group insurance policy or a pension plan or something like that. Again, she fought the urge to smile, convincing herself that such was not the case, that she and Riley would eventually find out what these benefits were.

"You shall each," Leeanah continued, "become one of us, to thrill in the presence of greatness and evil, because evil is good when applied in the proper way. Until you are fully indoctrinated, you shall study and be taught and, at the same time, share in the wealth that is ours for the taking as long as we worship almighty Satan."

Melanie looked about the room without moving her head. Why did the others remain so quiet, so impartial, so unaroused by what Leeanah was saying? Certainly, if the tenets she was spewing forth meant something, wouldn't there at least be an "amen" or "right on" from those gathered? Hoods covered their faces and she could not make out any features. Were they men or women or both? In time she would find out, surely, but just as surely her curiosity had been aroused to the fullest and she wanted to learn as much as she could.

Suddenly Melanie became aware that the others were filing back toward the door through which they had entered. Leeanah left the altar, moving toward her and Riley, while Synn ushered the others out of the chapel.

When he returned, he closed the door and locked it, hanging the key on a small peg next to the doorjamb. Riley and Melanie followed them up the steps to the main floor.

"You and your wife may go upstairs now and dress," Synn instructed.

"But we're—"

"Come on, dear," Melanie broke into Riley's offer of the truth. If they wanted to believe the two of them were man and wife, fine. Leeanah had said they'd been investigated but apparently the fact of their not being married was overlooked. Let them labor under the illusion.

"Leeanah and I will do the same," Synn went on, "and meet you at the front door. Unless you two would like to spend the night. We certainly have accomodations."

He laughed softly.

"No. I've got to be up and at 'em in the morning, Mr. Synn," Riley said jovially. "School waits for no man."

"I think you will probably be giving that aspect of your life up in the very near future, my dear Riley. And incidentally, do call me Sebastian."

"Very well, ah—Sebastian. But until I can afford it, I must get up and go stoke the fire so the little darlings won't freeze."

"I understand," Synn replied, smiling.

After they had dressed, Riley and Melanie hurried downstairs to find Synn and Leeanah waiting at the door.

"The car will take you back and I will be in touch with you very soon. Your instructions must continue now." Synn took Riley's hand in his and shook it warmly. He glanced at Melanie and stepped nearer. Embracing her, he bussed her on the cheek.

She swallowed, inhaling his exotic cologne.

"Good night, my friends." Synn opened the door.

"Good night." Melanie and Riley hurried to the Rolls-Royce parked where it had been since their arrival.

Synn and Leeanah stood on the wide porch watching the automobile glide around the driveway and out of sight as it turned down the hill.

"Well, what do you think?" Leeanah asked throatily.

The Immortal

"I believe Riley Larson is the best one you could have brought to me. He'll do very nicely. He's just what I need if I am to continue."

PART TWO

GIVE AND TAKE

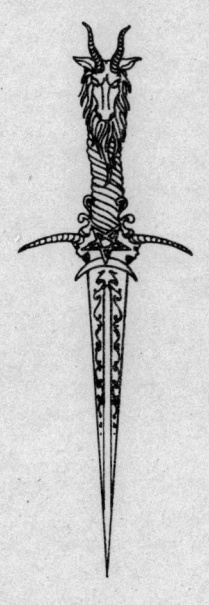

CHAPTER 6

Friday, November 14, 2:49 P.M.

Riley arose half an hour before his regular time to develop the film he had exposed the previous evening. Even though he took only a few shots and had been prevented from taking more of the brief ceremony in which he and Melanie participated, he was still eager to see the results.

After Grendel's walk, followed by a quick cup of coffee and a slice of toast, he dashed to the school to make certain the oil furnace was operating. He smiled when he thought of the fib he had told Sebastian Synn about having to *stoke* the fire. That would have meant shoveling coal, and Riley would never have taken a job which entailed something so strenuous.

By the time he checked the furnace, swept out the gymnasium and replaced several broken panes of glass, it was almost ten o'clock. Once he finished repairing two broken seat planks in the gym's visitors section, he would be free for the day. The work progressed smoothly and he was driving home by one thirty in the afternoon.

When he entered the quiet house, he found a note Melanie had left. She'd been called to work again today at the doctor's office. Deciding not to take her suggestion of making his own lunch, he went directly to the darkroom.

By two thirty, the eight-by-tens he had made of the shots snapped the night before were hung up to dry. At first he felt unhappy with his choice of pictures, considering he'd been interrupted after taking only three. But after looking at the coat of arms more carefully as well as a picture of the bookshelves, he decided his choices were perhaps not indicative of the wealth which the room exuded, but were, in themselves, more than intriguing.

When the prints were dry, he went into his office, turned on the desk lamp and grabbed his magnifying glass. The coat of arms photo happened to be lying on top of the small stack. It immediately arrested his attention and he began examining it.

The egg-shaped outline contained a rectangular shield that came to a small point along the bottom. It, in turn, bordered a diamond-shaped piece of inlay that was white with black markings. Above the outline of the shield, a goat's head, horns pointing upward, glared evilly into the camera's lens.

"That figures," he mumbled.

A banner, draped partway down either side of the shield, swept up and behind the animal's head. Faded lettering almost defied him to read the two words it formed, one on either side of the horned head.

He fumbled through the other pictures, withdrawing the close-up of the coat of arms. To a viewer's left of the goat, the letters *S-A-N* were followed by a blur, which he concluded after peering at it for several minutes, must have been another *S*. Diverting his attention to the opposite side, he made out the letters *F-I-N-E*. He wrinkled his forehead, trying desperately to recall whatever basic Latin he'd learned as a high school freshman.

"*Sans,*" he repeated softly. "*Sans* clothing. 'Without' clothing." Reporters tried to show off their knowledge every once in a while by using a well-known foreign phrase. *Sans* definitely meant "without." And *fine* was easy. It meant "end." Anyone who'd ever stayed in a theater for the finish of an Italian movie could figure that one out. "Without end." What was without end? The family line whose coat of arms bore the slogan? The goat's head? *Satan's* head?

Riley found it peculiar, and yet in keeping with what little he knew of Leeanah Thorndyke and Sebastian Synn, that the goat's head would be so prominently displayed in their home. Their home? What was their relationship? He figured in time he would probably learn, and thought it a waste of energy at present to examine different options open to them. The difference in their ages would hardly matter. Synn looked to be in his sixties or seventies while Leeanah couldn't have been much older than Melanie, if indeed she were that.

He refocused his eyes through the magnifying glass to the photo beneath. On either side near the top of the white diamond in the middle, two indistinct figures paralleled the lines. Again, he went to the close-up and found only part of one of the figures had been captured. What was there seemed to resemble an insect, surely a bug of some sort. Toward the botton, on either side of the diamond, were two sets of triangles, the tops of the bottom ones and the bottoms of the top ones touching, just as they had been on the knife handle. Riley felt his brow furrow involuntarily. Each set was centered in the middle of what looked like a darker blob. Had the triangles been red? Automatically nodding his head that they were, he picked up a marker pencil and wrote "red" next to the shapes. Their background, if he remembered correctly, had been black or very dark blue, or perhaps green. The notations were also made, lines drawn to indicate the color of each area.

As well as he could remember while the memory was fresh, he wrote in the other colors. That surrounding the white diamond with the black markings had been a deep, dark red—almost sanguine in tone. The bug-like shapes had last night escaped his notice, which had been riveted on the goat's head. The banner behind the head he recalled as brown with gold lettering.

Then he saw it. Toward the bottom of the photo showing the entire coat of arms, a druggist's mortar was represented below the point of the shield. A pestle rested within it, leaning to Riley's right. More letters were inscribed on the mortar. Moving the glass back and forth until it afforded as sharp a definition as possible, he began jotting the letters down: *S-I-C-I-T-U-R-A-D-A-S-T-R-A*. The ciphers, which were not broken into words he could understand or recognize, were meticulously printed on a band around the cup. What could they mean?

Riley stood, stretching as he moved away from the desk. "Hell," he said aloud, "what could any of it mean?"

Other than the goat's head, which he felt positive represented Satan just as it probably did on the knife, what would a couple of bugs, four triangles and some letters that seemed to form Latin words add up to? Where could he go to have them translated? He felt almost positive about *Sans fine* meaning "Without end." But what did the rest of it signify? Was it one word? Several words run together?

He crossed the room and picked up the tablet on which he had written the letters. Aimlessly walking out of his office, eyes fixed on the top page, he went to the kitchen and turned on the coffee pot.

"*Astra,*" he said aloud. "That's a car." But certainly not back in the days when coats of arms were in vogue. "Astroturf?" He shook his head. "Adastra. Could that be one word? *Sicitur adastra?*"

The telephone rang and removed the words from his mind. He went to the livingroom.

"Hello?"

"Riley. Andy McLain."

"How you doin', Andy?"

"I'm doing fine. But what are you doing?"

"How do you mean that? This instant, I'm studying a photograph I made. With my life, not too much has changed since I last saw you. I'm still working at the school—"

"That's not what I mean. Can you handle as assignment for me?"

Riley paused for two or three seconds. He didn't want to give the impression that he was eager. "Sure, I guess I can. What's cooking?"

"It's for a feature a couple of weeks down

the road. I feel that the new tax structure just passed in your district is a harbinger of things to come. Can you do a little leg work out there and maybe tie it in with a look to the future as to what might happen if the same idea is adopted by the federal and state governments?"

"I'm way ahead of you, Andy. I've already done an article not that far removed from what you just suggested. In fact, I can knock it out without much effort at all."

"Don't go too far overboard. Call your congressman and a couple of state representatives. Turn in a voucher with the article. I want to go big on this."

"Same money?"

"Same money but expenses thrown in, too. Fair enough?"

"Sure," Riley said, a sudden thought surfacing. "You said you got good response on the spook story I did. Right?"

"Yeah. All sorts of mail and telephone calls. Why?"

"Melanie and I attended a rip-off the other night and I thought an article concerning charlatans in different occult fields, like phony mediums and fortune tellers, might make a good fellow-up. What do you think?"

He was met with dead silence and pictured Andy chewing on a pencil, which he usually did while thinking.

"Gosh, I don't think so, Riley. It sounds good and all. But let's hold off on it. Maybe next September or for the Hallowe'en issue."

Riley paused for a second before he spoke. "All right."

"Hey," Andy said cheerfully. "Don't get depressed on me. You've been rejected by better editors than me. Besides, you're not the type to get selfish and want a lot of money. Or have you changed?"

"No. I haven't changed. It was just an idea, but I guess its time hasn't come yet. Ah, do you want any artwork with this article?"

"Something on the politicians you interview. How about one of the high school where you work? If that's where it's starting, people might be interested in knowing that, too."

"Okay. You said a couple of weeks. I'll get something to you in ten days."

"By the twenty-fourth. Fair enough," Andy said and hung up.

He went back to the kitchen, turned the coffee off and poured a cup. It was nice of Andy to call and make the offer. Though way down deep, Riley knew he wrote well, he wasn't ambitious when it came to driving himself like a slave to make the big bucks. If they ever happened to come his way, he'd collect them in his own style and not by hustling.

The phone rang again and he went back to the livingroom.

"Hello?"

"Riley? Andy again. I got to thinking about your proposal. I want to go for it. Make it a feature lead like the first one. Play up the fakes and phonies. Incidentally, what happened to the hundred I gave you?"

"Believe it or not, I've still got it. Want it back?"

"No. Consider it a bonus. Deal?"

"Deal." He heard Andy click off. Thoughts of Sebastian Synn suddenly filled his mind. What had he said? Something about receiving rewards beyond his and Melanie's wildest imaginings? Well, Riley had never dealt in big bucks before but within ten minutes he had given two assignments worth fifteen hundred dollars, and neither piece would take much effort to write. If he could average fifteen hundred a day for maybe three days a week, that would be a mighty comfortable living at the end of a year.

"Don't be foolish," he chastised himself. The school article came because he lived close to the system and actually worked for it. Andy had called him because of that and the fact of his story on the weird rite he had witnessed causing a bigger than normal ripple at Andy's office. If all anyone had to do to succeed was join a group like Synn's or kiss the devil's ass, there would be hardly anyone going to church and everybody would be millionaires.

Riley returned to his office after warming

his cup of coffee, planning to study the photos until Melanie arrived home.

Vicki closed her books and jumped when she looked up to find a young man sitting across from her, boldly staring.

Before she could tear her eyes away from him, he spoke. "I think you're in my English Lit class, aren't you? Werner's class? Eleven o'clock? Room—"

"I'm in that class," she said, "But I don't—" she stopped herself. Why smash the guy's ego by saying she had never noticed him before? He certainly was handsome enough. If she'd been sitting in the public library or in a restaurant, she wouldn't even have acknowledged his question. But here in the school library, with both of them carrying books and obviously students, the surroundings and scenario seemed right for her to react in a normal, healthy way. She smiled inwardly. The guy was a hunk. Black, piercing eyes, which matched his equally dark hair, were set deeply into a square face. His broad shoulders and arms looked well-muscled. Although she couldn't see his waist, she was willing to bet what she had left from the money Riley had brought last Saturday that it was narrow and he was built like a wedge.

"Yes?" he asked when she didn't continue.

"But I don't see why you waited until now to speak to me," she lied, covering up the blunder she'd almost made.

"Too busy, I guess. I'm Ed Allen. English major par excellence! Budding poet, I hope."

She turned away. Another damned writer. What was there about her that always seemed to attract this type? "That's nice," she said softly, putting her books and papers together in her briefcase.

"Why do I sense that for some reason you're suddenly turned off to me or something about me?" He stared levelly at her.

"It's nothing about you, Mr. Allen." She spoke brusquely.

"Call me Ed. Edward Arthur Allen the Third. But call me Ed, please?"

Vicki caught her breath. Edward Arthur Allen? The Third? Could he belong to *the* Edward Arthur Allen family? The multimillionaire financier? Raising her eyes to find him grinning broadly at her, she blushed and dropped them again.

"The same," he said, accustomed to having his name open doors and bring recognition from the most stubborn people.

"Well, Mr. Allen," Vicki decided she had to do something or succumb to his handsomeness—"if you look at me closely, you'll see I'm a few years ahead of you. Maybe not in college but in life and living, and damn it— I hate to say it—age."

He laughed softly, standing when she did, and moved around the table. Grabbing for her coat, he held it for her. "Hey, call me Ed.

What difference could a couple of years make? Besides, from where I stand, anyone who is in college is a peer and peers should be acquainted. Don't you think—ah, I'm afraid I didn't get your name."

She turned to face him, only to find his face scant inches from hers. Fumbling with her buttons, she covertly observed him. Nineteen. Maybe twenty but certainly no older. She was twenty-nine. The idea of being picked up by a guy of nineteen was ridiculous.

"Hey," he protested, "I'm not asking you to marry me or date me or anything. I haven't even asked you to have a cup of coffee, which was my intention all along. What do you say? How could a cup of coffee be misconstrued as anything other than what it is, for crying out loud?" When he grabbed his heart and faked a deep sob, she burst out laughing.

"One cup of coffee. All right? No strings. Just coffee."

"If I told you my intentions were strictly dishonorable, would you still consider?" He leered and took her briefcase.

"Are you always this crazy?"

"Only when I'm awake. Usually I just lie in bed and snore—if I'm alone, that is."

Vicki stopped at the thinly veiled suggestion. "I'll take your word for it." She continued walking, slipping her hand through the arm he offered to her.

The Immortal

* * *

When Melanie entered, her open-mouthed smile brightened the living room though the only light splashed in through the open door of Riley's office.

"You'll never guess what happened to me today!" she cried excitedly, taking her coat off and hanging it in the closet near the front entrance.

"Don't tell me," he called from the other room. "Let me guess. The doctor dropped to the floor with a heart attack right in the middle of an emergency and you took over, saving both the patient and the doctor. Right?"

"That's funny. Real funny. Nothing like that at all. However, it involves the doctor."

"If he wants to take you on an ocean cruise while his wife stays at home with the kids, don't go, Mel. He's after your *bod*. Believe me!" He crossed the living room to her and they embraced.

"Wrong again. Don't ever go on a TV quiz program. You'd embarrass yourself. Doctor Cushing wants me to do oil portraits of his wife and three children. Three hundred bucks apiece. Imagine that, Riley. Twelve hundred bucks worth of commissions. In one day. From one person. Woweee!"

He frowned.

"Judas Priest," she snarled. "Just becuase I get a fucking chance to make some money, you get pissed off. What's wrong?"

Riley turned away. "Did you think about

Synn at any time today, and what he said last night?"

Melanie sobered, shaking her head. "I was too occupied. I got called in late and was busier than a one-armed paper hanger all day. Then tonight, right before I left, the doctor said he wanted to talk with me in his office. At first I thought he was going to can me or tell me to forget coming back, that I was totally imcompetent. But then, he laid the commissions on me. Why? Why should I have been thinking about Synn and last—" She stopped. A querulous look clouded her face. "Oh, my God!" she finally managed.

"I didn't think of it either until just a little while ago—when Andy called and offered fifteen hundred skins for two articles he assigned to me. Between us, that makes twenty-seven hundred dollars in one day. A little unreal, don't you think?"

"Jesus Christ! Riley, do you think there's something to this Synn guy and what he said?"

"It sure seems a little more than coincidental. I tried to rationalize it but now that pretty much the same sort of thing happened to you, I believe we'd better back off and take a good hard look at the whole business."

"Yeah. Yeah. I think you're right." She was obviously upset by the day's strange turn of events. "You know, one or the other would be good news. Both are great news.

The Immortal

But when I think of last night, a chill runs up and down my back."

"I know what you mean." Then the two of them prepared their evening meal in silence.

After they finished the dishes, it was Melanie who spoke first. "The one thing that sorta bugs me is all the fucking around I did with different religions and shit when I was going to college. Christ, I even tried transcendental meditation. I looked into religions that were centered on drugs, blowing my mind while screaming for help from some sonofabitch who just stood there making notes about my reactions. I even went with a couple of stargazers who wanted to take me to some farm in Iowa, no less, where I could feed the hogs, watch them procreate and sell flowers in a dump called Dubuque."

"What's your point?"

"This is the only system that ever seemed to give results overnight. I wonder if Synn gives trading stamps as well. The bastard could clean up."

"I want to show you something." He stood and left the room, returning with the photos he had pored over most of the afternoon. "What do you make of these?" He handed her the pictures and the magnifying glass.

Melanie examined them quietly, recalling how upset she'd been when he began taking them, breathing a sigh of relief when he had to stop as Leeanah returned with Sebastian Synn in tow. After looking at each one in detail several times and for most of fifteen minutes, she laid them aside. "So?"

"So, can you make out the Latin?"

She picked up the photo that showed the complete coat of arms. "I guess the top one means '*without end.*'"

"'Hell, I figured that one out by myself." He offered her the piece of paper on which he had written the letters printed on the mortar.

She studied them for several minutes. After checking with the photograph, she looked up. "I thought maybe you had fucked up and didn't leave spaces between the words, but I see from the picture that they sort of run together. Maybe they're more separated on the actual item and the angle of the photo makes them look run together."

Riley coughed. "You might have a point there. Where could I find information about coats of arms? Doesn't every sign mean something? Isn't there a heraldic code whereby one can understand what everything signifies?"

Melanie shook her head. "Damned if I know. Why don't you try the library?"

"Hawthorne? You've got to be kidding. They'd think a coat of arms was a jacket for an octopus. I mean an expert. I don't want guess work. I want the answers and right answers at that." He smacked the photos in her hand with the backs of his fingers.

"Why? What do you think it means?"

The Immortal

"I don't know. All I do know is that a guy who has this thing hanging in his home told us he worships Satan and can arrange just about anything. Last night he virtually promised us riches, and today we've got commissions for twenty-seven hundred dollars that didn't exist yesterday. We saw his sacrificial knife up close, which I took pictures of, though he doesn't know it. The goat's head on it and one of the coat of arms are identical."

"What's this other stuff?" Melanie, looking again at the picture, pointed to the bug-like figures and triangles. "What's the significance of these? I didn't look that closely last night. You've written in here that the triangles are red. Were they?"

"No. I just made that up because I thought it would lend a little mystery to the overall situation. Good Lord, Mel, stop and think about it. This guy seems to know a hell of a lot more than anyone else I've ever encountered. How about you?"

She nodded slowly. "It does seem that way. If he'd asked us for money, I'd say he was in it for the dough gotten from people like us."

"That's just it. What *is* his angle?"

Melanie shrugged. "Does he have to have one?"

"It usually goes with the territory."

She bit her lip. "Do you think he wants our souls for Satan?"

Riley shook his head. "That goes with the assumption we've got souls. Is that all you can think of?"

"Right at the moment, yes!"

"What do we do when and if we hear from him again?"

"I rather like the idea of having people coming to me with cash in their hands and asking me to paint pictures for them. Like it? Hell, I love it. I think I want to find out more about what it is he has to offer. How about you?"

Before Riley could answer, the phone rang, splitting the silence between them. "Hello?"

"Riley?" the throaty voice asked.

"Yes."

"This is Leeanah Thorndyke. Sebastian would like to see you and Melanie tomorrow night at ten o'clock. Is that possible?"

He made a face at Melanie, waving his free arm and hand up and down. "Let me check with Mel," he answered matter-of-factly, clamping his hand over the mouthpiece. "It's the boogey man's girlfriend. He wants us there tomorrow night at ten. What do we do?"

"We go." She didn't hesitate.

Riley brought the phone back to his ear. "That sounds good to us, Leeanah." His tone was even. "I'm not certain if I can find the place, though."

"Don't worry about that. We'll send a car to pick you up. Until then, *ciao!*"

"Yeah, 'bye." He spoke into a dead phone. She'd already hung up.

Melanie looked at him half expecting to see him smile, but instead found a frown creasing his face. "What's wrong, Riley?"

He didn't answer right away. "I guess I just never saw myself as the type who would deal in the black arts to further myself."

"Is that what we're doing?"

"At this juncture, I'd say that's exactly what we're doing. How do you feel?"

"Horny. Want to make love to me, Doctor Faust?"

He smiled, then laughed. "Sure, why not?"

Taking her extended hand, Riley led her toward the bedroom, trying at the same time to erase the thoughts of Sebastian Synn from his mind.

CHAPTER 7

Saturday, November 15, 9:51 P.M.

Vicki could not understand exactly how it had happened. Complexities had followed her simple date with Ed. They spun through her head in turn as she tried concentrating on her orgasm, which was about to explode. The circumstances which led to going to bed with Edward Arthur Allen the Third hammered at her, interrupting her enthrallment.

After they drank four cups of coffee yesterday afternoon, he had suggested they eat, which they did, and that he take her home, which he did, agreeing to leave only when she consented to help him with his English Literature assignment the following night. He arrived at eight o'clock, briefcase in one hand, a bottle of Beaujolais Nouveau in the other.

They began the evening by opening their books, quickly laying them aside after opening the wine.

Ed increased his frenzied pounding on her

lower body and she retaliated with thrusts of her own. He was young. And he was good in bed. He was too young for Vicki but she didn't care about that at the moment. Grasping at shreds of thoughts and memories concerning his seduction of her, she smiled at the symphony of sensations building within her. He never would have succeeded in bedding her if she had not suddenly become aware of her own needs. She had not been with a man since leaving Riley, much too long to go without enjoying that special something men possessed. His kisses had aroused an animalistic need buried within her and she had responded savagely, taking both Ed and herself off guard for a moment. Quickly recovering, they had practically run to the bed, yanking off their clothes, throwing themselves into each other's arms as they fell sideways on top of the bedspread.

It hadn't taken long for Vicki's instincts to react, and before he had touched her love mound, she was wet and ready for him. Now, in seconds, it would end and she would spiral back to an acceptable, normal level of being. She wanted him more and more. Perhaps this was only the beginning.

Suddenly, Ed's body tensed, his muscles tightening as he erupted inside her. Then her own explosion tore her apart and she clung to him, desperate in her attempt to make every sensation of that second last for an eternity.

Several minutes later, he raised himself to find her weeping. "Wha—what's wrong, Vicki? Did I hurt you?" His concern was genuine, the arrogant pretension of youth gone from his voice.

Shaking her head, she said nothing, simply extending her arms to him.

He lay back on top of her, unmindful of the dampness between them, and hugged her. "Are you all right?"

"Oh, yes, Ed. Yes. Everything is all so right," she murmured and began nibbling his ear.

Saturday, November 15, 10:27 P.M.

The Rolls-Royce glided toward the Chicago skyline, its destination to the north where most of the bright lights would be avoided. In the back seat, isolated from the hired driver by the glass partition, Riley and Melanie continued their bubbling conversation about the last two days. Yesterday's gains had been added to by an offer of a full-time job on the Hawthorne News wherein Riley would be his own boss, make his own hours and working terms for $18,000 a year, and still be able to do all the freelancing he chose. That amount doubled the income he now made with the school system, and from the manner in which the publisher had talked, the time involved wouldn't be much different working for the News than by being a part-time janitor.

Melanie on the other hand, had had three telephone calls from women referred to her by Doctor Cushing's wife, Phyllis. Neither Melanie nor Riley could believe what was happening to them—the sudden influx of money into their lives. Not that it had been enough to make a dent in the national debt, but to them, the unexpected promise of over twenty thousand dollars within one day's time, was a miracle of sorts.

They suddenly had become aware of the telephone. Every time it rang, both ran to answer it. When an insurance man called, having picked their number at random from the city directory where it was listed, they both became giddy with laughter. The incident had brought them back to earth, where they firmly set both feet, promising they would not become wasteful with their newfound ability to make money.

"How long do you suppose it will be before we can afford a car like this?" Melanie ran a hand over the leather armrest between them.

Riley turned his head a bit to look at her. Forty-eight hours before, their arrangement still had been working. Now, all at once, everything seemed to be changing. Where he and Melanie had been content to sleep together and satisfy each other's physical needs, glad to be independent in every other way, they suddenly found themselves greedily totalling up the new financial figures. He hoped it was only a happy game and nothing more. He'd grown quite used to being alone, as much as Melanie's presence allowed him to believe that. A thought crossed his mind. Might she be planning a more involved relationship—like the one they'd been heading toward when she first moved in with him? He hoped not. Since Vicki and he had split, he'd come to realize how marriage seemed to ruin so many good friendships. He never wanted to lose Melanie as a friend. Still, he didn't want to feel obligated, to have to ask her if he could go to the bathroom, or change shirts, or do anything at all—yes, even bed down with another woman if he chose. He knew that primarily it had been her idea for each of them to go their separate ways emotionally, but now she was beginning to talk in terms of 'we' and 'affording' and expensive things like the rented Rolls-Royce in which they were being taken to their benefactor.

Was he really their benefactor? Was Synn directly or indirectly responsible for the good fortune that had spilled all over them in the last day or two? It seemed strange that after he promised them riches beyond their wildest dreams, they both would suddenly have more money rolling in than either of them dreamed possible. And neither had done anything much to achieve it. True, Riley had suggested to Andy the idea for a follow-up article on phony mediums, but Andy had at first rejected it out of hand. Then, within a few ticks of the clock, he had called back saying to go ahead, making it a double assignment. Riley shook his head. What was this Synn guy capable of? What would he do for someone he really knew and liked? After all, the two of them had just met the man and offers already exceeded twenty thousand dollars. What would tomorrow bring?

"I'm sorry, Mel," he said. "What did you say about the car?"

"I was just thinking out loud. Do you think we'll ever own something like this?" She ran her hand over the leather again. "Christ, it even feels expensive."

"And it is expensive. We think we've had a lot of money thrown our way and still it would barely buy the motor for this heap. Or maybe the four fenders and back seat." He shrugged. "I don't know if either one of us will ever get much more than we've been offered. Beside, money tends to spoil people. It changes them."

"Fuck," she whispered. "I'll take a chance on changing. If I've got money and somebody doesn't like it, they can go piss up a rope! I'll find new friends. Friends who can appreciate me the way I want to be."

He smiled ruefully. "See what I mean?"

"Shit!" She turned away and stared out the window.

His thoughts went back to Sebastian Synn, who seemed to take care of his friends. What, however, would he do to a nasty neighbor who, in Synn's estimation, crossed him in some way? Riley thought he might be growing a bit paranoid, attributing to anyone the ability to produce good or evil spells. For all he knew, Synn had nothing to do with anything that happened and would be as surprised and elated as they at the good fortune befalling them.

The Rolls-Royce made the one-hundred-eighty-degree turn and again the lights of Synn's mansion merrily beckoned the automobile forward. The chauffeur jumped from the driver's seat and hurried around to the right side, ushering them out of the passenger compartment.

Before Riley could ring the bell, the door swung open and Leeanah greeted them. "Good evening, Riley. Good evening, Melanie. How delightful to see the both of you again." She stepped back, offering the hospitality of the house, allowing them the freedom to enter.

After taking their coats and hanging them in a closet, she led them to the library. Once their eyes had adjusted to the gloom that greeted them, they saw Sebastian Synn seated at the large desk toward the rear of the room.

Melanie touched Riley's arm and they faced each other with questioning expressions. Redirecting their attention to Synn, they hesitated before approaching the desk.

He didn't seem to notice their presence, including that of Leeanah. The telephone he held bobbed back and forth. He spoke quietly, yet the pink tone of his skin betrayed his excitement about something, perhaps even anger, though his face seemed completely unemotional. After several long, embarrassing minutes, he hung up and stared at the top of his desk.

"He threatened me." The words came softly, a certain evil quality hanging on each of them.

"He didn't," Leeanah commiserated with him evenly, stepping around the couple to hurry to the desk.

"Oh, but he did. Doesn't he realize he's signed his own—"

"Riley and Melanie are here, Sebastian," she broke in.

"Oh, dear." Synn stood, then moved around the desk, rushing toward them, arms extended. "My friends. How are you this evening?"

"Fine," Riley said, accepting the warm handshake.

"Melanie. Sweet Melanie," he cooed, embracing her.

"I hope you forgive my inhospitality. I should have been finished with that call long before you arrived. I'm absolutely shameless as a host. Please forgive me."

"There's nothing to forgive, Mr. Synn," Riley was on his best behavior.

"Remember—Sebastian," Synn reminded him and looked to Melanie to assure her that she too was to be on a first name basis with him.

Leeanah moved two chairs opposite the couch. Synn took Riley by one arm and Melanie by the other, showing them to the settee. Once they were seated, he and Leeanah took the chairs.

"Tell me," he said, "how have things been going since last we saw one another?"

Riley glanced at Melanie before fixing his eyes on their white-haired host. "I don't know quite where to begin."

After their good news had been shared, Synn sat back, a satisfied grin brightening his face.

Riley studied him for several minutes. "You knew, didn't you? You had something if not everything to do with this—these things that have happened to us. Right?"

Synn held one hand up, palm facing the couple on the couch. "Not really. It's just that you have received a sample of things to come. Once you two have completely given yourselves to Satan, totally dedicated your every breath of life to him, then—then things will truly begin to happen. What has happened to you in the last day or two has been

good but hardly anything to rave about.
Wait. Study. Give yourselves to *him* and the
world will be yours."

"But at what price?" Riley asked, feeling
Melanie's hand restraining his arm as he sat
forward.

"Price? There is no price other than your
unwavering devotion to the Prince of Darkness."

"Couldn't that be quite a price? Selling
one's soul to the devil?"

Synn laughed. "Do you really think you
have a soul, Riley?"

Riley could feel his face reddening. How
many times had he questioned the idea
himself? He peered into Synn's eyes. Instead
of finding anger or hostility or even indifference, he felt he detected a warmth, a
friendliness. Certainly there was depth to
this man's personality which couldn't be
plumbed by one quick glimpse or even
extended study.

"I'm sorry, Sebastian," Riley said. "I
guess I'm too pragmatic when it comes to
receiving things for nothing."

"But is it for nothing? Don't you have to
write articles for your friend—ah, what did
you say his name is?"

"Andy." Riley preferred to keep his
friend's last name out of the conversation, at
least for the time being. He had almost let it
slip earlier when telling about everything
that had happened, but thought better of it

then as now, especially since Sebastian had asked for it.

"Yes, Andy," Synn repeated the name softly. "But you do have to produce to get money—as does Melanie if she wants to receive her commissions. Am I not right, my dear?" He turned his attention to her.

She nodded but elected to say nothing.

Leeanah sat forward. "Do you think we should share with Riley and Melanie the incident on the telephone?"

"I was just about to, my dear," Synn agreed, turning to acknowledge her. "The conversation I was just finishing when you two arrived, was with a rival of sorts. I guess that might be the proper way to identify him. Collingsworth. Judd Collingsworth is a homosexual who dabbles in the black arts. He is a charlatan and a fake. His boyfriend had been introduced to me a year ago, but learned of Collingsworth quite by accident, going to him when he discovered they had sexual aberrations in common and deviate personalities to match. At any rate, the two of them are attempting blackmail by threatening to expose me to the authorities. They want money and goods *and* my absence from Chicago."

Leeanah reached out, taking his hand, squeezing it in a reassuring manner.

"Thank you, my dear," he whispered.

"What are you going to do, Sebastian?" Melanie asked when an uncomfortable silence followed. So a couple of homosexuals were trying to get a little extra dough by blackmail. She looked up to stare at Synn. "Why don't you just report them to the police and have them arrested?"

"I have no proof. Besides, I prefer dealing with them in my own way." He scrutinized her face for a long time before diverting his attention to Riley. Then, ignoring her, he inquired, "Would *you* be willing to help me?"

Riley shot a quick glance at Melanie whose eyes remained fixed on Synn. "What kind of help?"

"Actually it would be most enjoyable from your standpoint. But it would be the most powerful assistance anyone could give me at this time."

"What would I have to do?" Riley was quietly uneasy.

Melanie studied Synn, expecting him to ask Riley to rub the faggots out.

Instead, Synn turned his attention directly to her. "Are you the jealous type, Melanie?"

She swallowed and looked at Riley, not taking her eyes from him. "I don't know exactly what you mean by jealous. If you mean where Riley is concerned, I can honestly say I don't own him and he doesn't own me. We can do pretty much whatever we want to do without explaining anything. Just—"

"That's excellent," Synn chortled. "I

The Immortal

thought from the first moment I met you two that you were totally honest with each other and I was absolutely correct." He turned to Leeanah, who stood.

She smiled at Riley, holding her hand out to him. He took it and Synn did the same to Melanie. When the four of them stood facing each other, Leeanah took Synn's free hand and motioned for Melanie to take Riley's. Once they had formed a small circle with their joined hands, Leeanah closed her eyes.

"Oh, Prince of Evil, witness that we are joined as one to form a coalition against those who would harm you through Sebastian. In what we are about to do, help us, so that it is the strongest remedy we can invoke. We act in your name. We live in your name."

Melanie had automatically bowed her head when Leeanah began speaking, and now looked up to see Synn and Riley with theirs bowed like Leeanah's. Wondering if any of them would have to die in his name, she lowered hers again.

"We will, with your help, Riley," Leeanah continued, "perform a rite—a great rite—and Sebastian will be given the power and strength necessary to fight those two."

Melanie coughed quietly, clearing her throat.

"And you, sweet Melanie, will be given the opportunity to witness this while Riley and I perform."

"Come," Synn ordered complacently. "We will prepare to go to the chapel." He led them from the library, up the wide, spiraling staircase to the second floor room where they'd been taken on their first visit.

When everyone had dressed in robes, the four met in the hallway and Synn led the small entourage back down the steps to the first floor, through the foyer and to the out-of-the-way door in the rear corridor.

Once they stood in the room at the bottom of the steps, Riley's eyes flitted over the curved walls. Egg-shaped. Did that fact tie into the egg-shaped coat of arms? The thought of the picture he had sent to the library of the University of Chicago in an effort to learn more of its heraldic history, crashed into his mind. Would Synn know that? Could he find out that sort of thing? What would the consequences be if he did learn that Riley had taken pictures before meeting him and sent them to an expert in the field of heraldry?

Riley wiped away the thought. Suppose either of his hosts could read minds. Instead he fixed his attention on the altar before which they stood. Behind it he could see Synn moving toward the one visible door, which he unlocked, and left the chapel. After several minutes, he returned, a group of hooded people following him subserviently.

Unable to see any of the newcomer's faces, Riley eyed the table and the items resting upon it. To one side, the gold-handled dagger lay pointing toward the far edge of the altar. Directly in front of him, a golden plate engraved with a pentagram and other esoteric symbols, lay in the center. Opposite the knife and next to the plate, a length of knotted cord coiled around a short chalice. Black candles resting in golden holders graced the ends of the altar, three to each side. Off to his right, he saw a blood-red cloth covering something apparently only a few inches in length. Certain the pentagram on the plate matched the white one on the floor, he stopped taking note of his surroundings, fixing his attention on Leeanah and Synn, both of whom stood on the far side.

"We are about to begin," Leeanah said directly to Riley and Melanie, ignoring the rest of the coterie standing behind them. "When I ask you to join me, please do so. Melanie, you will cooperate by *not* interfering in anything that happens from this point on. Do you both understand?"

Riley felt Melanie's quick glance toward him, but did nothing other than nod. Melanie followed suit and an awful silence descended on the small group.

"Concentrate with me," Leeanah commanded.

Riley watched Synn and Leeanah close their eyes. He turned to Melanie and shrugged, wondering what was being concentrated on, and thought of the last two days. If this was what brought about money so easily, perhaps it was best to cooperate. Maybe tomorrow *would* bring him the means to buy a Rolls-Royce or be independently wealthy.

After what seemed an endless time, Leeanah spoke again and Riley opened his eyes. "Oh, Lord of Darkness and Evil," she intoned, "help me in this ritual. Make me humble enough to obey you and wise enough to accept your rewards. Help my partner in this ritual as well. When I receive the cord, it is for him and me. Between us we shall make a sign you will accept."

Synn picked up the knotted coil and turned to Leeanah who was untying her robe. As it dropped from her body, Riley gasped at her breasts. Taut, standing erect, they barely jiggled when she turned her back to Synn. He wanted to shout a warning when Synn raised his arm and brought the knotted cord down across Leeanah's backside. She didn't whimper or make any sound as the whipping went on. Turning her front to Synn, the flagellation continued.

When it stopped, Riley breathed a sigh of relief. What a shame. And what a stupid thing to do—whip a beautiful body like that. Even more stupid was having a body like that and subjecting it to any type of punishment. He looked closely at Leeanah and saw no welts, just a pink glow which hadn't been there before.

The Immortal

A soft shuffling brought his attention to the people behind him. Melanie turned enough to see what was happening. Their hands joined, the people were moving about the altar in a circle, dancing backwards. *Widdershins!* When he turned to face the altar, Synn was binding Leeanah's hands and arms behind her.

Riley felt a twinge in his groin. He was being aroused by Leeanah's nudity now that she was bound, helpless. He wondered if perhaps he was capable of strange sexual practices—an idea he had never before entertained. Maybe he'd explore it with Melanie.

The rope tied securely, Synn brought it up around her neck and left a piece dangling in front. Picking it up, he led Leeanah around the altar to where Riley and Melanie stood.

The dancers stopped.

"Baphomet! Elohim! Satan! Hear me! Grant our wishes this night and make our ritual a pleasing one to you and us!" He stopped in front of Melanie; Leeanah stood before Riley. "Riley," he said quietly, "take off your robe."

"What?"

"Take off your robe," Leeanah whispered.

"But—"

"You said you would help. Take off your robe." Leeanah fixed an icy blue stare on him.

Riley wondered how aroused he was. His penis jerked spasmodically. If he were fully aroused, his penis standing erect, he would be embarrassed. Melanie would be embarrassed, and probably Synn and Leeanah would never speak to him again. He dropped his eyes which locked on Leeanah's pubic area.

Slowly his hands came to the sash and pulled it. The robe fell open. He slipped out of the sleeves, not daring to look down.

"That's fine. Good," Synn approved. "Very nice."

"Wonderful," Leeanah whispered.

Riley stared at them. They were both gazing at his groin, his manhood erect in front of him.

"Follow us, Riley," Synn said and led Leeanah back to the altar. "As I say a prayer and create the necessary talisman, you and Leeanah will copulate, focusing that energy into a cone of power that will allow me to seek justice against my adversaries. Do you understand?"

Riley nodded, glancing at Melanie whose face reflected her fascination with the whole epic ritual and her lover's expected copulation with another woman.

Leeanah turned her back to Riley and told him to undo the knots. When she was free, she lay down on the altar and held out her arms to Riley, who climbed up and dropped to his knees. Her legs spread, he forced his erection inside her body, amazed at her tightness. Slowly, his motion met with hers and

The Immortal

they pumped in unison, their breaths coming in short gasps. Somewhere nearby, he sensed Melanie's presence. Would she be angry? Then, all too soon, it ended. Riley felt himself withering, dying within Leeanah's body. When he tried to withdraw, her arms around his neck held him firmly.

"Not yet," she whispered. "When Sebastian finishes, then we will part."

He nodded, holding his breath when her vaginal muscles began contracting and relaxing in a pumping rhythm of their own. He felt himself being aroused again, figuring he could go for most of a night with somone like Leeanah.

"Satan," Synn intoned solemnly.

The people answered in monotone, "Satan."

"Hail!"

"Hail!"

Synn stopped for a moment, dropping something into the chalice.

"Now," Leeanah said, pushing Riley away.

He withdrew and suddenly felt cold, the room's chill first making itself known to him. She followed him off the table, rubbing against him as they stood next to the altar.

"Elohim," Synn said loudly.

"Elohim," the dancers responded, shuffling backward again.

"Baphomet."

"Baphomet." They increased their tempo, exhibiting for the first time a degree of emotion.

"Arehail!" Synn screamed, singsonging the word in a sudden frenzy.

"Arehail!" the dancers shouted, mimicking the song, and came to a dead stop.

Silence flowed in to fill the room once the echo of the brief litany subsided.

Leeanah circled one arm around Riley's waist, pulling him nearer the altar. The people moved in closer, bringing Melanie with them. When the gathering surrounded the table, Synn raised his other arm to grasp the haft of the dagger with both hands. In a slow arc he brought it down toward the chalice.

Riley leaned forward, straining to see what was in the cup. It looked like a couple of small white figures. Wax figures. The blood-red cloth caught his attention and he noticed that it was now flat. The figures in the chalice must have been under it.

Leeanah reached for the cup, dumping the waxen dolls onto the surface of the altar. Synn continued his downward curve, the dagger slicing through the air until it hovered over the images' heads. After a second of hesitation, he plunged the point into one.

Raising his arms, he repeated the gesture with the second wax head. Moving them until they were side by side, Synn placed the sharp edge of the blade over the necks of the dolls and cried out, "*Now!*"

The Immortal

The heads, sliced cleanly from the bodies, rolled a few inches away. Not a sound could be heard in the room. Riley saw each person's attention riveted on the decapitated waxen figures.

A trickle of blood dribbled from the stump of each neck.

CHAPTER 8

Sunday, November 16, 2:53 A.M.

"You asleep?" Riley asked softly.

Melanie stirred, rolling over to face him. "Sort of. I guess I was dozing off. Can't you sleep?"

"I think I'll be able to when I put my mind to it. It's just that I was kicking around everything that happened."

"Tonight?"

"Yeah."

"So tell me, Riley. Just how was Leeanah?" The mood and timbre of her voice seemed light, almost carefree. The manner in which she asked the question showed she was not jealous, nor had she even entertained the thought of envy or insecurity or even paranoia where the other woman was concerned.

"You really want to know?" He did his best to duplicate the lightness in her voice.

"Not really." She sat up, reached out, and turned on the nightstand light. Instantly, shadows clung to the bureau, to the wooden valet where Riley's pants hung, his shirt draped across the form, to the chair at the foot of the bed. "If having had sex with her bothers you, don't think about it. I'm not jealous. You know that."

He reached out, stroking the back of her hand. "I know."

"Then what's bothering you?"

"The whole of the thing. Do you think that was really blood that came out of the dolls?"

Melanie shrugged. "I rather doubt it. If you believe it, I think you might be giving too much credence to Synn's powers."

"Could you see any fluid inside the figures before he chopped the heads off?"

Lips puckered in thought, she pictured the scene for an instant and shook her head. "I don't recall seeing any. If there had been, we should have seen the white bodies get even whiter when the stuff drained."

He nodded. The red liquid had just materialized at the place where the heads had been. How could Synn have done that? An illusion? A magician's trick? A little sleight of hand to impress the novices into accepting his beliefs more readily? It might have worked for some but not for Riley. Or Melanie. In no way would they fall for theatrical tricks of Synn's intentions. Too bad, too. He sort of liked the guy even though he didn't know much about him.

The idea of their monetary gains over the

last few days came back to bang at his mind. Still, Synn didn't claim he'd engineered any of it. Too modest? Riley doubted that. Sebastian Synn struck him as the type of person who would brag about the slightest accomplishment—no matter how small or insignificant.

"How do you think he did it?" Melanie wanted to know.

"You've got me. I'm sure if we'd pressed him, he'd have told us it was actually blood from the victims he was concentrating on. Wouldn't that have been cute?"

"Are you going to ask him?"

"Ask him? Ask him what? 'Hey, Sebastian, old buddy? Did you rub out those two nerds who were bugging you?' I rather doubt he would admit or deny it—either way."

"You're probably right. Are you going to go back?"

Riley didn't answer immediately. An idea had been forming in the back of his mind. He had to have four hundred fifty dollars for Vicki every two weeks. That was nine hundred bucks a month. Thus far he had not had too much of a problem putting that amount together—although it irked him when he had to hand it over to her. She was slated to graduate in a year and a half. Eighteen months and he'd be free. He had calculated the total at sixteen thousand two hundred dollars. What he would like to do with his newfound influx of big dollars, was to lay aside the necessary amount of his obligation to Vicki and then get on with his own life. But would that be possible if he severed relations with Synn?

"I guess," he said after several minutes of consideration, "I'll have to if I'm going to be a big success as a writer. What about you?"

"Hey." She poked him in the ribs with her elbow. "I didn't get laid tonight in front of a bunch of people. I can go back and hold my head up high."

He smiled. "What about those others? Who do you suppose they are under those hoods?"

"Yeah. I was sort of wondering about them, too."

"How come they were right there when Synn needed them?"

"You're starting to sound like a character in a horror movie or something. Synn knew we were coming. More than likely he arranged for them to be there at the appointed time."

"But suppose we'd balked?"

"Balked? Balked at what? If we hadn't shown up or agreed to go ahead with the— the—the ritual, I suppose he would have screwed Leeanah himself or had one of the others do it while he played with his dolls."

"Uh-huh," Riley agreed. "That makes sense—I guess."

"But you're not convinced, are you?"

"Well, they were there the last time, too.

Both times, he went to that door and just let them in. Like they were holed up back there waiting to be called."

"That's silly. The doorway probably leads to an outside entrance that the members or whatever they're called, use. That's a pretty spiffy house. I know I wouldn't want people tracking through it, messing it up, if it were mine."

"You're probably right." He leaned over to kiss her goodnight.

She turned out the light just as the telephone rang and in the same motion clicked in back on.

"Who the heck do you think that is?" Riley was peeved.

"Why don't you answer it and then we can go to sleep. I know I don't have to work tomorrow, but I don't want to sit up all night either. What the hell time is it?"

He slipped into a robe as the phone continued jangling in the living room. "Almost four o'clock."

Melanie slipped down beneath the blankets and closed her eyes. She could hear Riley talking to someone—speaking in hushed tones—but a certain air of exigency hung on each word. Excitement, urgency in his voice, was unusual in most instances. It would take something really special, even extraordinary to get him excited by just telling him something on the telephone. Besides, who would be calling at this hour?

Synn? Could it be Synn? Maybe Leeanah. Poor baby probably couldn't get to sleep for thinking about Riley's performance tonight. She smiled. Watching them had to have been one of the most erotic things she had ever witnessed—two people making love like that —right out in the open. But had it really been love? Leeanah referred to it as a great rite, and Sebastian explained that by doing it—fucking like that in public—they would create a cone of power, or some such nonsense, to help him get even with his enemies. Melanie giggled under the covers. "Let's fuck and get even with someone," she murmured aloud, her voice muffled by the pillow and blankets.

"I've gotta go," Riley murmured, coming back into the bedroom.

"Go? Go where? For Christ's sake, Riley, it's four in the fucking morning. Does Leeanah need another humping?"

"That was a cop on the phone."

"A cop?" Melanie sat up in bed, her breasts standing upright, prickling in the cool night air of the room as the blanket slipped from them.

"Yeah. Some Lieutenant Hongisto wants me to see something. Apparently he read my article on the ritual. Said that maybe I could lend a little expertise to the scene of a crime."

"Expertise? On what?"

Riley shook his head as he danced around

on one foot, pulling on a sock. "He didn't say. All he did say was that maybe I could help. I asked if the press had been called in yet. And he said no."

"So?"

"So, maybe I can get an exclusive and get a byline in the Trib or Sun. At any rate, I told him I'd get there as soon as possible."

"There? Where?"

"Someplace north of here and west of Naperville. This Hongisto is from the Chicago department but was called in by the locals. Apparently, he's special."

"Now, he's trying to make you *special*?"

"I sorta liked what he said on the telephone. He said he could do his job better and more quickly if he consulted experts in different fields."

"Jesus Christ. What the hell are you expert in?"

"That's the strange part. He didn't say."

"And you're going to just go tripping off at four o'clock in the morning and go visit this turkey?"

Riley nodded, buttoning his shirt.

"You're crazy. You know that? Where's my laid back, 'I-don't-give-a-fuck-about-anything—especially-money' Riley Larson?"

"I've got an idea how to get out from under the nine bills a month I've gotta come up with for Vicki. It'll take some concentrated effort, but with a little luck and a few days like we just had, I figure I could be clear of it in a month or two."

Melanie's eyes popped but she said nothing.

"I'll get back as soon as I can." He moved toward the door.

"Hey, Riley," Melanie called from the bed.

"Yeah?"

"Be careful. You don't know what you're walking into."

"Hongisto said there would be half a dozen police cars and state trooper cars around. There's lights all over the place."

"Just be careful," she admonished again.

"If I don't see any police cars, I don't go in. Fair enough?"

She nodded and turned out the light next to the bed.

Riley slowed when he came to the intersection on Highway 59 and turned left. Hongisto had been explicit in his directions, and when he saw a squad car on the side of the road, its lights flashing crimson in the pre-dawn black, he slowed. After explaining to the officer who stopped him that he was to meet Lieutenant Jules Hongisto, Riley eased the rusty Toyota along a dirt road. After driving for a few minutes, Riley saw a sign: "Beware of the Thing," written in old English letters. He smiled grimly as thoughts ran through his mind about what the *thing* might be, and who could have thought of such a dumb idea. It had to have been someone on the weird side. He quickly dismissed the opinion, recalling what he had been involved in earlier.

In the distance, Riley could make out the belching brightness of red, white and blue lights flooding the night. Four police cars and one sedan without emergency lights were parked at different angles, and he could make out the figures of uniformed policemen moving about, waggling flashlights.

Once he had stopped the car and gotten out, he headed toward the house. Reminding himself not to touch anything for fear of spoiling evidence, Riley walked up onto the porch. The house appeared to be made of brick and the windows on either side of the front door were barred with ornate grillwork which seemed most impenetrable. A grilled door hung open to one side of the heavy oak door, which leaned halfway open. Riley pushed it open further and stepped inside.

Several men stood huddled in the center of the entryway. The tallest, a giant in an overcoat, towering over the rest, looked in his direction. "Yes? What is it?"

"I'm Riley Larson. I'm looking for Lieutenant Jules Hongisto."

"I'm Hongisto." The large man stepped around the others to approach Riley. "You made good time, Mr. Larson. I'm glad you agreed to help because we've got a strange one here. Come with me." He motioned for Riley to follow and led him into a room off the entry.

Kerosene lamps and candles feebly attempted to light the room and foyer. "No electricity?"

"None. Can you imagine? In this day and age, too." Hongisto made a sweeping motion with his long arm.

Riley followed the extended hand, which more closely resembled a small ham. Paintings hanging between pillars caught his attention. One of a man bound and gagged, green eyes bulging from his head, blood dripping from five bullet wounds carefully arranged on his face, hung askew. Riley was riveted. After several seconds, he turned away only to be met by similar works of horror. Another depicted a woman, torn asunder from the crotch upward, her arms and legs held out, while her eyes strained downward toward the grotesque shape of a demon of some sort. Others, just as bizarre, held his attention in turn as he scanned the walls.

He sucked in his breath when he dropped his eyes. Skulls littered the floor—skulls of various sizes from what appeared to be adult to infant to miniature lay in piles or were scattered about.

He looked up to see Hongisto studying his reactions. "What the hell is going on, Lieutenant? What kind of charnel house is this?"

Hongisto shrugged his wide shoulders, palms of his huge hands open. "There, son, you've got me. I don't know if we have another clown who goes for boys like we had a few years back or what."

Riley instantly recalled the furor caused by stories of the arrest and trial of a single man who had murdered young boys and men after ravishing them sexually. He had also seen several news stories and documentaries on what the police dubbed "serial killers," wondering if that was what they had uncovered here. But why would they have called him? What did he know of serial killers and the like?

Hongisto smiled slyly. "You're trying to figure out why I called you. Am I right?" He chuckled good-naturedly.

Riley felt at ease with the big man who stood at least four inches taller than his own six feet and must have weighed close to three hundred pounds. Thinning hair complemented rather than detracted from his rough, tough face, which seemed to have earned each line and crease the hard way. Riley felt he could like this man if they had an opportunity to get to know one another. "That's about it, Lieutenant."

"I have a pretty good memory. In fact, you should play trivia games with me sometime. I'm a whiz. Only guy I've heard of who's tougher than me is a columnist who writes about trivia. A baldheaded fella. He's tough. But then, I digress. I read your article on the occult that appeared in the supplement that comes with my Sunday newspaper. At the time, I found it interesting and never thought I'd be investigating something like this." Again he swept the room with his arm.

"I don't understand." Riley's face screwed into a puzzled expression.

"I'll get to it. I'm rather thorough in my investigations and in my talk. I want to make certain you understand."

Riley nodded.

"I've been on the force in Chicago for almost thirty years and I've seen and heard of some pretty strange stuff. I even helped a psychiatrist once who thought—no, that's not fair to him because he convinced me of the idea—that one of his patients had the spirit of Hitler locked up inside him. That's pretty far-out stuff, huh?"

Riley nodded, wondering what the man was leading up to with this kind of oblique talk.

"I didn't think too much of your article when I read it but I filed it away in my memory bank and when I saw what's in the next room, I thought of it immediately." He picked his way over the skulls on the floor and walked to a closed door in the far wall. Motioning Riley to follow, he opened it, stepping through.

Riley walked after him. "Are these all real skulls, Lieutenant?"

Hongisto stopped, turning to frame himself in the doorway. "No. Most if not all of them are plastic replicas. Why someone would want to collect imitation skulls is beyond me. But then, I'm glad they're phonies and not the real thing because I wouldn't want to go around trying to determine who belongs to which head and so forth. It could be a real pain in the neck."

Riley smiled. He liked Hongisto even more since the man showed real humor with his last remark. When the detective turned back into the room, Riley continued after him and stopped, holding his breath at what he saw.

A white pentagram, not unlike the one in Synn's mansion and the blurred one he had taken pictures of and described in his article, was centered on the floor. Although he couldn't say for a fact, he felt the words and esoteric symbols surrounding and contained within the five-pointed diagram and accompanying circles, were the same as those he had seen in Synn's egg-shaped chapel. This room, however, was square.

"Seem familiar?" Hongisto asked.

Riley nodded, curious to know what the police really wanted of him, not about to offer anything for which he wasn't asked. "Yeah," he mumbled, "it sure does."

"Take a look at this over here," the lieutenant said and walked across the room to a brazier that seemed to be at least three or four feet across. "What do you make of this,

Mr. Larson?" Hongisto pointed to the interior.

Riley followed his outstretched finger and swallowed. Feathers. Burned and charred feathers—just like he had found in the church ruins and about which he had written.

He looked up at Hongisto. "So?"

"So it seems to be very much like the scene you described in your article, Mr. Larson. Where did that incident take place? You were rather vague about it."

"On purpose, Lieutenant. I felt that whomever I had accidentally seen wouldn't want any whereabouts or identities known, and wrote about the location and a few other things in an abstruse, indirect manner."

"That's a nice choice of words." A broad smile came across Hongisto's face. "I can tell you're a writer just by your use of words. I wish I had the ability. Perhaps when I retire—"

"Do you think there might be a tie-in between what I saw and what this place is all about?"

"There might be," Hongisto replied simply, "and then there might not be. Let me show you the rest. Do you have a strong stomach?"

Riley spun about to face him. "What do you mean? The sight of skulls—even plastic ones is almost enough to do a normal person in. But my stomach doesn't react too

The Immortal

easily, if that's what you mean. Why?"

"Let's put it to a test." Picking up a kerosene lamp as he left the room, he started up a narrow staircase, Riley right behind him.

"I assume," Riley said, "you're going to contact the press soon."

"Not really. In fact, I'm going to ask you not to write about this. I know you're not a regular reporter so your job or your income isn't in jeopardy if I ask you to keep quiet."

Riley thought of the job offer with the Hawthorne News. He hadn't accepted yet and there certainly was no reason why he should have to start there loaded with a prize-winning story. He made a mental note to call Tom Byron, the publisher. Life and the news reporting business just didn't work that way. If this big fella wanted him to be reticent about this case, reticent he'd be. The one thing he didn't want was to have Detective Lieutenant Jules Hongisto angry with him.

"How about a promise of an exclusive when you're ready to open up, Lieutenant? You know, a reward for cooperating and all." He looked at Hongisto, expectation in his facial expression.

"That seems like a fair exchange. I'll tell the boys downstairs." Hongisto opened a door and stepped inside, holding the lamp high to allow as much light as possible to fill the room.

Riley stepped in and stopped short. Lying on the bed, the bodies of two naked men were sprawled next to each other, as if they were sleeping on their backs. Their heads were gone.

Riley stared. Finally, after several long seconds passed, he tore his eyes from the gory scene and looked at the lieutenant. "Where are—?" He couldn't finish.

"Over here," Hongisto said. "There's one on each side of the bed."

"When—when did this happen?" Riley couldn't look at the bed or the severed heads.

"That's the strange part about it. A call came into the downtown headquarters around 11:15 P.M. last evening, informing them of a grisly murder out here. We called the police in Naperville and they investigated. They called back and I was sent out because of my experience in handling several —different type cases. As to when? The doctor has tentatively established the time of death at about 10:30—give or take an hour. He'll get more definite as times goes by."

"But—but who did it?" Riley suddenly realized Hongisto was humming. "Lieutenant?" He tried to break into the man's reverie.

"Oh, I'm sorry, Mr. Larson. That's a nice song. 'As Time Goes By.' Did you know the black fella who played the part of Sam in *Casablanca* couldn't play a note on the piano?

S'true. Dooley Wilson. Nice actor. Good movie. They don't make 'em like that any more." Hongisto looked at Riley as if he'd rather be playing a serious game of trivia than investigating a gruesome case of murder.

"Do you have any leads yet, Lieutenant?" Riley rephrased the question, hoping to get a bit of information.

"I had the M.E. boys wait until you got here before removing the bodies. However, this is the strange part. According to the lab boys, there aren't any fingerprints in the entire house, other than two sets. We're assuming they belong to the deceased men. Isn't that rather strange, Mr. Larson?"

Riley nodded slowly. "Gloves?"'

"Maybe yes, maybe no. I don't see anyone sick enough to perpetrate a crime like this being so neat they'd wear gloves. Another thing," he said, stepping around to the far side of the bed, "is the strange condition of the men's faces. Look at this." He motioned with a sausage-like forefinger at the floor.

Riley stepped closer to see better what he was indicating, and froze, rooted to the spot. The man's face was caved in, in a triangular shape, as if something had been shoved into it. Riley shook his head, trying to dislodge the idea fermenting there.

Synn had stuck the dagger blade into the heads of the two waxen images before severing their heads. Riley had thought the gesture purely symbolic. Melanie agreed when they talked about it later. But here, here in the flesh—make that dead flesh— were two male bodies whose heads had been severed and whose faces had been punched in by some unknown means. Unknown to the police maybe. But he thought he knew better. Should he tell Hongisto? Maybe the lieutenant would have him locked up for being a nut case himself. What would that accomplish? As far as he knew, the police had only called him in to look and comment. Certainly there could be no suspicion on their part that he'd had something to do with this. Why would they think that? Still—

"Lieutenant, I hope you don't think I had anything to do with this. Do you?"

Hongisto threw his head back and roared, his laughter totally out of place in the shadowy murder room. "Of course now, Mr. Larson. As I told you on the telephone, I usually consult experts in the different fields of which I know nothing. Granted, I've looked into many mighty strange things but I'm beginning to think that this one is going to be a winner in the Strange Sweepstakes. *The Hongisto Horror Show.*" He chuckled again. "Because of the things you wrote about, I felt you might be able to give me some input. Can you?"

Riley studied him. Short of giving him Sebastian Synn's name as the remote-control murderer of these two men—obviously the ones referred to last night when he and

Melanie arrived—what could he say? "I really don't think so, Lieutenant. I'm just a writer. I don't know that much about the occult and what have you. Just to satisfy my own prurient curiosity, who were the two men here?" He jabbed a finger toward the cadavers, wondering if one's name might be Judd Collingsworth.

Hongisto laughed. "I love the way you talk. 'Prurient.' What's that mean?"

"Actually, it can mean 'lewd' but basically its a wanton or restless craving. I guess my curiosity is restlessly craving the information."

"I can't tell you who they are. We know, of course, but we have to notify relatives first. However, I can tell you they were a couple of homosexuals. The older one was a college professor at one time and the younger one his servant. I suppose lackey would be more in keeping."

"And they dealt in the black arts?" Riley was trying to establish beyond a reasonable doubt, for himself and Melanie, that these were in fact the same two men about whom Synn had been raving. He wished he could ask if one actually was Judd Collingsworth, but knew if he did his own involvement might be betrayed—and that he didn't want.

"I would think that the rooms downstairs would more or less confirm that, wouldn't you, Mr. Larson?"

"I suppose so, Lieutenant. Is there anything else you'll need from me?"

"I can't think of anything other than the location of the other site. I really do appreciate the fact that you saw fit to come out here at this awful hour." Hongisto turned, leading the way from the murder room.

Once downstairs, Riley wrote out the directions. "The place has been cleaned up by whomever. Don't forget my exclusive."

"Perish the thought. I seldom if ever—no make that never—go back on my word. You can put that in the bank." He smiled broadly. "Do you know who used to say that a lot on TV?"

Riley couldn't believe the guy. A grisly double murder upstairs, bizarre artifacts and weird rooms downstairs, and this overgrown excuse for a police detective wanted to play trivia. Believing it better to humor him than incur his dislikes, Riley dutifully played straight man. "Who, Lieutenant?"

"Robert Blake as Baretta. Good show. A little fanciful at times but pretty good. Did you know he was Little Beaver in some of the Red Ryder movies? Nice actor, that fella."

"I'm going to hold you to that exclusive, Lieutenant."

"Be happy to be of service to you. I can reach you at the same number I called you at earlier?"

"That's right." He knew the police could get anything they wanted—even an unlisted

telephone number in the middle of the night.
"I'll be in touch."
Riley left the house, the eastern skyline a rosy-yellow glow as the sun struggled to rise for another day. Once behind the wheel, he yawned and turned the ignition key. Bed would feel good and he was thankful Melanie wouldn't have to go to work today. He'd take the day off as well to catch up on his sleep. Once his mind and body were rested, he'd have to have a long talk with her about what he'd seen and how it probably tied in with what they'd done the previous night.

Sunday, November 16, 9:20 P.M.

After sleeping seven hours, Riley rose and ate everything Melanie prepared for him. For the rest of the afternoon and well into the evening, they discussed each thing they had learned at the mansion and what he'd been exposed to by the police.

"If only Hongisto had said who the murdered men were, we would know for certain."

"I can understand why he didn't tell you. There wasn't anything with a name on it that you might have seen?"

"There was a row of mailboxes, but which one belonged to their house, I have no idea. I noticed them when I left. The cop was gone when I drove out of the lane so I checked for the name Collingsworth, but most of the boxes just had numbers and no names. Who knows?"

"Hongisto does."

"But I feel here," Riley pointed to his midsection, "that one of the dead men was Judd Collingsworth."

"You really believe that what you saw was the handiwork of Sebastian Synn, don't you?" Melanie shook her head, her hair waving as she did. "For some reason I find the whole thing a bit tough to accept. It seems almost like a fantasy rather than something that actually happened."

"Hey, Mel, you weren't there. The one guy's face looked like a huge knife had been jabbed into it—just like the wax dolls that Synn had on the table."

Melanie shuddered again. When Riley had described what he had seen and how he thought the men were murdered, she had visibly trembled.

"Think about it. Synn said the two guys were queer, that they were trying to run him out of Chicago, that he wanted to get even, then stabbed the heads of two dolls before slicing them off. Incidentally, do you have a handle on what time we were in the egg-shaped room?"

Melanie furrowed her brow. "Yeah, I got to thinking about that before, when you said this giant-sized package of trivia portraying a cop said the coroner put the time at eleven or so. We were in there from about 10:30 until eleven. Of course it might have been longer, but you blew your wad early and I guess the rite could have taken all night if your staying powers were better." She laughed lightly.

"Not funny, Mel. The coroner hadn't definitely fixed the time. He only said it was within an hour or so on either side of 10:30 last night. But the strange thing is, the cops were notified downtown in Chicago at 11:15. What time did we leave there?" He stared at her intently, the burden of unwanted knowledge weighing heavily on him.

"There I can be exact. It was about ten past eleven when we walked out of the front door. I remember looking at that huge grandfather clock in the entranceway. In fact, if you want to be absolutely precise, it was eleven minutes after eleven."

"Eleven eleven, huh? Do you think Synn called the cops? You know, sorta bragging that he could do something like this, wanting them to be in on it as soon as possible."

"That would really be weird." Melanie jumped as the phone rang.

"I'll get it." Riley stood and hurried to the living room, wondering who might be called at 9:30 at night. After Hongisto's summons that morning, he decided speculation was fruitless and picked up the phone.

"Hello?"

"Riley? This is Leeanah. Sebastian apologizes for not beginning your indoctrination last night. He would like to make it up to you this evening. In fact, we'll send for a car and have it leave this instant. You can be here within two hours. Is that all right?"

"Just a minute, Leeanah," he said loudly enough for Melanie to hear in the kitchen. Motioning for her to join him, he clamped a hand over the mouthpiece. "Do you want to go back there?"

Melanie shook her head, slowly at first, then with more conviction.

"I think we'd better cool it for a while," he agreed hoarsely.

She nodded. "Tell her we've got the flu or something and we'll get in touch with them."

"Leeanah? Gee, I don't know what to say. I didn't sleep at all last night. And now, both of us have the flu or some bug. Can we postpone it?"

"Were you thinking of me, Riley?" she asked coyly.

"Not all of the time," he answered carefully, "but yes, I guess you could say I was. Will it be all right if we hold off for the time being?"

There was a long pause. "Yes, of course that's all right. Sebastian and I will call tomorrow and check with you to see how the two of you are getting along. Good night."

"Good night, Leeanah." He hung up.

"Did she buy it?"

"I don't know. But I think we might be in trouble of some sort. If Synn has the power to do what he did, what sort of chance do we have?"

"Christ, you're overreacting, Riley. What have we done to incur his wrath? Nothing. Besides, he doesn't hate us."

Riley frowned. "Not yet, he doesn't. What'll he think if we quit? You know an awful lot of money came our way in a few days."

"He'll probably think of us as a pair of ingrates and find a couple more suckers to do his fucking for him." She grabbed Riley's hand and pulled him toward the bedroom. "Come on, I'm pooped. Let's get to bed and see how we look at everything tomorrow."

Grendel raised his head, watching them walk into the bedroom, and got to his feet. When he reached the door, he curled around, lying down in front of it.

"There, see," Melanie said before closing the door. "Grendel will protect us."

Riley smiled. "Right."

"What are you thinking about now?"

"Huh? About Hongisto."

She smiled at him, stripped to her bare skin, and crawled into bed.

"He's quite a guy," he mused. "The type of cop people try to capture on paper and in the movies but seldom if ever pull off.

G'night." He kissed her before turning out the light.

Outside the door, Grendel lay, his eyes flicking back and forth in the darkness, sensitive to his master's uneasiness.

CHAPTER 9

Monday, November 17, 12:30 P.M.

Melanie stayed in bed the next morning after Riley got up to go to work. His duties at school were finished by 12:30 and he hurried home, anxious to talk with her, to see if she'd arrived at any conclusion about what their decision should be. If they quit the cult, or group, or however Synn referred to it, Riley felt reasonably certain they could walk away without any consequences. Synn seemed to have no idea that the police had called him, which in itself was a coincidence that still left him reeling. To be sure, it was only speculation on his and Melanie's part that the victims were the men Synn had referred to and harangued against. If indeed they were the same, attacked by some sort of magical tactics, Riley felt he and Melanie would be much safer having absolutely nothing more to do with Sebastian or Leeanah—Leeanah with whom he had copulated.

Her face filled his mind. She had to be one of the most exotic and beautiful women he'd ever seen. Probably the most arresting features of her remarkable appearance were her eyes. Those cold, blue orbs seemed to pierce any protective element erected by whomever she happened to look at, stabbing one right to the core.

He shuddered and looked up when he approached the Toyota. Within ten minutes or so he would be with Melanie and they would make their decision.

As he drove along, thoughts of Leeanah kept intruding, interrupting his flow of impressions about the decision he knew they had to make. Would she influence Synn? Influence him to seek retaliation against them? When he touched his turn signal lever, he found his hand shaking. Could Synn actually do what he claimed? Had he said in so many words that he would kill the two homosexuals who were, according to him, blackmailing and trying to chase him from the Chicago area? Riley couldn't think straight. Still, the mere implication of such powers might well affect the most pragmatic person's mind. Or had Riley merely inferred that Synn somehow murdered the two by long distance, jumping to such a conclusion when he saw the decapitated corpses lying next to each other on that bed? True, the condition of the one face he had seen, punched in by some triangular-shaped object, seemed to be the way it would appear if a gigantic sharp knife had been thrust into it. He had seen the round little balls of wax, representative of heads, on the dolls Synn used in the ritual, their front sides penetrated by the dagger blade. All Riley did was transfer the idea to the actual dead men. Could he be wrong?

He turned into the driveway of "Worthless Acres" and shut off the motor. Still seated behind the steering wheel, he stared ahead. If he were wrong, perhaps he and Melanie would be throwing away the opportunity of a lifetime by telling Synn and Leeanah to get lost. He did want to be free to write that novel without having to feel he was being pressured into making extra money for Vicki. All he wanted was the chance to live his own life in his own way. That wasn't much to ask. Or was it? If he could manage to put aside the necessary funds to simply dole out Vicki's amount each month, that aspect of life's hassle would be finished. But did he and Melanie want to commit themselves deeply to someone like Synn? And was it merely Synn with whom he was concerned? There was at least one other entity involved who apparently controlled everything, for whom Synn passed out favors to those who wanted them and were willing to pay the price.

He slipped from behind the wheel and hurried to the front door. The cloudless sky, a pale blue, reminded him how choice such November days could be, and that it wouldn't be long—perhaps as soon as tomorrow—before slate winter clouds would cover the sun for days on end.

Grendel stood at the door, tail wagging, tongue lolling from one side of his mouth, ready to leap up and greet him. Accepting the slobbery kiss, Riley called out, "Hey, Mel. You here?"

The door to her studio/bedroom opened and she entered the living room. Her coarse hair, more wild than usual, seemed to accentuate her state of mind, highlighting the frightened look in her eyes.

"Hey, what's wrong, Mel?" He crossed the room to take her in his arms.

Clinging to him, she held tightly for several minutes before answering. When he pushed her back to look more closely at her, she said, "I had a phone call from Leeanah."

He waited, expecting her to continue. She didn't. "And?"

"She wasn't too nice in the way she asked, no, make that ordered the two of us to be there tonight."

"Ordered? Oh, come on. Are you sure she *ordered?*" He suddenly found himself wanting to defend the woman. The memory of lying on top of her, the fantastic sensation he had experienced when she began working her vaginal muscles, crowded his reason aside, making his head swim.

The Immortal

"Yeah, goddamn it! Ordered!" Melanie pulled away from him. "That bitch said we'd better be there or be prepared to pay the consequences. Can you imagine the fucking gall of that whore?"

Riley fell into the easy chair and looked up at her. "She was serious when she said it?" His reason returned, clearing his head. What he had just felt seemed almost too real—as if he had actually been coupled with the woman again.

"Riley? What the fuck are we going to do? Jesus Christ! What a mess. You got any ideas?"

"Maybe Leeanah has a thing for me?" he suggested, hoping Melanie would not think he was being facetious.

She screwed up her triangular-shaped face. "Thoughts like that went through my mind earlier. I even went a couple of steps further."

"How do you mean, Mel?"

"I put myself in her place. Suppose I had let Synn fuck me the other night and he didn't want to come around any more after that. What would I think?" She paused and sat down on the couch before continuing.

"You tell me."

"I don't have many options open. Maybe I'd think Leeanah was insecure and didn't want Synn to see me any more."

"What you're really saying is that she thinks you might be jealous of her?"

"Precisely."

He stretched and got to his feet. "Any coffee?"

"I just made some." She stood also.

They moved into the small kitchenette and took mugs from the shelf. After pouring coffee, they sat at the table.

Riley sipped his, pondering. "That's a distinct possibility, I suppose."

"You suppose? What other reason could there be?"

"How about the big changes we experienced a few days ago when we suddenly had money being offered to us like we were the greatest couple of artisans to come down the pike in years? Maybe Synn and Leeanah don't like to be used and made chumps of by a couple of ingrates like you and me."

Melanie drank more coffee while she kicked the idea around. "I guess that's a valid argument. But—"

The phone rang. Color drained from her face.

He stood. "I'll get it. Take it easy, will you? It's just the phone, for crying out loud."

Picking up the receiver on the third ring, he spoke cheerfully. "Hello?"

"Oh, Riley," Leeanah's voice sang in his ear.

He felt his crotch react. "Hi, there, Leeanah. What's up?"

"I'm glad to hear you're sounding better.

The Immortal

From the way Melanie talked you were on your deathbed."

He turned to look at her in the kitchen. Apparently she told Leeanah he was still sick, as they had done last night. "Oh, I'm coming around a bit. I don't really feel that swift yet. Why?"

"Sebastian and I want the two of you here tonight. Please, don't say no. It's vital."

Riley hesitated for a second. "I don't think I can say right now how I'll feel tonight. Can I let you know?"

He didn't like the silence on the other end. "I'll call you back later this afternoon, Riley." The definitive click sounded threatening and he gingerly replaced the receiver.

"I see what you mean." He poured more coffee into their mugs.

"What did she say?"

"Not much. Just that she and Sebastian want us there tonight."

"Did she buy your story of not feeling a hundred percent yet?"

His brow knitted. "I don't know. Maybe. She said she'd call back later this afternoon."

"Why don't we get the fuck outta here? Go someplace and maybe they'll forget about us."

"Where can we go to get away from Synn and his tricks?"

She stared at him. "You really believe he killed the two men you saw."

"I don't know what else to believe. We both saw what he did to the wax dolls. I saw two men who had been done in, in exactly the same way. And the best part, or maybe the worst, depending on how you want to look at it, is that there weren't any fingerprints other than their own in the whole house."

"But couldn't they belong to the killers?"

"Hongisto seemed relatively confident that tests would show they belonged to the victims."

"What are you going to do the rest of the day?"

"I've got to get going on that first story for Andy. I know I've got time but if I waste it now, I'll be under the gun in a few days, sweating it out. How about you?"

"I was just getting my camera ready. I'm to see Doctor Cushing's wife and children after I get finished with work tomorrow."

"They're not going to sit for you?"

"No. That's sort of old-fashioned, anyway. It's fun but old-fashioned. I'll take a slew of pictures and use them to capture the best features of each subject. It works."

"Hey? What do I know about portrait painting?"

They went to their respective rooms to work, the only sound in the small house coming from Riley's portable as he pecked out the story of the new tax structure.

Two hours later, she came into his office carrying her camera.

"Can you look at this?" She handed it to him. "I think the shutter isn't working properly."

Spinning about in his chair, he took the camera as the phone rang. They looked at each other. "I'll get it," he said. "You're sick now. All right?"

She nodded.

He got to the phone on the fourth ring. "Hello?"

"Riley? I'm glad you answered. I didn't want Melanie to be the one. I—I miss you, Riley."

An involuntary smile crossed his mouth. "You do, huh?"

"Yes. I—I—I want you again. Do you know what I mean?"

"I believe I have a rough idea."

"Can I expect to see you tonight?"

"What about Melanie?"

"What about her?"

"She's still ill. In fact, more so now then when you spoke to her earlier."

"She can stay at home. Can't she?"

"I don't think that would be very nice of me. Do you?"

"I'm afraid I don't understand."

"She took care of me when I was ill. Now that she's sick, I can't very well go running off letting her lie in bed, can I?"

"Are you all right now?"

"I'm feeling pretty good. Better than when I talked with you before."

"That's good. I wouldn't want to see you ill—or *hurt* in any way."

He felt his skin crawl when she said the word "hurt," wondering what kind of threat it implied. "I'm positive everything will be back to normal tomorrow, Leeanah," he assured her softly. Just about to say something further when she didn't speak, he heard the click of her phone breaking the connection. For a full minute he stared at the instrument in his hand, then slowly, deliberately replaced it in the cradle.

He went back to his office, repeating the conversation for Melanie who had gotten her camera operating in the meanwhile.

"Do you think we're really in trouble, Riley?"

Sitting down heavily in his desk chair, he sighed. "I don't know. I really don't know. Maybe. Maybe not."

"Do you think they'll try to retaliate because we're being a couple of shits when it comes to their invitations?"

"I hope not. Good Lord, Mel. What are we doing? Simply saying no, we don't want to come to their house to play spooks any more. That's all. It's nothing to kill people because of, or try to harm them."

"But look what they did to those two queers." She shuddered.

"We don't know that for a fact. Truth of the matter is, I doubt if we ever will. Not unless they decide to tell us or we learn the names of the victims."

"I guess you're right. What are we going to do then?"

"We'll just stay home. After all, you're suffering from the flu and I'm recovering from it and taking care of you at the same time. It's plausible."

"Plausible, *shmausible*. I just hope we don't wake up tomorrow morning with our heads cut off."

"I think you're being silly, Mel." He grinned inwardly at the manner in which they had reversed their attitudes. Last night he had been the concerned one, while she was greedy and realistic. Tonight found them on opposite sides.

"What do you want for supper, Mr. Serious Thinker?"

After they finished eating, Riley decided he'd retire early since he still felt the results of having lost Saturday night's sleep. Shortly before he was ready to turn the lights out, the phone rang. Melanie froze, remaining silent.

"I'll get it." He hauled himself out of bed and went to the livingroom.

"Hello?"

"How's Melanie?" Leeanah asked, a hint of sarcasm in her voice.

"Actually, she's in bed. I think she might be sleeping and I don't want to disturb her."

A pause followed. "I'll call you tomorrow

to see how she's doing, Riley. I don't want to go on without seeing you."

"You make that sound like a threat."

"A threat? To whom?"

"To yourself."

He could picture her smiling in her seductive manner when she didn't answer.

"I didn't mean it to sound like a threat to anyone, Riley. It's just that I felt something the other night when we performed the great rite. I shouldn't and I know it's wrong to think of it as a self-satisfying experience. It was supposed to have been done to concentrate the cone of power for Sebastian's sake, not to give either of us pleasure."

"Did it work?" Riley was suddenly aware that perhaps the whole episode was a bust because Leeanah had enjoyed having sex with him. He knew that he had liked it. Besides, he might find out more about the murders.

"The cone was established and as far as we know, the ritual reached a successful conclusion. Why do you ask? Are you really that interested?"

"In some ways, yes. What was the purpose of it?"

"I can't say. Perhaps if you ask Sebastian, he'll tell you. I'm not at liberty to divulge anything."

"I might just ask him sometime."

"Perhaps you could tomorrow night—if

Melanie is feeling up to letting you come here by yourself."

"Why by myself? I won't even consider coming unless Mel comes along."

"I didn't mean anything by that, Riley. It's just that we're—er—I mean—I'm not interested in Melanie. Perhaps Sebastian is. I really don't know. I will hope that you both can come tomorrow night. Just the sight of you would almost be enough to satisfy my hunger."

Again, he found himself smiling involuntarily. It was crazy even to think that a luscious woman such as Leeanah could find him attractive. Still, Melanie had fallen for him. But she had said she loved his mind as much as his body and anything else that might be in season. What about Leeanah? Was she simply after a sex kick? Just what did the woman want?

"That's nice of you to say, Leeanah," he mumbled, embarrassed at having to acknowledge the compliment without returning it.

"I'll be in touch with you tomorrow, Riley. Until then—" She didn't finish the sentence other than by laying the receiver in its holder, breaking the connection.

Riley felt disappointed. He thought Leeanah might have said good-bye in a foreign tongue, or at least murmured something highly provocative and suggestive. Still, he felt the unfinished farewell seemed highly significant in itself.

He returned to the bedroom to find Melanie sound asleep.

Tuesday, November 18, 7:00 A.M.

When Riley awoke the next morning, she was already up and dressed, ready to leave for Doctor Cushing's office.

"I won't be home until late," she announced as he sat up in bed.

"Where will you be?"

"The doctor's house. I'm to take pictures of his wife and children tonight. He said he'd bring me home afterwards. Will you be all right?"

"No, *Mommy!* I will be *afraid* in the dark if I'm *awone.*"

"Then, my dumb little boy, turn the lights on. See you whenever," she called over her shoulder, sweeping out of the room.

He got out of bed, stumbling to the window. It was still dark outside. "Seven," he muttered, looking at the alarm clock. It would take her the better part of an hour to walk to the doctor's office and open it by 8:30. Shaking his head at her idea of physical fitness, he took a quick shower but decided to forgo the shave, opting to give his facial skin a rest for a change. While drinking several cups of coffee, he allowed Grendel to run loose outside, knowing the dog would return at his call. After locking him in the house, he got in the Toyota and left, not hearing the telephone ring as he backed onto Lily Cache Lane.

Riley felt lucky. There was hardly any work facing him when he arrived at the school and those tasks that required his immediate attention were quickly disposed of. By 11:45 he had finished and was heading homeward.

After parking the car, he walked toward the front entrance, breaking into a trot when he heard the telephone ringing. The click he heard when he grabbed the receiver annoyed him. Why couldn't people wait an extra ring? Maybe they did. Well, if they wanted him badly enough, they'd call back. He slipped out of his jacket, his light windbreaker catching his attention, which he pulled off the hook. Jamming his hand into the pocket, he withdrew the feather, stained brown from dried blood. How could he have forgotten it?

Should he tell Hongisto? Why?

"Lieutenant? I've got a bloody chicken feather. Do you want to see if it matches any of yours?"

Still, he'd been curious as to what kind of blood was on the feathers the police found at the double murder scene. His curiosity was piqued again now that he held a similar item in his hands. What could he do with it? Give it to Hongisto? If Synn did have powers beyond reality and belief, it would be foolish of Riley to jeopardize his own position by casting suspicion on the man. After all, he knew who was present at the old church that night. This feather belonged, as it were, to Sebastian. The ones the police had, as far as they were concerned, belonged to the dead men.

Whom could he find to analyze the bloodstains on the feather? A laboratory outside of Hawthorne had been built and opened to escape the high rent of downtown Chicago. From what he'd heard, the lab did an excellent business, utilizing a delivery and pickup service to the Loop.

He looked up the telephone number, and, after confirming the fact the laboratory could indeed analyze it, slipped into his heavy jacket and was out the door. The phone rang again as he backed out of the driveway.

Thirty minutes later, he returned, knowing the technician to whom he had given the feather would call as soon as the results were known. At least he had lucked out by hitting the lab on a slow day. Once his jacket was hung up again, the phone rang.

"Hello?"

"Riley? Tom Byron."

He frowned, remembering his promise to have gotten back to the publisher of the Hawthorne News yesterday. Somehow, everything that happened had pushed the thought right out of his head.

"Tom? I'm really sorry about not getting back to you. Just tying up some loose ends before reporting for duty." He laughed just enough to let Byron know he was embarrassed. It wasn't the best way to impress his new employer.

"I—I don't know how to tell you this, Riley. My accountant gave me some bad news today. I have to withdraw the offer."

Riley stared at the mouthpiece. Was he kidding? Things like this didn't happen. Not in real life. He had been offered a job. A good job. One that was going to allow him the opportunity to live a life most people merely dream about. Now it was being withdrawn without even a chance for him to try it.

"I don't understand, Tom. What do you mean?"

"There's no way I can afford eighteen thousand a year for what would amount to a part-time employee. My accountant—"

"But—but—" What could he say, except thanks for the offer. If the man wasn't about to hire him, that was that. It was a simple fact. "What about freelancing? Can I still freelance articles and handle special assignments for you, Tom?"

"Why—why I guess so. That's built into my budget as far as I know. It's just that the eighteen *thou* wasn't. I'm sure you understand. Maybe in the future. I could plan on it more soundly and then—"

"Have you got any assignments for me now?"

There followed what grew to be an uncomfortable pause. Then, Tom Byron spoke. "Not right now. When I get something, I'll call. Fair enough?"

"Yeah, sure. Thanks for at least making the offer, Tom." Riley hung up the phone.

Rotten luck. Just when things were about to fall into place financially for him, he was suddenly back in the ranks of freelance writers. Not that he didn't appreciate his freedom, but now his newly formed plans were no longer viable.

"Oh, well," he muttered, walking toward his office. "I've still got an assignment to finish and another to start."

No sooner had he sat down than the telephone rang again.

"Hello?" he answered guardedly, not quite certain who would be calling at this time of day, hoping it wasn't Leeanah or Sebastian.

"Riley? Andy McLain. How you doing?"

He couldn't believe it. Both articles had been cancelled—and by the guy who had assigned them to him. When he asked about the possibility of a kill fee, Andy had hemmed and hawed, finally admitting that he couldn't pay him anything. The customary fifty percent of agreed-upon fee for writing something that wound up in the

The Immortal

wastebasket was definitely not available. Riley had wanted to scream at him but decided against it, knowing that down the road he might need the likes of Andy McLain and even Tom Byron. Right now, he felt like going to the Rescue Mission in Hawthorne and belting down a bowl of free soup. He felt as if he hadn't a friend in the world.

When he saw Melanie, he knew she had been crying. "What's the matter?"

"Of all the stupid, rotten, fucking, no-good goddamned luck," she fumed, home again where she could blow her stack if she wanted.

"What happened, Mel? Come on, simmer down. Tell Uncle Riley all about it."

"Doctor Cushing and his wife are getting divorced. No marriage! No portraits! No commissions! Son of a bitch! Even the other three called in today and cancelled theirs. God damn it!"

Riley began laughing bitterly. He quickly told her of his own losses that day, sobering after he finished. "Oh, well, easy come, easy go."

She stared at him. "Do you suppose Synn and Leeanah are flexing their muscles, showing us they can control our lives—our destinies?"

He collapsed in the easy chair. "I—I don't know. That's a possibility, I guess. I never once thought about it. I guess I was too upset even to remember where the good fortune came from in the first place. Well, now it's gone. As far as I'm concerned, that fries it. I'm through with Sebastian Synn and Leeanah Thorndyke."

The phone rang.

He glared at it. "It's probably them, calling to chortle over our losses."

"I'll get it." She went to the phone. "Hello?" She paused and looked at Riley, motioning for him to come. "It's for you."

He took the receiver frowning as she merely shrugged when he asked quietly who it was.

"Hello?"

"Mr. Larson? This is the Field Laboratory calling. I've analyzed the stain on that feather you brought in earlier."

"Oh, right. What did you find?"

"It's chicken blood. What were you expecting?"

"I don't really know. Thank you. Send me your bill." He hung up and explained to her what the call was about.

They talked for several hours, realizing at ten o'clock that they hadn't eaten. Just as they were about to sit down at the table, the phone rang once more.

Riley stormed over to it, ready to tear it out of the wall. The telephone had suddenly become a monster. It had taken away everything they had gained in the last few days. There was nothing left for anyone to take.

He grabbed the phone and barked, "Hello?"

"Riley, this is Leeanah. What kind of day have you had?"

"I think you know, Leeanah. Why don't you just write me and Mel off your books? The way I look at it is we're even after today. We don't need you and you shouldn't want us if that's our attitude."

"Riley. You'd better decide to rejoin us or —or else—" She let the sentence hang, ominous, unfinished.

"Or else what?"

There was a muffled conversation on the other end and suddenly he heard Sebastian Synn's well-modulated voice.

"Riley. Stop this foolishness. What you have lost can be regained a thousandfold. A millionfold. If you will only reconsider."

Riley glared at the receiver and slammed it into the cradle. For the first time in the last twenty-four hours he felt in control of his own life and destiny.

When the line didn't respond to Synn's clicking of the bar, he turned to Leeanah. "It's gone dead. Obviously our friend has hung up."

"What do you intend doing?"

"I must have him here—soon. Or it will be too late. We must make a sacrifice tonight. Prepare yourself."

Leeanah bowed slightly and turned to run

up the curving staircase. In minutes, she descended, dressed in her robe. She ran lightly down the hall to the door and entered, rushing toward the egg-shaped chapel. When she arrived, Synn already stood behind the altar, the acolytes surrounding him. She pushed her way through the group to stand next to him.

"Select one," he muttered without taking his eyes from the small doll-shaped, waxen image in his hands.

Leeanah took the hand of the young man standing nearest her. "What is your plan?"

"It is Riley we want. Without Melanie to confuse him, we will be able to attain our ends." He dropped the figure into the chalice.

Leeanah slipped out of her robe, lying down on the cold black altar. The young man took off his robe, displaying a well-muscled body, his only attire a spiked collar clamped around his neck. Lowering himself, he plunged his erection into Leeanah while Synn began mumbling prayers to the dark forces of the nether world.

CHAPTER 10

Wednesday, November 19, 1:59 A.M.

Vicki rubbed her eyes. Tired. Exhausted. Why had her history professor announced an unscheduled test for the next day? At least he had given them notice, which was more than most of the other teachers did. Her study habits had been interrupted—too much time with Ed ever since they had gone to bed last Saturday. Now, she found herself paying the price for letting her schoolwork slide in preference to making love with him.

She looked at her alarm clock. Two in the morning. The only redeeming feature of her situation was that the class in which she would be given the test didn't convene until ten. If she got to bed by three, she could still sleep six hours and have an hour to wake up, shower, and get to school.

Looking at the notes left to review, she decided that another thirty minutes' work would enable her to go to bed. . . .

* * *

Synn waved the knife over the waxen image. The doll, its small breasts and simulated dress showing a definite female outline, lay on the altar, having already been dumped from the chalice. On the altar in front of him, Leeanah lay on her back, accepting the ministration of her sixth partner since they had begun the ritual. For some reason, Synn was experiencing trouble concentrating the cone of power to the fine point of control he needed. For the better part of four hours, the rite had gone on. He wanted to be so exact on this one. The results would be baffling—even to one who might know what had been the cause of the phenomenon.

"Master? Are you here with me? Help me! I am so close to accomplishing my task. Help me, I beg of thee!"

A low moan swept through the egg-shaped room, whistling along the wall, never diminishing, gently traveling the full circumference until the peculiar sonance filled the chapel.

Synn wiped tears away with a silk handkerchief. "Thank you, Master. I know you are here. Leeanah, hold the seed within yourself. I am ready."

His head motioned to one of the hooded people standing opposite the altar. A man stepped forward, sliding a small brazier closer to the center. He threw back the constraining folds of his robe, exposing his nudity, adorned only with a spike-studded collar around his neck. Withdrawing a taper from a container on the altar, he lighted it from one of the black candles and held it in front of him, his eyes fixed on the writhing flame.

"Light it." Synn growled the order in a whisper that heightened the almost tangible expectation flooding the room.

The man dropped the lit end into the brazier igniting the coals and incense, bluish clouds of smoke curling up, then down to engulf the altar and the coterie standing about it.

Vicki coughed. Her throat was dry. Thirsty. She was thirsty. Get a glass of water. She finished reading the last section of the final page of her notebook and stood, hurrying to the kitchenette. The first glass was followed by a second and most of a third. She felt flushed. Could she be getting ill?

Synn raised the small waxen figure over his head, waving it back and forth.

Suddenly dizzy, Vicki grabbed the edge of the counter. The glass slipped from her trembling hand, shattering as it hit the small square of tile flooring. The room spun crazily about.

"*Master!*" Synn cried, the words constricted by the same emotion running rampant through the group. "Deliver unto me the person known as Riley Larson. It is his wife who prevents me from gaining my end. Rid the world of her. Take her and do with her as you will. Destroy her earthly body and take her soul for your own. I need Riley Larson. If I am to exist any longer, bring me Riley Larson. Send him to me. Help me acquire my ends and I shall be yours forever and ever. Hail, Satan! Hail, Baphomet! Hail, Asmodeus!"

The group moaned, mumbling as the black deities were called on to grant Sebastian's desire.

An evil smile distorting his smooth, high cheekboned face, he dropped the waxen image into the flaming brazier.

Vicki coughed, choking on her own spittle as she fought to regain her balance. Dizzy. She had never been so dizzy or unsure of her footing before in her life.

Stumbling, half falling across the room, she barely caught the back of her chair at the table, collapsing onto it. She felt as if she were burning with fever. Wave after wave of dry heat washed through her as if she had no moisture in her body at all. As if the room were overheated, the building on fire. As if she herself were burning or being burned.

Fire?

"Oh, my God," she managed. "The building's on fire!"

The Immortal

The searing pain began in her chest, radiating in all directions, growing in severity the farther out it reached. She felt as if the rays of the sun were being focused on her through a magnifying glass, burning through her thin blouse and bra to her skin, through it to her flesh, searing to the bones of her rib cage. Her arms, her hands, her back, her stomach all burned. What was going on?

She tried moving. She had to get out of the room. Out of the building. Something was burning. She had to escape. The pain in her chest and breasts grew more intense, maddening her as she felt it could get no hotter. Yet it did.

Dropping her head, she stared at her breasts, watching flames leap from within her. She tried to scream. Nothing. She had to move. Get to the bathroom. Turn on the shower. Get in. Douse the flames. How could she be burning like this? She could not move anything. Her arms. Her legs. The flames leapt out farther, extending at least twelve inches in front of her now. Bluish-white, they sizzled, tantalizing her with their reality. Why couldn't she move? Why couldn't she scream?

Why couldn't she simply stand up and run to the shower or into the hall? Surely everyone in the building knew by now it was on fire.

She watched the flames leap and cavort,

dancing in her lap, reaching down to burn her crotch, scorching her skirt, her panties, until they were ashes. When the fire touched her soft skin she wanted to scream but still no sound would allow itself to be born.

Horrified, she watched the flames corkscrewing from her chest, jumping about, consuming her flesh as they raced away from her charred breasts to her shoulders and arms, down toward her hands. Raising her head, she stared straight ahead. Tears? Was she crying? She must be. The pain was so great she had at least to be crying because of the agony. She couldn't scream for some reason but knew she had to be crying.

She felt the fire creeping up her throat toward her face. Unable to move her burning arms and hands to repel it from her head, she sat upright, perfectly still as it inched up her throat, past her chin, to her mouth, her nose, her eyes, her hair. When the chair collapsed, weakened by the holocaust, Vicki crumbled into a heap, her untouched legs falling beneath the table.

For several minutes, it continued to rage, consuming every fibre that had been her body, arms and head. Then, little by little, the satisfied conflagration danced less vigorously, withering here, dying out there, until one lone sentinel-like tongue of flame pirouetted in the greasy ashes that had been Vicki Larson. Then, it, too, died out, and the room was quiet.

The Immortal

* * *

Synn watched the wax doll as it melted, wiggling from the intense heat of the charcoal. Its legs, hanging over the edge of the brazier, fell to the top of the altar as the last speck of wax sputtered in a sizzling pool before evaporating.

A thin smile creased Synn's lips. "Satan! Baphomet! Asmodeus! Hear me! Go to Riley Larson. Destroy what is his. Make him believe in you and force him to come to me. Now. In your names I obey and serve you for all eternity."

He turned to look down at a spent Leeanah, bending toward her. She took his proffered hand and stood, exhausted from her four-hour sexual marathon, yet happy to have been of service to Sebastian.

Melanie nudged Riley who snored too enthusiastically to allow her to sleep. Grunting, he turned over, facing her back. His arm circled her upper body and he instinctively cupped one of her breasts. Melanie smiled in her half-awake state and drifted off.

Riley fondled the breast and froze when it disappeared, slipping from his manipulating fingers. What had happened? It was gone. All of it had apparently gotten away from him. Even the nipple, which he had been gently twisting between his thumb and forefinger. How could that be? Where had she gone?

He opened one eye and shuddered. The other flew wide involuntarily. Where was he? His bedroom was gone. His bed was gone, having been replaced by a single, metal framed one. He shivered from the cold. It was an uncomfortable pallet with a thin mattress and insufficient covering—especially inadequate for sleeping alone. What the *hell* was going on?

Propping himself up on one elbow, he looked around. Other beds were ranged along the wall against which his was aligned at a right angle, and opposite as well. It looked like a dormitory. But—

Other people who had been lying down, snoring, suddenly all sat up as if someone had directed them to do so. Thin, emaciated faces stared at him. Wild, disheveled hair stuck out in all directions from each head. Yellow, broken teeth lined their open mouths. Slowly slipping from their beds, they began moving toward him, laughing in a quiet, mad way.

Riley shrank back toward the metal headboard. He had to get away. But how? He didn't even know where he was or how he had gotten here—wherever this was. Looking about wildly, he saw a door next to his bed and leapt toward it. It had no knob, only a round opening where the latch mechanism should have been. The hole was worn smooth from years of fingers being inserted to pull the door open. He did the same, feeling the prickly sensation on his neck and back of someone reaching out to stop him. Flinging the door back, he faced another just like it. Opening that another confronted him, then a fourth, fifth, sixth were thrown open only to be replaced by duplicates. After encountering more than a dozen, all the while pursued by the outstretched hands of the thin madmen, trying to stop him but never quite making contact, his animal instinct for survival took precedence over all else.

Finally, the last one opened to reveal a short corridor, another door at the end. Rushing toward it, he threw it open to face another and another and another. The herd of lunatics was still advancing behind him and he frantically tore at the old doors, slamming them into one another as he yanked them open. Then the last one fell from his bruised hand and he stepped through, the crowd of men retreating, moaning as though they had lost a prize, or a friend.

Riley watched them retreat toward the room where he had awakened as they closed the doors behind them. Turning, he found himself in a similar room. There were women here. Not men. Women. Old women. Haggard women. Ugly women who stood at the side of their beds as if waiting for him, turning to face him, gesturing with their thin, bony arms and skeletal hands to come to them.

He savagely shook his head from side to side. Was he going mad? As insane as these people had to be? Then he saw her. Melanie. Standing at the far well, nude, her breasts standing out, the nipples staring directly at him. He motioned her to come to him. Slowly, tantalizingly walking toward him, she stopped when he started for her.

They had to get out of this madhouse. Where were they?

He looked down, sucking in his breath. Her legs weren't the same. Her hips flared out from her tiny waist but ended in straight stick-like appendages with white socks and patent leather shoes on feet too small for her.

When they were close enough to embrace, they did, but when she pulled away, he yelped. It wasn't Melanie. It was Leeanah Thorndyke. He looked down. The legs and feet hadn't changed, nor had the body. He was aware that she and Melanie had similar figures. Only the face and hair were different. What matter? He needed a woman back in the dormitory from which he had come, to take to bed, to keep him warm.

Grasping her hand, he turned, erupting through the circle of women. He had what he needed. When the doors to the women's area were closed behind them, he turned to find Leeanah smiling at him.

"What's a nice girl like you doing in a place like this?" He heard himself thinking it

a stupid line, but he had to start a conversation with her sometime, some way.

"*Why, I thought you knew. I'm a nymphomaniac from West Virginia. Really, I am!*" She flirtatiously batted her eyes, smiling seductively at him.

"*That's fine. You're just the one I've been looking for tonight.*"

They ran through the other doors more quickly than he had before, to find the original room completely empty.

"*Here.*" He pointed to the bed next to the doorway. "*This is mine.*"

She slipped onto the bed, slowly lying back, keeping her eyes fixed on him. When he lay next to her, they embraced and Riley dropped his free arm and hand to her legs. Cold. They were icy cold. Like marble. Poor thing was as chilled as he. Moving his hand up toward her pubic hair, he felt her tense when he fondled her.

"*Sir!*" she exclaimed. "*Just what kind of girl do you think I am?*" He saw her hand coming but couldn't move, and thought the sound should have been more of a clapping noise than that of glass breaking. Just a tiny sound, almost inaudible.

Riley grunted again in his sleep and turned over, Melanie doing the same. She threw an arm around him. In minutes both were sleeping dreamlessly.

* * *

Grendel, lying outside the door, raised his head when the two of them turned over. His eyes darted about the darkness. Something was in the room with him. A half whine, half growl rumbled from deep within his huge chest. Raising himself on to his front legs, rump on the floor, he waited.

A tiny crash came, just like the others he had heard. Almost a continuous tinkle of noise came from Riley's office. The dog stood, hair on end along his neck and back. His tail hung motionless as he took a tentative step toward the small room. Another sound, a bit louder, but not sufficient to awaken his master.

He stood outside the room now—his way partially blocked by the door that stood ajar. Stepping closer, ears alert, he sifted all the normal night noises from those which had attracted his attention in the first place. The growl ceased, replaced by a whine—pensive, curious, plaintive. He took another step. The noises stopped.

He sniffed, sorting out different aromas emanating from the room where his master spent so much time. Nothing. He could detect nothing out of the ordinary.

Another little crash, a sprinkling sound of broken glass. Just barely audible.

The growl joined the whine again and he took another step, his nose pressed against the door. It swung open a few inches, enabling him to step closer. He bumped the door again. It swung in farther. Now he could enter without touching the door or the frame. The growl stopped. The whine ceased. The dog entered the black office.

When Grendel had completely passed into the room, the door swung shut soundlessly except for the click as the latch caught.

PART THREE

THE JUDAS GOAT

CHAPTER 11

Wednesday, November 19, 1:30 A.M.

Riley lay on his back, staring at the dark ceiling. Melanie still slept, curled into a ball, her back to him. He had slept well but recalled having the weirdest dream—the strangest by far in a long time. Dreams had always fascinated him and he even took time to read up on them at one point, but didn't pursue it to the diligent extremes to which some people went—writing down each detail when they awakened. Still, the dream he remembered having last night contained enough basic symbolism to let him understand most of its veiled meanings.

The room in which he found himself with male inmates of an insane asylum had to have represented his own current circumstances. Wanting to find some way to keep warm meant he was not very satisfied with his life at the moment. Did that include his relationship with Melanie? His obligation to get enough money together to satisfy Vicki?

His investigation of the church ruins and subsequent meeting with Sebastian and Leeanah? He felt his relationship with Melanie was as stable as anything he could ever hope for and yet, could he be unhappy with her? Was he that enamored of, and intrigued by, Leeanah Thorndyke?

He recalled the woman he had seen in the second dormitory—after opening all the doors which represented problems he must overcome to instigate any change he might want to bring about. At first she had been Melanie and then, as can only happen in dreams, she became Leeanah. Leeanah! He sat up, fumbling in the darkened room for his pack of cigarettes.

After lighting up, he coughed and settled back into thinking further. Leeanah was a special woman. How could he judge based on the little he knew about her? She had class. He couldn't deny that. She certainly knew tricks about making love that Melanie had not yet learned. He wondered how she had developed the ability to work her vaginal muscles that way. His groin reacted as he thought of the powerful sensations she had evoked that night.

He snuffed the cigarette out. It didn't taste good at all. At this rate, he'd quit before the holidays. At least he might feel better if he did.

His mind wandered, touching on Melanie, Leeanah, Sebastian Synn and the events

The Immortal

that had taken place since they met. He opened his eyes wide, wondering about the strange feeling he had had when Synn touched his scrotum and penis that first night. He thought at first he'd been jolted with a tiny shock of electricity, but decided that was a bit far-fetched. If Melanie had felt such a thing, he was certain she'd have mentioned something about it. There were just too many strange, unexplained things that had taken place since they came in contact with the couple.

Nudging Melanie's back, he gently awakened her. She stretched and sat up.

"You know I don't have to go to work today. I was planning on sleeping in until I woke up," she said yawning, reaching for the ceiling at the same time.

"I'm sorry. I wanted to ask you something. Remember the first night we went to Synn's mansion? And he touched our crotches during the initiation rite?"

"Yeah?" She yawned again.

"Did you feel anything?"

She laughed. "No, Riley. I'm totally dead in my vagina. No feeling whatsoever. Yes. I felt something. Like a little electrical shock or something. Why? Did you?"

"He must have been wired or something but I didn't see anything in his hand. Did you?"

She thought for a moment. "I don't recall. Why?"

He explained about his dream in an effort to understand if and how it had brought memories of that first night to mind.

"I will say this, Riley. You've got one pisswhistler of an imagination." She laughed.

"It may seem like that, but I know dreams reflect what we think subconsciously and usually tell us something, but in code. Do you know what I mean?"

"Yeah. You prefer Leeanah to me. Right?"

"No. That's not right. I think you both were probably symbols of my feelings for Vicki and the situation I'm in because of having been married to her at one time."

"What about the funny legs?" She turned to look intently at him.

"They sorta looked like Little Orphan Annie's legs, seeming to indicate an infirm or unsteady or weakened foundation."

"Foundation? Of what?"

He shrugged. "I don't know. Certainly you're pretty rock solid in everything you do."

"But I turned into Leeanah. What do you know of her?"

He thought again of those vaginal muscles, quickly shaking his head to rid himself of the image. "Nothing, I'll grant you. Maybe she was a symbol of something I want."

"Such as?"

"I don't know." He threw back the covers

and reached for his robe. "I'll make coffee. You going back to sleep?"

"Now that you've got me wide awake, you want to know if I'm going back to sleep? No, Riley. I'll get up and clean the house. Maybe paint it. Shingle the fucking roof and be ready to have you hump me into never-never land tonight." She threw back the covers and stood, stretching her body once more before slipping into her robe. When she turned she found herself alone.

By the time she entered the kitchen, Riley already had the pot on the stove.

"Did you close the door to your office last night?" she asked, sitting at the table.

"No. I said it should be opened during the winter to let the hot air circulate better. Why?"

"It's closed now." She roughly rubbed her hair.

"I didn't close it. You must have." He went to the living room. "I do think we should leave it open, though. It's chilly in here this morning."

He stopped at the thermostat and checked. The one needle was set at sixty-seven degrees. The other, which indicated the room temperature, showed sixty-four degrees. He listened intently. The furnace was not running.

Reaching out, he wiggled the knob back and forth and relaxed when he heard the furnace rumble on as the oil pot ignited. He crossed the room to his closed office and opened the door.

Jules Hongisto pawed through the purse he held, his back to the pile of white gray ashes behind him. The peculiar smell of grease frying hung heavily in the one-room efficiency apartment. Grease frying? It was the best and only description that came to his mind. He had seen enough and heard enough and smelled enough for any fifteen or twenty people during his years in the Chicago Police Department, and had investigated one other case of spontaneous human combustion. It hadn't been pretty. This one was downright sickening.

He turned around. The legs of the woman still lay under the table. He was glad the building manager didn't come in with the officer when the door had been opened earlier. For some reason, the stench of burning grease had been much stronger in the hall, which initially prompted the manager to summon the policeman on the beat.

"I saw the pile of ashes and the legs, Lieutenant," Officer Rodney Whett said when Hongisto arrived. "I kept everyone out and put a call in for you."

"Why me, Officer?" Hongisto wasn't flattered.

"I thought, based on what I know about

you, that you'd be the best one to call."

"You're probably right, son. But in the future you'd better go through proper procedures and channels. I won't say anything this time."

Then he'd dispatched the officer to the hallway to keep the curious from looking in. He wondered about the phenomenon confronting him. The other case he had investigated involved an old woman, grossly overweight and an uncontrollable alcoholic. Jules had read up on the strange occurrence known as spontaneous human combustion and incorporated a lot of the information into his report, but wondered about the intelligence of his superiors at the time when they ordered him to take out those details and pass it off as an accidental death. He remembered how impassioned he'd become when the coroner called it death by misadventure, caused by a fire of unknown origin.

He looked at the pile of ashes. A Victoria Larson had lived here. Was this what remained of her? According to the manager, she was a student at the University of Illinois Circle Campus in Chicago—an attractive young woman in her late twenties or early thirties. Certainly not the type of person to be a victim of spontaneous human combustion. According to his information, they were usually overweight, in their later years—although there were reports of younger victims—and heavy drinkers, primarily of gin. There were, naturally, isolated cases of teetotalers, but, like younger victims, they were not the norm at all.

How had this woman died? His hand closed on a billfold in the purse and withdrew it. The identification card held his interest. Victoria Larson. Age twenty-eight. Birthdate July 20th, 1958. Height 5 feet 6 inches. Weight 118 pounds. In case of emergency contact Riley Larson.

Hongisto froze. Riley Larson? The same man he'd met the previous Sunday morning? Such a coincidence. Could it be the same? Certainly Riley was an unusual first name. He'd never met anyone with it before, but then, there were a lot of things Jules Hongisto felt he didn't know or hadn't yet experienced. What could Riley Larson be to Victoria Larson? A brother? Maybe. A relative of some sort? Probably. A husband? He shrugged, reaching into a pocket for his own notebook. Fumbling through the pages, he stopped when he came to the penciled name of Riley Larson and compared the telephone number with the one written below the same name on the woman's identification card. They matched.

Hongisto shook his head. The wonderment of coincidence brought a wry smile to his face as he walked to the telephone across the room.

* * *

The Immortal

"Hey, Melanie! Come here! For crying out loud! What the heck happened?" Riley cried as he opened the door and stared at the disaster zone that had been his office as recently as the previous evening.

She came up behind him. "Holy shit! What the fuck happened in here last night?" They stared at the overturned desk, the litter of contents strewn everywhere. The typewriter dangled in the middle of the room, tied to the overhead light fixture by its electrical cord.

"I—I—" he stuttered, trying to find the words.

"Christ, no wonder its cold in the house. The goddamned window's smashed." She pointed to the window overlooking Lily Cache Creek that flowed less than two hundred feet behind the cottage. "Jesus! What happened? I didn't hear a fucking thing last night."

"Neither—neither did I." He managed after several moments. "Where is Grendel? How come he didn't bark his fool head off?"

"Here, Grendel!" She turned back to the living room. "Come on, stupid. You fucked up as a guard last night, but come on out wherever you're hiding. Come on, boy!"

"Grendel!" Riley ordered. "Come!"

Nothing. No response of any kind.

"Hey, Riley," she called out, entering the office. "Look! There's no glass in the room. Now that's what I call strange."

"I don't follow you." He came into the

room, facing her as he turned. He saw the color drain from her face and began to turn around himself when she stopped him.

"Don't turn around, Riley. Jesus Christ! I'm going to be sick." She gagged, vomiting up the coffee she had just drunk.

He turned to see an animal—white—a white dog nailed to the wall by its paws, tongue and tail. He froze, staring at it. "Grendel? Grendel!" Rushing over, grabbing the huge head hanging down, he tried to raise it. Examining the face of the animal, its eyes bugging, he released it as if it had become too awful to touch. "Jesus Christ!" he moaned. "Who the hell would have done something like this? Jesus! Jesus Christ! Aw fuck!" He began pounding the wall on which the dog had been crucified head downward, weeping in anguish over the cruel death of his loyal friend.

Melanie stepped up behind him, embracing his shoulders without trying to turn him around. After several minutes, she ventured, "Are you sure it's Grendel? Goddamn it, Riley, he was *black*. Black as the ace of spades and not white. How could the son of a bitch turn white, for Chrissakes?"

"I—I—I don't know," he choked. "Somehow, Grendel saw something—something pretty bad, and it must have scared him. Frightened him so badly that he turned white. But why did they have to kill him?"

"I don't know, Riley. Just what the fuck

did go on in here last night? We didn't hear anything. At least I didn't. Did you?"

He shook his head.

"Come here." She tugged on his arm, turning him away from the animal's body. "Look over here. There's not a piece of glass anyplace in the room."

He looked uncomprehending, his pained, dumb expression eliciting an embrace from her. "So?" he sobbed over her shoulder.

"So how the fuck did they get in? It looks like they went out through the window but how the hell did they get in?"

Riley stared at her, understanding at last. How *had* the bastards gotten in? He broke free of her embrace and went to the front door. Locked and chained. He checked the back door to find it the same. The rest of the windows in the house were locked, with storm windows securely in place. Nothing, other than Riley's office, was out of order.

Returning with a claw hammer, he pulled the nails from Grendel's carcass which fell to the floor in a heap. Unable to control the flood of tears, he dropped to his knees and hugged the great head once more. Then he struggled to his feet, the animal lying across his arms, and went outside where he gently laid it down next to the back steps. He'd worry about burying it later.

Just as he reentered the kitchen, the telephone rang and he heard Melanie answer. "Hello? Yes. He's here. Just a moment."

She looked at him as he entered the front of the house, a puzzled expression on her face. "It's for you. The police." She handed him the receiver.

"Now what? Hello, this is Riley Larson."

"Mr. Larson? This is Lieutenant Jules Hongisto. I—I hate to bother you. But you were so helpful to me Sunday, that I was wondering if I could impose on you again?"

Riley bit his lip. "I don't think so, Lieutenant. I have a problem here that I've got to solve."

"A problem? Maybe I could be of service?"

"It's a little out of your jurisdiction, Lieutenant."

"It sounds as if it might be something for the police. Is it, Mr. Larson?"

"If it turns out that it's for the police, I'll call. Good-bye." He took the phone from his ear, only to replace it when he heard Hongisto shout.

"Don't hang up, Mr. Larson. Please. I need you to identify a body."

"A body. Whose body?" He disliked the long pause that followed his question.

Then Hongisto said, "Do you know a Vicki Larson?"

Riley sat behind the wheel of the Toyota before turning the key. As he did, tears filled his eyes and he blinked them away to back out onto Lily Cache Lane. He wanted Melanie to come with him. But she'd refused, saying that whoever had broken in last night wouldn't come back in broad daylight. She finally convinced him, insisting she could take care of herself and beat the living shit out of whoever killed Grendel if they were stupid enough to come back. For some reason, he knew it was just what she would do if they did return to the scene of their crime.

Crime? Was it a crime to kill a dog? He didn't know. But he had loved Grendel more than anything in the world—especially after Vicki left and before Melanie came into his life. Why had they killed him? What had he seen to turn his coat white?

Riley sped onto the Interstate and joined the traffic bound for Chicago.

Melanie watched him back away from the garage toward the lane. She wanted time to clean up the blood and debris in his office before he returned. The shock of finding such chaos, then the dog's body, had shaken them both. Soon after, when Hongisto called with news that Vicki was dead, she feared momentarily for Riley's sanity. But he quickly recovered, agreeing to meet Hongisto at Vicki's apartment. After he hung up, he demanded that Melanie accompany him.

She refused from the outset, aware he was thinking of her. But he was becoming overly protective and she wanted no part of that at all. At length, she convinced him to meet the lieutenant alone while she cleaned up the mess. He reluctantly agreed and, after a quick shower, he left.

Melanie turned to walk into the office when the phone rang again. "Hello?"

No answer. She could hear breathing that became short and almost raspy after she spoke. "Hello?" she repeated. "Who the fuck is this?" She waited and then—

"Melanie? Is that you?" It was a smooth, well-modulated voice.

"Yes, who is this?"

"I'm sorry. You took me quite by surprise. I was expecting Riley to answer. This is Sebastian. Sebastian Synn."

"Oh, Sebastian. How are you? I'm sorry for the way I greeted you. We've had a trying morning."

"I see."

She felt for some reason he was being condescending in the way he acknowledged her mention of an unusual morning.

"Is Riley there?"

"No. He's gone."

"I see. Where?"

She looked at the mouthpiece. *Nosy bastard*, she thought. "He got a call about his former wife. Something's happened. He had to go to identify her body."

Her statement was met by a long pause. Then, "I understand. I had no idea he'd been married before. How long have—you and he *are* married, aren't you?"

"No. We're just a couple of moderns living in sin, according to the old way of thinking. Why? Why do you ask? Is it important to you that we be married?" She bit her lip. He sounded a bit confused. What could it matter to him whether they were married or not?

"No, of course not. After all, Leeanah and I aren't married and still we share the same house and—" The sentence hung, unfinished.

She wondered if he were about to confess that they shared the same bed as well, but listened as he continued talking.

"I have a suggestion, Melanie. I would like to have lunch with you. I think there are some things which need clearing up. I would like an opportunity to explain the different things that have been happening."

She didn't speak immediately. What did he mean? Could he have had something to do with wrecking Riley's office and killing the dog? It seemed possible. But why would he want to explain? That made no sense at all. She felt reasonably certain he'd had nothing to do with Vicki since he hadn't known of her existence. Besides, he wasn't stupid enough to openly admit complicity. Yet if that were the case, then Vicki was murdered, and she didn't think Hongisto had referred to her death as a homicide.

Their losses? Was he going to admit he had somehow arranged the run of good luck she and Riley had enjoyed, only to revoke it after they made excuses about not going to any more meetings? If that were true, she'd like to hear his explanation—to hear how he arranges such things. Most important of all, she'd like an explanation as to why she and Riley were selected in the first place. Did Leeanah flip over him when she came to the house that night? Was Synn trying to ace Melanie out so Leeanah could have a clear field? It hardly made sense, but then neither did anything else which had taken place since Riley saw Synn lying on that altar in the church ruins.

She swallowed and replied, "You're sure it's just lunch you want?"

"I promise. We'll talk and when we finish, you'll understand a lot more than you do now. I promise."

"Where and when?"

"Why don't I pick you up about 12:30?"

She quickly calculated how much work she would have to do to be ready at that time. "Make it one o'clock and you've got a date."

"That'll be fine, my dear. Until then—"

The line went dead and Melanie hung up. She'd have to hurry if she wanted to straighten Riley's office, clean up the blood, shower, and be ready by one.

When she finished the office, she paused in front of the typewriter, back on its table again. Amazed that it still worked when she plugged it in, she sat down, rolling a piece of paper into it.

The Immortal

"Dear Riley,

If you come back and I'm not here, don't panic! Sebastian Synn called and invited me to lunch. He said he wanted to explain everything that has been happening. I'm just curious enough to want to find out what the fuck he's talking about. I'm sorry about Vicki. Don't forget that I exist and that in my own dumb way, I love you. I'll see you when you get home or vice versa.

                              Melanie"

CHAPTER 12

Wednesday, November 19, 11:01 A.M.

Fearful of his meeting with Lieutenant Jules Hongisto, Riley deliberately slowed his pace until he merely shuffled along the sidewalk in front of Vicki's apartment house. What had happened to her? She had been healthy the last time he saw her, less than two weeks before. Was it a heart attack? She had no history of problems with her cardiovascular system—other than the one of heartbreak which he apparently caused. That was a foolish way to think. They'd had their differences, especially the last few months before she left. But for him to assume blame was ludicrous at best. Something had happened to Vicki—something totally unexpected, which he was about to find out from Hongisto. Hongisto, the bearer of bad news.

Pulling the lobby door open, he entered, electing to walk up to the fourth floor rather than take the elevator. Prolong it. If he took it slow, the mistake might well have been corrected by the time he arrived. The freshly painted walls of the hotel-turned-efficiency-apartment-house did nothing to brighten his own outlook.

He pushed open the staircase door and entered the hallway. At the far end he saw a uniformed policeman standing outside her door. Nothing had been remedied. He would have to identify her body and talk with the police. Had she met a violent death? Was that the reason the cops had been called in? In seconds he would know.

Nearing the door, he sniffed, slowing his walk. Someone was frying something. He wrinkled his nose; the smell actually offended him.

"Hold it, buddy," ordered the policeman on guard, stepping in front of him.

"I'm to see Lieutenant Jules Hongisto." Riley sounded confident.

"Oh." The officer stepped aside, reaching out to open the door. "Lieutenant?" He pushed it open wide.

Riley caught his breath. The smell was coming from Vicki's apartment.

Jules Hongisto suddenly loomed before him as if materializing out of thin air.

"Mr. Larson." He offered a gigantic hand.

Riley took it, noting the fact that his own hand, not exactly small, could almost be hidden from view if the policeman's closed completely around it. "I wish I could say it's good to see you again, Lieutenant, but under the circumstances—"

"I know. I know. It's awful. Sometimes I simply hate my job. Especially when I have to tell a nice fella like you something bad."

"What happened? How did Vicki die?" He recalled how slow Hongisto had been in telling him on the phone, searching for the right words—words that would inform and yet be gentle. He eventually succeeded, but not before Riley anticipated the very worst and almost cried on learning she was dead.

"Come in and sit down, Mr. Larson. May I call you Riley?"

"Sure. Of course." Aware that after several minutes the greasy smell was barely noticeable, he moved to the small couch Hongisto indicated, wondering as he sat what the blanket lying near the table covered. It certainly wasn't the body. Much too small for that.

Hongisto took a straight chair, positioning it in front of Riley in such a way that the table, blanket and whatever was under it, were blocked from his sight.

"Have you ever heard of spontaneous human combustion, Riley?"

He stared at the detective. "What? I don't think I understand what you're saying."

"Spontaneous human combustion is a rare and mysterious occurrence in which the human body is apparently consumed by fire from within." Hongisto stopped, waiting for the bizarre definition to register.

Riley's eyes widened. "Are you saying that Vicki burned to death?"

"In a manner of speaking, yes. Have you ever heard of this?"

Riley shook his head vigorously.

Hongisto cleared his throat as if preparing to address a group. "Cases involving this type of phenomenon have been reported and filed for centuries. It occurs infrequently. When it does, it is so strange and baffling that the authorities are usually thrown in a dither, trying to determine first what happened, second how to refer to it, and finally, how to report it. You can imagine superiors frowning and questioning a law officer who says the deceased burst into flames and just burned up."

Slowly, mutely, Riley nodded, but said nothing, waiting to hear more.

"Modern doctors and pathologists refuse to acknowledge that this sort of thing can happen. Still, it does. This is not my first case. However, I will say that this one, Victoria Larson's death, does not fit the norm."

Riley's eyes flickered. "What do you mean? Did Vicki burn to death? Where? Here? And what do you mean, 'doesn't fit the norm?' How is it different? Do you think someone did it to her?"

Hongisto shook his head, holding up his hands. "One at a time, Riley. I know you're upset. Let me explain everything I know about this and then you'll know as much as I do. Fair enough?"

Riley sat back. "Go ahead, Lieutenant."

"Even though doctors refuse to admit something like this can happen, there are certain facts they turn their backs on—evidence that cannot be otherwise explained or understood. What I mean about this case not fitting the pattern is that normally, the victim is an older woman, usually much overweight and almost always an alcoholic. In most instances, the drink they consume is gin.

"But," he went on, "Victoria Larson was a *slender, young* woman. From what I have already learned from the manager and the papers on the table, she was going to school and seldom socialized—very serious about her schoolwork. Is that right?"

"I guess." He really didn't know what Vicki's habits had been since she started school, although she told him on one or two occasions she was doing well. It would have been like her to invest time and effort into gaining her security. A lot of good it would do her now.

"As I said before, this is not my first case. It *is* my second, though. There was a woman who died in the same way some fifteen years ago right here in Chicago. She fit the requirements, so to speak. Heavy, lived alone, drank a lot of gin, up in years. She burned up completely. The only thing left was her right leg."

"Burned up completely? Come on, Lieutenant. I know better than that. Even bodies that are cremated have bones and things left." Riley glared at the giant as if accusing him of being condescending.

"I know that, Riley. This is one of the bits of evidence that defy explanation. A crematorium burns at twenty-five hundred degrees Fahrenheit. That's awfully hot. Still, there are quite a few bones that won't burn up completely during the four hours it takes to consume most of the body. In the case of spontaneous human combustion, the length of time is considerably shorter. In some recorded instances—minutes."

"Minutes?" Riley was astonished. "Come on. You're putting me on now. Why, that would mean a lot hotter fire than in a crematory. Right?"

"Exactly. The fire seems to be extraordinarily intense. Let me backtrack for a minute. I said the usual victim is an older woman, overweight, addicted to alcohol. Now, your wife doesn't match those facts, does she? There have been other instances, such as a nineteen-year-old secretary dancing her heart out in a public dance hall, suddenly bursting into flame right on the floor in front of a lot of witnesses. There was no source of fire near her and she burned to death before anyone could do anything to help. A fortyish woman was consumed in

The Immortal

front of her family in California quite a few years ago. She didn't have the essential requirements either. There have also been male victims—rare, but recorded."

"And you're telling me that Vicki simply burned up? Who saw it? I assume you have witnesses."

Hongisto stood. "No. No witnesses. Just the evidence always found at the site of death whenever spontaneous human combustion takes place. You notice the smell? It reminds me of burning grease. Look at the ceiling." He pointed upward.

Riley cocked his head back. A dark circle, looking exactly like a huge soot mark made by a candle held too close to a surface, marked the ceiling over the spot where the blanket lay on the floor. He dropped his eyes.

"Is—is that—is that Vicki—Vicki's remains?" he stammered, indicating the blanket. His hand and arm trembled noticeably.

"In a minute, Riley. You see—"

"No, *you* see, Lieutenant. Look here!" he jumped from the couch, and rushed to the table, banging his palm on it with a loud smack. "If Vicki died as you say she did and the temperature was as high as you claim it was, why in hell didn't her notebook here burn up? Or the table? Or the apartment? Come on. Tell me. You've got all the answers to this one."

Hongisto crossed the room to confront

him, carefully positioning himself between the distraught man and the blanket. "That's just it, Riley. There are some things connected with a case like this that defy explanation. Usually there is a charred circle on the floor where the burning body falls. If the ceiling is low enough, there will be a mark just like this one overhead. A paper item can be as close to the fire as two or three feet and remain untouched. Why? I have no idea. No one does. But that's the way it happens. In one case that took place in the eighteenth century, a noblewoman died in the same way and her legs were completely untouched. Even the silk stockings she wore were intact. That's another piece of unexplainable evidence. The legs can sometimes be spared completely. Strange isn't it?"

Riley stepped back. He felt as if he were choking—strangling on the information, suffocating from the idea of Vicki dying in the horrible manner which had been described. He looked up into Hongisto's compassionate unsmiling face.

"Where's her body now, Lieutenant?"

"There is no body, Riley. If you want to look, I'll show you but it won't be nice. I promise you that."

Riley thought for a split second. It was the idea that it was Vicki. They had been friends, husband and wife, then friendly adversaries in the game of "make a buck to live." But he didn't hate or even dislike her.

The Immortal

In a peculiar way, he still loved her. He owed it to her to look. He had to, to satisfy his own desire to believe Lieutentant Hongisto. He nodded toward the blanket.

Hongisto shrugged and stooping down, pulled the cover back.

All that remained of Vicki Larson was a pile of dirty gray ashes. A bit of bone stuck out of the low mound and a piece of leathery material lay to one side, half-covered with the fine powdery dust.

"What's that?" Riley, hand shaking, pointed to the grayish-black thing partially exposed beneath the pile of ashes.

"I'm not certain, mind you. The medical boys looked at it and they said it might be her liver. They'll know more when they get it to the lab. I—"

"That's all? That's all that's left?" His voice choked and cracked while tears burned, fighting to be shed for Vicki.

"No. I said before that sometimes the legs are left untouched. That's what happened here." Hongisto threw the blanket back all the way.

Riley gagged. Vicki's legs, clad in white socks and a pair of slip-on shoes pointed under the table. Both had been burned off just below the knee. He peered closely through his tears, then turned away. "Lieutenant?"

Hongisto mercifully covered the remains. "I'm sorry, Riley. It's not very nice. It's awful. I thank you for doing this. It must be very difficult."

"Let me ask you a question, Lieutenant. If the medical experts don't recognize something like this and you do, how will you file your report?"

The detective smiled ruefully. "I'll call it what it is. The coroner will probably fill out the death certificate with something like: 'accidental death by fire of unknown origin,' or some such poppycock. Nine chances out of ten, he'll deny my report in theory and wind up accepting it just because the facts are so obvious and apparent. It's rather empirical of them. That's a nice word, isn't it. Empirical. It sorta rolls off your tongue. Well, I'm sure you know about it, right, Riley?"

Still shaken, Riley nodded slowly. Just what was going on in his life? First, he finds his office a shambles—caused by what, he had no idea. How could his heavy desk have been overturned without making a sound? The window had been broken outward, with no way for anyone to have gotten in. Why hadn't he and Melanie heard it? And Grendel —Poor Grendel had turned white. Why? What could have so frightened him? And the worst of all was finding his faithful friend crucified to the wall. Again, why hadn't they heard pounding? The nails were large and couldn't have been simply pushed through his flesh. They must have been driven in

The Immortal

with a good-sized mallet or hammer.

He looked up to find Hongisto perusing his notebook. Should he tell this man? An arm of the law? In view of Vicki's strange death— He stopped. Could—could Synn—Synn and Leeanah have been responsible for this— this murder? Because it would be murder if they had been involved with something that caused Vicki's death. But Hongisto said he had seen other cases like this. No, not cases. Just one. Yet he had apparently read up on the subject because he talked so knowledgeably about it. Still, how would he react if Riley did tell him about his office and what happened to Grendel? Would he try to connect it with Vicki's death? What about the two decapitated homosexuals? Would or could he tie the three crimes together? Were they related?

Riley thought for a moment longer. He knew Synn had been angry with two men— who seemed to fit the description of the two who had been murdered. Then Hongisto called Riley to ask if he knew of any information that might help in the investigation. The pentagram on the floor of one room in the murder house matched what he'd seen in Synn's mansion and the partially obliterated drawing in the ruined church. Was that the only reason Hongisto had called him—the similarity to the pentagram he described in his article?

He glanced at the tall man again, to find he

was being studied by him. Did he suspect something about his and Melanie's involvement with Synn? If Synn were a murderer would the two of them be involved? He shook his head. He was being paranoid. As far as he could tell, Hongisto was sincere and genuine. He didn't strike Riley as the type who would play cat and mouse with anyone. Rather, he seemed almost too direct.

"What's wrong, Riley?"

"Wrong? I'm still a little shaken, I guess. I think I'd better get out of here. Are you finished with me?"

"Sure. I can get a hold of you any time I want, can't I?"

"You make that sound almost threatening, Lieutenant. I'm not under suspicion, am I?" Riley cursed himself for asking. He really was paranoid.

"I don't know of what. Were you paying your wife alimony?"

"That's the second time you've said that. You mean my ex-wife, don't you? I told you on the phone that Vicki and I were divorced."

"I know that, but I guess I'm old-fashioned. I consider two people married forever until death separates them. I guess I'm silly that way. *Were* you?"

"Yeah. I had to support her until she finished her education."

"How much a month?"

"Nine hundred."

"How long did you have to go before she graduated?"

"About eighteen months."

"I don't see you as the type to kill someone for fifteen or sixteen thousand dollars, Riley. Besides, I don't think any human being is capable of burning another in this manner. I believe this one will go in the books just as I said a few minutes ago."

"I can go then?"

"Sure. I'll get in touch if I need anything. Is that all right?"

"Of course. Good-bye, Lieutenant."

Hongisto said good-bye as Riley opened the door and stepped into the hallway. The officer there stepped aside and Riley hurried to the stairwell. The stench of burnt grease seemed much stronger in the hall for some reason, and he didn't want to stand waiting for the elevator. Tears came to his eyes again now that he knew the source of the odor. He wanted to vomit—to heave his guts out in her memory. What a Godawful way to die. He didn't think he'd ever forget the sight of the small pile of ashes that had been Vicki Larson, his friend and ex-wife. Not ever.

Melanie smiled at Sebastian Synn who sat opposite her across the table they shared at Queen's Restaurant in Hawthorne. She had jokingly suggested it, thinking of it as a bright, open place—one where she wouldn't feel threatened by her host. But he graciously accepted the idea and they entered shortly after 1:30. The room was almost deserted and she noticed that Synn seemed to feel more at ease once he saw the emptiness of the place.

After ordering a light Chablis, they looked about the room, Melanie feeling most uncomfortable with him. She seldom if ever felt strange around men, but for some reason she could not quite unscramble in her mind, she didn't feel the least bit safe or assured with Sebastian Synn. The intrusion of the waitress bringing their drinks was welcome.

When she turned to face him again, he was looking over her shoulder at the couple seated directly behind her chair. She'd never really had an opportunity to observe him at close range, though she'd been as near to him as this at the mansion. But there the lighting was always so subdued that she'd seen only highlights of his face and features. There was a marked degree of handsomeness about him. Instantly, she revised her opinion. If Sebastian were to be described in a word, it would have to be attractive—no, pretty? Pretty? Men weren't pretty, were they? Beautiful? Maybe, but when she looked at him, she saw the fine cheekbones which balanced his face in perfect symmetry. His eyes were penetrating and forceful but direct. She decided she'd never want him very angry with her because he would probably melt her on the spot with a withering glare. His lips were not full, but rather skimpy in their development. The white hair was probably prematurely turned, but from what color? His eyebrows were equally as white. She glanced at his hands. No hair on them at all. Strange, to say the least.

Did he know she was studying him? Lifting her glass, she slowly sipped the wine, scrutinizing him more minutely. When she looked closely at his complexion, she choked.

"Are you all right?" A gracious smile was on his face.

Dabbing at her lips with the napkin, she quickly recovered. "Yes. It just went down the wrong way."

His gaze wandered back to the couple behind her and she continued surveying him. His skin was a network of fine lines. So tiny, so miniscule they were almost invisible. But sitting this close with the light just right, she could see them. Startled at the weird texture his skin seemed to possess, she found herself wanting to reach across the table to verify her conclusion. It should feel like a delicate parchment, she surmised, looking quickly away when she heard the couple behind her rise and his attention returned to her.

"The stupid oafs are leaving, finally," he said.

Melanie smiled inwardly. Did he think they'd have the place exclusively to themselves? When she turned, she found the room empty except for the two of them. There had been several tables occupied when they entered, with diners at various stages of completing their meal. But within the few minutes since they'd sat down, everyone had departed, leaving them the sole occupants of the room.

Not thinking too much of it, she brought her attention back to his hands. They too were covered with a network of lines like his face. Then she saw the ring. Large, obviously gold, it was engraved with a strange looking creature in profile. She looked up to find him staring at her.

"You like my ring?"

"I've never seen one like it before. May I?" She held her hand out to take his.

Congratulating herself when he extended his ringed hand to her, she thought she might begin trembling. A drop of perspiration formed between her breasts when she took his hand in hers. The skin felt just as she had anticipated—like delicate parchment —so fine she feared it might tear and bleed if she handled it carelessly.

The huge ring covered the entire joint on which it rested. The animal it depicted reared on its hind legs, tail winding between them. But instead of forefeet to match those in the rear, talons of an eagle or some bird of prey extended from the upper body. Wings and an eagle's head were mounted on the body. She looked up, a question on her face.

"It's a gryphon," he offered.

Could he read minds? If that were the case, she would be in big trouble. She looked at him quizzically.

"I don't read minds, if that's what you're wondering, Melanie. The gryphon is an unusual creature of mythology. Not too many people are aware of it. It's associated with wealth and power."

"Maybe that's why."

"I'm afraid I don't understand."

"If it's associated only with people of wealth and power, us poor riffraff wouldn't know about it."

He laughed, the sound so gentle and refined that she looked away.

"I've had it a very long time," he said. "I think it's beautiful."

"It *is* beautiful," she echoed, dropping his hand. He seemed open, unafraid of anything she might ask. She wanted to ask him about a lot of things. The coat of arms Riley had photographed the first night they went to the mansion came to mind. Maybe she'd get to that later. How did he make his money? Had he lived in Chicago all his life?

"Did losing the commissions to paint those portraits bother you?" He broke into her thoughts.

Startled by the direct question, she waited a few minutes before answering. She'd promised herself not to use her usual vernacular while with him. "Yes. Yes it bothered me quite a bit. To have them offered, to be almost ready to start, and then to learn the doctor and his wife were divorcing, well—let's just say I was rather upset." She thought back to her reaction at the time, her tirade and foul language.

"That was nothing, Melanie. I can make you a millionaire many times over, if you let me."

"You promised something like that before and then took everything away. At least, I'm assuming it was you who were responsible for Riley's job offers as well as my brief fling at being a successful portrait painter."

He smiled, dipping his head a bit. "I was. I gave and I took away. Both Riley and you had promised not to withdraw from my—my group. But you did. I had to demonstrate my power. Did I succeed?"

"Oh, yeah. You did that, all right." She bit her tongue to stop herself from asking if he had been responsible for the damage in Riley's office and Grendel's death. If he were, it would do no good to get him angry with her. Just what *could* he do? If it were possible for him to create disaster at a distance without raising a sweat, what might he accomplish against someone sitting a few feet away?

"I do want Riley back. I want you, as well, my dear. What do *you* want out of this life?"

She ignored the question. He wanted Riley first and her as an afterthought. That was the way it seemed. "Which of us do you want the most?" she challenged.

"I'm sorry. I don't understand."

"Even though Riley's not here, you've mentioned his name first and mine second every time you've referred to us. You just did it again. Is Riley more important to you than I am? That's all I want to know."

"My desire for the opposite sex is as strong as yours, my dear. I do not want Riley for something as unnatural or deviant as you're implying, if that is in your mind. It's just that his presence is extremely important to the group—to me at this time. Of course, your presence will enhance everything as well, but not in the same way."

"Explain that." Her tone was brusque.

"No. I won't. You'll just have to take my statements and promises on faith. If I say I need him, I need him. It is that simple. By the same token, if I say I can make you a millionaire many times over, believe it. I am not lying to you."

"You can really do that? Make me wealthy?" She looked at him, her head cocked to one side, wanting to believe but also wanting proof.

"Of course."

After several seconds passed, still skeptical, she looked directly at him. "What do I have to do?"

"Convince Riley to rejoin me. That's all. Bring him back to me—at the mansion. Join the group and take the necessary indoctrination with him. Then, unbelievable wealth will be yours."

She couldn't control the sly smile crossing her face. The idea of riches ricocheted in her brain. She remembered how indecisive she had been at first, while Riley was so cocksure. Then she'd gained his confidence and he lost his ability to make a decision where Synn and Leeanah were concerned. "I want to ask you about Leeanah. May I?"

"Of course."

"Does *she* want Riley?"

He laughed softly. "No. I rather think not. Why do you ask?"

"Well, the two of them—you know—that one night—ah—"

"The great rite used in focusing the cone of power?" He laughed again. "No, my dear. Do not be jealous of Leeanah. She belongs to me and does what I ask of her. Your relationship with Riley should not be affected unless you make it happen. Don't. Jealousy is so petty and unbecoming to people. I find it almost impossible to think of you as being jealous of anything."

"I'm not the jealous type. I just wanted to know what the setup was, that's all. If Riley wants to hump her and you say it's okay, who am I to stand in the way?"

"Besides," Synn added, "I'm going to make you rich."

She smiled.

The Immortal

"Will you bring Riley to me?"

"I need some proof."

"Proof?"

"Proof that you can do what you say."

He smiled, reaching into his inside coat pocket. Withdrawing a wallet-like leather container, he opened it.

She stared, her jaw dropping. Diamonds. Large diamonds. Huge diamonds—none appearing smaller than three or four carats—glistened under the lights of the restaurant.

"Are—are those—real?" she managed to stammer after several minutes.

Synn laughed. "Of course they're real. Take one."

"*Take* one?"

He nodded.

She reached out tentatively. One, larger than the others caught her attention. She recalled the story about the greedy child taking the biggest piece of cake and turned her attention to the smaller stones.

Synn's hand suddenly closed over the jewels. "Let me decide for you." He opened his palm to display the largest diamond.

Her hand shaking, she accepted it. It had to be worth thousands of dollars. Not just a few but many thousand. Maybe even—

"How valuable is this?" She couldn't take her eyes off the bright beauty.

"If you priced it at a reputable jeweler's, I think you would be amazed at that bauble's worth."

"And you're just giving me this?" Her voice was tiny.

"If you had said you wanted the whole case I would have simply turned it over to you. I am that generous."

"Is this all I'll get if I bring Riley to you?"

"I hardly consider this untold wealth. No. I promise you, you will become a multimillionaire shortly after Riley is delivered, and you demonstrate your sincerity toward me. I do not merely ask for loyalty. I demand it for the baubles I give."

"You're sure this gem is real?"

Synn threw a ten-dollar bill on the table and stood. "Come with me." It wasn't a request but an order.

She got up, meekly following him from the dining room. Even though they hadn't eaten, food was no longer paramount in her mind.

Outside, he pointed across the street to a jewelry store. "We can go there and have your diamond appraised. Come."

"What if," she said, hanging back, "you bought the services of the jeweler?"

"All right then." He was patient. "You choose the place."

She frowned. Was there another jewelry store in Hawthorne? She wasn't certain. After all, valuable gems hadn't been in her realm of thought until just a few minutes ago.

"Can I go in alone?"

"If you wish."

Without a word, Melanie left him standing on the sidewalk and crossed the street by herself. Entering the store, she approached the girl behind the counter. "Can your store appraise a diamond for me?"

"We have two gentlemen who could be of service to you."

"I want an estimate as to the worth of this jewel." She withdrew the diamond from her pocket and handed it to the girl, whose eyes widened when she saw the size of it.

"It'll be a few minutes." The girl turned to walk to the rear of the store.

Melanie impatiently admired the rings and watches in the different showcases until the young woman reappeared, an older man following her.

"This is a most exquisite gem, young lady." His every word was tinged with excitement. "Where on earth did you get it?"

Melanie cocked an eyebrow and stared at him for a moment. If he were in Synn's employ, the man was a superb actor. If not— She hesitated a moment. "It—It was a—a gift. How much is it worth?"

"This stone," he began, more to himself than to Melanie, rolling it back and forth between thumb and forefinger, peering at it through his loupe, "is for all practical purposes, priceless. Not that there isn't a price for it because there is. But you and I, young lady, do not have the type of money needed to indulge ourselves with stones like this. It's quite large. Between seven and eight carats, I'm sure. It's absolutely flawless. Even the Hope Diamond doesn't have the color quality this stone has. The Hope is blue-white while yours is waterfall clear. That's the most excellent of color quality—it's a D-color, I'm positive without even looking further."

"It's value?" Melanie whispered, suddenly in awe of everything the man had said.

"Conservatively speaking, and merely guessing, mind you, since I have no idea as to the going rate of the market, I would estimate the value at perhaps one million to one and a quarter million dollars. Of course, you would need someone with that much money and the desire to purchase, to realize the stone's value."

Melanie felt weak. Turning, she saw Synn on the opposite side of the street. He appeared to be smiling and touched the brim of his hat with his right hand in a salute.

She choked for an instant, realizing she had just promised to deliver Riley to Sebastian Synn for the price of the diamond the man behind the counter held out to her. Her hand shaking, she accepted it, and, clutching it, tightly, left the store.

CHAPTER 13

Wednesday Evening, November 19, 9:50 p.m.

From the moment Synn dropped her off at Worthless Acres, Melanie pondered the dilemma she and Riley were in, from which she suddenly found herself doubting they would ever extricate themselves safely. She felt like screaming with joy about possessing the gem, after Synn left without getting out of the car. He certainly was the utmost in perfection when it came to being a gentleman. Considering certain aspects of him which more than interested her—his complexion, white hair and eyebrows, supergentle manner—she might have welcomed at least an attempt on his part to make a play for her while they were driving toward Lily Cache Lane.

But he had said nothing out of the ordinary, done nothing remotely improper, and simply said good-bye when they reached the cottage. The Rolls-Royce had started without waiting for her to enter the house, and she stood there watching it leave. Even before going in, she knew Riley had not returned yet. The driveway was deserted.

She went to his office first to make certain everything there was in good shape. Wondering why he had not yet returned, she prepared a light supper for herself, making certain there were leftovers in the event he arrived home with a good appetite.

Worried, she wondered about his state of mind. It hadn't been enough to have found Grendel killed so horribly, completely changed in color, the cops had to call and tell him his ex-wife was also dead. She shuddered. Just what the hell was going on? Why hadn't he returned yet? It was midmorning when he left, with no word from him since, although me might have tried while she was having lunch—which turned out to be a glass of wine—with Synn.

She ate slowly, hoping Riley would walk in any minute. He hadn't by 10 o'clock. She felt her energy reserves waning and got ready for bed, which entailed taking off her clothes and slipping into a dressing gown.

Her hand, rolled into a ball and thrust under her robe, clutched the diamond Synn had given her as a show of faith, to prove he would make her wealthy. But at what price? Merely convincing Riley to rejoin the group seemed a totally inadequate service for such a treasure. Why did Synn want him to be a member so much that he would give up a jewel worth in excess of—she squeezed the stone even harder remembering the jeweler's words. It didn't make sense. Nothing made much sense to Melanie concerning Sebastian Synn.

Turning on the television set to watch the news, she dozed, falling asleep before the weather report came on.

Sleeping dreamlessly, she floated in a warm cocoon of comfort, hearing and not hearing the soft dialogue of the late movie. Then came the strange sound. At first she attributed it to the television and didn't stir.

Scrape.

She continued sleeping. Two people laughed, giggled and carried on a dialogue with traffic sounds in the background—a movie, she subconsciously told herself.

Scrape.

A man talked entirely too fast to be understood—something about gold—he was talking about genuine gold—not 14 karat gold, which was like adding water to your coffee and cream or something like that— something that passed in her semiconsciousness like a flash of light—something she didn't care about—

Scrape.

Her eyes opened. The sound didn't belong with the soup commercial playing when she looked at the screen. In fact, if she recalled correctly, that particular noise had accompanied the fast talker and his diatribe about gold as well. She frowned.

Scrape.

The sound had been going on with the couple talking and laughing as well.

Scrape.

It was coming from outside, she felt certain. Rubbing her hand over her face, attempting to awaken fully, she stumbled to her feet, holding the clenched fist with her diamond close to her breast.

Scrape.

What the hell was that?

Scrape.

Why didn't they keep a gun or something in the house? What could she use? A knife? That would mean she would have to get within an arm's length of whoever or whatever was making that noise, to defend herself. What were they after? The diamond?

Scrape.

Hurrying to the kitchen, she grabbed the oversize chef's knife and stood in the center of the room, not quite certain what she should do next. How could they be after the gem? No one other than Synn and the people at the jewelry store knew she had it.

Scrape.

The sound was louder here in the kitchen. What was going on? Now she was positive it came from outside. A panic-filled sense of dread washed over her.

Scrape.

Tiptoeing to the window over the sink, she

pulled the heavy curtain back slightly, peering through the slit she had made. Clouds blotted out any light from the moon and stars but she could make out a silhouette, a man digging. Digging?

Scrape.

Digging for what?

When he stood, turning to face the house, Melanie felt like screaming. She crossed her legs as an overpowering urge to urinate swept through her. She couldn't make out the face of the digger but he was coming toward the house. The back door. She held her breath, trying desperately to remember a prayer—any prayer—to anyone—to any god. It would help her—help her prepare to die if that was his intent. What had he been digging? Her grave?

When the figure reached the steps, it stopped and bent down. She strained to see what he might be doing. When he stood upright, something was in his arms. A lifeless shape. Something white. That much she could make out in the gloom.

Grendel? The man—Riley—was carrying Grendel! To the hole he had been digging in the back yard. Riley was burying the dog.

Hands trembling, she dropped the curtain and swallowed hard, both relieved and frightened at her reactions. Should she interfere? Help him? She knew he and the dog were special friends, while her relationship with the Labrador retriever was, at best, one of tolerating each other. Though she had walked him many times, Grendel aways preferred Riley. She found herself wondering if he felt the same degree of grief for Vicki.

Vicki. Melanie had almost forgotten about her death. Rudely reminded by the fright which confused her senses, she stepped back, replacing the knife in its wooden holder. Her left hand hurt. She looked at it, trying to figure out why it cramped so badly.

The diamond. She opened her fingers, stiff from having clutched it so tightly. It lay in her wet palm, reflecting what light filtered in from the living room.

Glancing out the window again, she saw Riley, head bowed, standing by the open grave, Grendel's carcass out of sight. He picked up the shovel and began filling the hole in a slow, steady tempo which increased until he was shoveling at a backbreaking pace. Once a little mound covered the last remains of the animal, he looked around and slowly walked toward the kitchen door.

At first, Melanie felt like running into the living room. Riley might think she was spying on him if he found her in the kitchen. But what difference did that make? She wanted to be there to condole with him, offer a shoulder if he needed one to cry on, or simply help him sort out his feelings. Why should she feel strange about standing in the kitchen when he entered?

His eyes lit up at the sight of her. Closing

the door, he strode over, enveloping her in a bear-like embrace, squeezing for a full minute before releasing her.

"Are you all right?" she asked, tenderly.

"Yeah. I'm fine. I'll make it."

"Tell me what happened. What happened to Vicki?"

While he made coffee, he repeated everything Hongisto told him, how Vicki had died, the peculiar circumstances found in a case of spontaneous human combustion.

"So, tell me." She subtly mimicked a Jewish grandmother when she realized Riley was handling the stress of both deaths much better than she would have. "Where have you been since leaving the nice policeman?"

He forced a smile. "I just drove around most of the afternoon and evening. I finally decided it wasn't solving anything and that at best, you and I had to get on with our lives. I'm not too much into the mourning scene and as far as I'm concerned, it's over and done with."

He poured each of them a mug of coffee and they went into the living room. When they were seated, he took a sip. "How was your day?"

Melanie gulped. Her moment of truth was at hand. She still held the jewel, deciding against showing it to him until the absolute right moment. She had to convince him to return to Synn. Synn. Probably the person responsible for Grendel's death. She had no idea how it had been accomplished, or why. What might the man's reasoning have been? But she felt quite certain that if Synn could give and take back so easily, kill two men by black magic or whatever means he used, present her with a flawles diamond worth God knows how much, he could damn well turn a dog white and nail the poor son of a bitch to the wall.

"I—I had lunch with Sebastian Synn," she started in a soft voice. She had to get it over with. Synn was too powerful for them to resist at this time. Maybe they could pretend to cooperate and then, at the right moment, get the hell away from him and Leeanah.

"You what?"

Melanie looked at him. He didn't seem upset. In fact, she felt he merely asked as if he hadn't heard her quite right. Was he so anesthetized by the deaths? He'd said they were behind him and he wanted to get on with their lives.

"He called right after you left and wanted to have lunch with me."

"What did he want?"

"That was the strange part. He said he wanted to explain everything that's been happening."

"Did he?"

"Well, in some ways yes and in some ways no. He came right out and said it was he who'd taken everything we'd gained away from us."

"You didn't jump to a wrong conclusion—based on what he said?" Riley stood, walked into the kitchen, and returned with the coffee pot. After refilling their mugs, he sat down again.

"I don't think I did," Melanie answered, having replayed her conversation with Synn while Riley poured the coffee.

"He didn't happen to mention if he'd rubbed out the two faggots Hongisto had me look at, did he?"

"We didn't talk about that. Why bring it up?"

He shrugged. "I don't know. The way Vicki died. The fact that Grendel turned white, was nailed to the wall, and we didn't hear anything just made me wonder. Who is Synn and just how powerful is he?"

"I don't know the answer to either one of those, but I know he's filthy rich and generous as—" She held out her hand, slowly opening it.

Riley watched her and whistled when he saw the jewel. "Where'd you get that?"

"From him."

"It's not real."

"That's what I thought, too, when he gave it to me. He had a whole caseful."

"How many?"

"Two, three dozen. This was the biggest."

"How do you know it's real?"

She told him about the jewelry store and the estimate of the jeweler.

When she finished, he stared at her. "What do you have to do to earn it? Or have you already performed?"

"That was a cheap shot, Riley. You may not like what I'm going to say but I've done a lot of thinking about it. Just don't say no without giving the idea some time. All right?"

He thew his hands up. "I have no idea what the hell you're talking about. But go ahead."

Melanie smiled. He had used the word *hell*. His cursing when they found Grendel this morning suddenly replayed in her memory. It had made her feel better to hear him use such foul language. She would have been concerned about his sanity if he hadn't reacted normally. How long could he restrain himself in a tough situation without giving vent to his anger?

"I'm not certain about Synn and what he can actually do, but I think the two of us should go back to his group. At least for the time being."

He stared at her. "You're kidding, right?"

She shook her head, her hair tossing from side to side. "Look, Riley, what if he did kill those two queers? What's to prevent him from doing the same to us?"

"We haven't threatened him in any way, Mel."

"I know that." She was hoping not to blow the opportunity to get Riley to agree. "But what if he gets pissed at us for not going back? Then what? Does he chop our heads off in some ceremony where we aren't even present to defend ourselves? Face it, the man plays rough."

"Rough? That's putting it mildly. Was he responsible for Grendel?"

She shook her head. "I didn't mention it and neither did he. But he didn't push for more information when I told him we'd had a trying morning."

"What do you mean?"

"He just sort of accepted it, like he knew what had taken place. But suppose he did have something to do with it? You and I didn't hear a goddamn thing last night, yet this morning your fucking office was wrecked and Grendel—" Her voice drifted off without finishing.

He nodded. "I suppose you're going to tell me Vicki died because of him, too."

"You gotta admit it's a pretty strange way to die."

"But Hongisto explained all that."

"Look, put yourself in Synn's place for a minute. You want to get rid of a couple of rivals, so you take care of them good—in a real strange, bizarre way. We were there, Riley. We saw what he did. Then, quite by chance, because of the article you wrote, you were called by the police to look at a murder scene. A pretty goddamned strange murder scene, too. You said so yourself."

"I know that. But if he did kill Vicki, why? We weren't married any more. Why kill her? He didn't even know her."

Melanie shrugged, withholding her theory on that. Synn hadn't known she and Riley weren't married. When Riley almost corrected him that first night at the mansion, she had jumped into the conversation and the subject was dropped. Synn had been shocked—at least that was how she interpreted his reaction—when she answered the phone this morning. Later, after he dropped her off at "Worthless Acres," she came to the conclusion he hadn't been expecting her to answer. He hadn't expected her ever to be around again. He'd thought *she* was Riley's wife and may have wanted to get rid of her to reclaim Riley without any interference.

His main interest was Riley. He'd said as much. But why? He wouldn't answer the question in the restaurant. Could it be he tried to kill Melanie without mentioning her name, referring to her as Riley's wife? If that were the case, then poor Vicki had been murdered by mistake. Melanie was the intended victim.

What could they do? What could *she* do? Go to the police? What was the likelihood of them believing her? Even this unusual guy Riley had met—Hongisto. There was no one to whom she could turn. No one who could

The Immortal

help get the two of them out of this situation.

One thing she did know was that she was frightened. Frightened for her own safety. And Riley seemed to be the key to it. If she could deliver Riley to Synn, she would reap untold wealth, according to him, and hopefully be allowed to live her own life without further interference. She hated having to be a *Judas goat* where Riley was concerned but what other choice did she have? If Synn wanted him that badly, she felt reasonably certain he wouldn't be in any danger. She also suspected that Sebastian would have his own way whether she cooperated or not. She might as well profit if she could. Riley would undoubtedly hate her for betraying him, but in time she hoped he'd realize it was for his own good as well as her safety. If she could convince him of that when the time came, perhaps he wouldn't feel bitter toward her.

"I don't know if Synn had anything to do with Vicki's death or not." She hoped he wouldn't detect the lie in her voice. "Whether he did or not is immaterial. It's the two other incidents that have me convinced."

"You really believe he did Grendel in?"

"I wish I didn't. And I'm sure he took care of his competition with that 'cone of power.' Jesus, Riley, I'm scared. On the other hand, we don't know anything about him. Maybe we're barking up the wrong tree. But one thing we do know is that he's generous to a fault. Why don't we take advantage of our position, join him, get what we can and get out while the getting's good?"

"Assuming we could get out whenever we wanted," he put in softly.

"Does that mean you'll go with me?"

"Hey, look. You're not the only one who's scared. You didn't see Vicki or what had been Vicki. Even if Synn didn't have anything to do with *her* death, the two men who lost their heads and Grendel—Grendel dying —are enough to convince me, too. Let's go for it."

Melanie stood, crossing to him. "Come on, I want you to show how you feel about me right now. I was scared to death you might say no and I'd have to join Synn on my own and maybe do something against you with him."

Taking her hand, he led her to the bedroom. "Could you? Do something against me?"

He partly closed the living room door and turned her to face him.

"You know how I feel about you, Riley Larson." She began unbuttoning his shirt, helping him out of it, dropped to her knees, undoing his belt, opening his pants which she pulled down until he could step out of them, and then slipped off his shorts.

The Immortal

When she stood up, he embraced her. She thrilled, feeling him stir against her lower abdomen. He opened her gown and gently pushed her toward the bed. Slowly falling backward, she caught herself with her arms, lowering her body to the mattress. He lay down next to her, tenderly embracing her.

Their mouths locked briefly before he left hers partially open to explore her body in its entirety. His tongue caressed her breasts, leaving a damp trail behind, circling in toward the erect nipples that waited expectantly for his examination. He tongued them, carefully teething each into a frenzied state of excitement which coursed through her body, centering in her lower extremities, focusing on the mound of her womanhood, which alternately tingled and ached under the soft reddish hair.

Melanie arched her back, anticipating Riley's entrance into her. Pulsating shocks like electrical charges, rippled up and down the full length of her body as she trembled, waiting.

His tongue continued its slow, maddening journey down to her navel where it pushed inward, searching for the extra touch to excite her even more. It continued unerringly past, over her gently rounded lower belly, toward the reddish hair. Nuzzling below it, he kissed feverishly for a moment before tearing his lips away, raising himself up on both arms, one leg thrown over her.

She spread hers, inviting him to enter. As he lowered his body, she reached out, taking his firm penis in both hands, guiding it toward her vagina. She sucked in her breath with a tiny gasp as he penetrated, his erect penis slipping into the lubricated hollow. In seconds their animal-like rhythm was established and they built to a savage symphony of mutual fulfillment.

Gradually, inevitably, a crescendo of satisfaction reached its climax in both of them. As their intensity of feeling lessened, they lay coupled together, his erection withering, her breath coming slower.

By midnight, he was gently snoring, but Melanie lay on her back staring at the blackness around her. She wanted to feel some pang of regret, while instead an unknown logic, one she had never before experienced, hammered at her, telling her she had done the right thing, was doing the right thing, and had one more step to take before closing her eyes for the night.

She slipped from beneath the covers and put on her dressing gown. Tiptoing out of the bedroom, she closed the door without making a sound, turned on a lamp and went to her purse lying on the end table next to the couch. Opening it, she fumbled through the contents and pulled out a card on which Sebastian had written his unlisted telephone number.

The Immortal

She dialed quietly for fear of waking Riley. It seemed the ringing of the telephone which blasted in her ear could be heard through the entire house. After several endlessly drawn out minutes, the receiver was picked up on the other end and a quiet voice spoke simply, "Yes?"

"Sebastian?"

"Yes."

"This is Melanie. I believe Riley will be coming along with me."

"That's fine, Melanie."

"When will you want to see us?"

"Tomorrow evening. I'll have a car stop by for you."

"May I have Riley drive us there? It hardly seems fair to impose on you all the time. Or we could follow your driver, since I'm not certain how to find your home."

A pause followed before he answered. "That will be fine. Yes, then if for any reason either of you had to go somewhere, you would have your own automobile in which to travel. On occasion, I must go into the city to transact business and what have you. I'll send the limousine tomorrow evening."

"We'll be ready at that time, then." The note of finality in her voice told him she did not want to talk any more.

"Very well, my dear. You have done magnificently. You will be rewarded beyond anything you can think of. Until tomorrow night." He sounded gleeful as he hung up.

For a long time, Melanie stood staring at the silent receiver in her hand. Had she done the right thing? In time they both would know.

CHAPTER 14

Thursday Evening, November 20, 10:45 P.M.

Melanie covertly watched Riley drive, his eyes fixed on the taillights of the Rolls-Royce. They'd carried on a spasmodic conversation since leaving Worthless Acres, and she still hadn't determined his state of mind. Was he the slightest bit enthused about meeting Sebastian and Leeanah again, or simply being cooperative to humor her? After admiring the diamond she showed him last night, it hadn't been mentioned further. Might he be the slightest bit jealous? Maybe he was suspicious. She dreaded the latter idea. If he were jealous, it was a new facet of his personality—one she'd never had reason to suspect ever existed. And she knew him better than anyone. Better than Vicky had.

Every once in a while she noticed a tiny grin on his lips, as though he might be thinking about the future and how it would change for the better because of his renewed association with Synn. Certainly, the fact that money might lie in their futures had already been aptly demonstrated. She could feel the diamond in her purse. That was real.

A tremor rippled down her spine at the thought of the price she was willing to pay to hold onto the gem, just the beginning of what Synn had promised. Again, she glanced at Riley. A broad smile animated his features in the half-light of the dashboard.

"What's so funny?" She almost jumped at the sound of her own voice.

"I was just thinking. We were fools to have considered not following through with Synn. It was stupid to turn down a fortune just because he decided to do away with a couple of fags. Whatever he believes in— however he does what he does—I'm ready to accept. Why fight it? He said we'd cash in. Then, like a couple of self-righteous, religious idiots, we almost blew it. If he can kill people by remote control, never once be suspected, and get away with it, I'm ready to side with him and not against him. Do you know what I mean?"

She looked out the window, then back at him. "I guess I do. It's sorta scary when I think about the whole thing. I could just go to pieces. Are you certain this is what we should do, Riley?"

What was wrong with her? Now she was sounding like she *didn't* want him to go. That would mean losing the diamond and everything else. If they suddenly shot off the

Interstate and up a ramp before the driver in the Rolls knew they were gone, what would Synn do? She shuddered, not wanting to think about it. Much better to cooperate, at least for the time being, get what they can and study the situation from the inside. Once they knew more about the overall operation, they could better figure out how to get away from him. Perhaps they would discover his weakness—if he had one.

Riley turned, glaring at her. "Of course it is. I'm not going to be a hero and fight this guy. He has too many tricks up his sleeve. I say we go along with him and get filthy rich, if that's how he wants it. And you know? For some dumb reason, I think Vicki would be proud of me." He laughed.

Melanie looked out the window at the lights of the suburbs flashing by. What were the people in those houses doing? How would they react if they knew there were a man and woman living nearby who could work magic, performing feats beyond the scope and ken of any one of them? The fact that she and Riley did know made the two of them different, she guessed. Would they learn how to kill people from a distance? Make people rich? She wondered how he did it all. Simply command it? Pray to the devil for it? Make a few threatening phone calls? How did Sebastian Synn regulate and control the fate of people he barely knew?

When she focused her attention on the car

ahead of them, she realized they were close to the mansion. In seconds, they turned off the darkened street, passing through the pillars that marked the driveway to the great house atop the slight rise.

The Rolls didn't stop, continuing through the portico, disappearing back down the drive. Riley brought the Toyota to a halt opposite the doorway through which they had entered on the two other occasions. The first time, Melanie had been in awe. The second time, she had anticipated the start of their indoctrinating sessions. Instead, they took part in a weird ceremony where Riley fucked Leeanah in front of everyone. Now she was fearful, an awful anxiety coursing through her, warning her. But it was too late. They were getting out of the car. What would happen when Synn confronted them?

Riley rang the doorbell. She turned. The rusty Toyota looked so pitiful, so out of place under the roof of the entrance. What were they doing here?

The door opened.

Sebastian, a broad, friendly smile on his face, stood with arms wide. "Welcome, my friends. Welcome back to my home."

Riley returned the smile with a wide grin, and Melanie wondered if she were reacting in the same way. Her body, arms, and legs, felt numb. Was she actually smiling? Putting on a happy expression?

She watched Riley accept Sebastian's

embrace and stepped forward when he extended his arms to her. Once held, she thought how absolutely soft he seemed under his lounging jacket. Then she was being placed at arm's length.

"Melanie, you have no idea how proud I am of you. How grateful." The tone of his voice was soothing, caressing.

"I—I'm glad you're happy, Sebastian."

"Come. Come in," he urged, standing back to make a sweeping gesture with one arm. "Leeanah will be with us in a moment. How have you been since we last saw each other?"

Melanie watched Riley hem and haw, searching for the right words to answer the questions without telling everything. Apparently, he didn't want to embarrass their host and themselves by mentioning the double murder, Grendel's death, the destruction of his office, or Vicki's horrible death.

Looking up, she found Synn observing her closely as he held the door to the library open for them to enter. Her skin crawled. She could detect nothing in his eyes. Now that she thought about it, she hadn't been able to see the slightest emotion in those eyes at the restaurant the day before. Where were the windows of his soul? Or had the devil already collected his debt for the dark abilities Sebastian possessed?

"If you will wait here, I'll hurry Leeanah along," he murmured graciously and left them.

Riley went to the coat of arms on the wall. "I still wonder what all of this means? *Without end?* What are the meanings behind the symbols on it?" He turned to face Melanie.

She shrugged. "You haven't heard from the U?"

"It's only been a little over two weeks since I sent the pictures. I also sent one of the knife."

"Sh-h-h-h." Melanie hurried to the couch. "I hear them coming. Sit down, Riley."

He moved toward the divan, walking slowly, deliberately, as if he wanted to be caught out of his seat.

The door opened, and the exotic perfume Leeanah wore preceded her into the low-lit library. Without a word, she rushed to Riley, kissing him on the mouth. Synn stood back, watching approvingly.

Melanie felt stupid, foolish. It was a brazen display at best. Was Leeanah truly after Riley? Had Melanie fallen into a trap to deliver him for Leeanah's personal needs? Her doubts wavered when the woman turned to her, extending her hand.

"Melanie, how absolutely marvelous to see you again. I've missed both of you. I'm so happy that you're going to join us and begin your indoctrination."

She turned away, floating to a small table at one side of the door.

"Please," Synn invited, "sit down." He

motioned toward the couch. They took the suggestion, after which he sat in a chair opposite them as at the two previous meetings.

Leeanah returned, carrying a tray. After offering it to Melanie, who took the glass nearest her, Leeanah stepped in front of Riley who also took a glass. Synn took the remaining two, handing one to Leeanah after she had put down the tray and taken her seat.

Synn held up his glass. "To you. Riley—and Melanie. May your wishes be fulfilled, your desires become reality, and the entire world be made yours."

Melanie sipped the drink after bowing her head in acknowledgement of the sweeping toast. The thought that he could probably deliver flashed through her mind. She wanted to laugh giddily but fought the urge.

They talked about nothing in particular for several minutes, merely filling time. Then Synn stood.

"We have a light supper prepared for the four of us. Come, my friends, we'll break bread together and further solidify our relationship." He took Leeanah's hand, helping her arise.

Riley got to his feet and did the same for Melanie, winking at her as he did.

When they stood in the hall, Synn released Leeanah's arm, gesturing for Riley to take it. Riley exchanged Melanie's for Leeanah's proffered hand. Synn stepped to Melanie's side, staying her movement by placing a hand on her shoulder.

She watched Riley escort Leeanah down the hall toward an open door and through it.

When they were alone, Synn spoke. "You did magnificently, my dear. I couldn't be happier. You'll be amply rewarded—now and forever."

She wanted to ask him how. How would she be rewarded? More gems? Money? Property? How? She felt so goddamned mercenary. Had she truly betrayed Riley? From the look on his face when Leeanah kissed him and Synn offered him her arm, she doubted it. He looked like he had died and gone to heaven. What, then, bothered her so much? The inability to put a tag on Synn? Categorize him? Maybe that was it. She didn't know. She'd want to discuss the whole thing more fully with Riley once they got home. Home? Wasn't it supposed to be where the heart was, according to the old saying? Or perhaps it was a song. No matter what the source, she suddenly thought of her "home" being a dining room down the hall, chatting with another woman.

She readily took the arm Sebastian held out to her, hurrying to get to where she'd find Riley.

Three ornate chandeliers, set at regular intervals in the oak-beamed ceiling, lighted the large room. When they entered, Melanie saw Riley and Leeanah standing near a credenza laden with food. No one else was in the room. Melanie frowned. Something bothered her. Something she could not quite put her finger on. But what?

Synn helped her select some of the enticing food. When her plate was loaded with escargots, pate de foie gras and delicately scented sukiyaki, she made her way to the table where Riley and Leeanah had already taken places. When she sat down she felt as if she might be intruding on a private conversation. However, Leeanah warmly included her in the dialogue, when Melanie quickly realized they weren't talking about anything personal.

Instead, once Synn had joined them, Melanie concentrated on Riley, seated directly opposite. Something about him troubled her. His eyes. His eyes weren't focusing. At least, it appeared to her as if they weren't. In fact, he seemed to be intoxicated. Riley? Never. On more than one occasion, she had seen him sip a single glass of wine for over an hour. He had always claimed to dislike the feeling of losing control of his body and mind. The idea of slurring words, staggering about, not being able to function normally didn't suit him. He wanted to be one hundred percent there, all the time. If he were to drink, that percentage dropped drastically.

Yet Melanie was almost willing to bet he'd

had too much. But when? He was stone cold sober when they arrived. He had one glass of wine in the library and the glass standing next to his plate wasn't touched. What should she do? Yell out to him? That wouldn't be wise. Not with Synn and Leeanah so close to her. What then? What could she do? Had Riley been drugged?

She desperately replayed the scene in the library. Leeanah had gone to the small table near the door, poured four glasses of wine and returned. Melanie remembered because she'd admired the gown Leeanah wore, comparing it to her own slacks and blouse. She'd felt like a "one" compared to Leeanah's "ten." But to the best of her recollection, she had seen no covert movements over the glasses. She, along with Leeanah and Sebastian had drunk the same wine. What was affecting him, then? Perhaps whatever it was had already been put in the glass before they arrived. Mentally picturing Leeanah offering the wine, she remembered taking the glass closest to her. That was normal. Leenanah then turned the tray for Riley to take a glass—the closest one. Had she maneuvered the glass to him that had been drugged?

"Hey, Melanie, come back to the party."

She looked up to find a clear-eyed, bright-looking Riley staring at her along with their host and hostess. She felt absolutely stupid. Idiotic. Was she? Had she somehow misin-

The Immortal

terpreted his condition? She must have, since he looked normal now.

"I'm sorry," she ventured. "I guess I was daydreaming. What did you say?"

"I didn't say anything. Sebastian suggested we stay over. Spend the night and begin our studies in the morning. That way, we'll save a lot of time. What do you think?" Riley flashed his toothy grin.

She felt trapped. What could she say? *No, I don't want to. They might whack our heads off during the night. I don't sleep well in strange beds.*

If she agreed, she'd want to stay awake all night, just to be safe. Maybe she and Riley could sleep in turn, one keeping watch at all times. That might work.

"I guess it'll be all right. I don't object, although we don't have anything with us." She looked at Riley, turning to face Leeanah as she sensed the woman's gaze on her.

"I'm sure we can supply you with anything you might need, Melanie." She reached out one hand to take Riley's, touching Melanie's at the same time with the other.

"Of course," Synn said expansively. "Anything you need will be yours for the asking."

Melanie fixed her stare on him for a moment, positive he meant every word, turning away when he looked at her.

"And now," he continued, standing, "I think it might be wise if we all retired. I'm rather sleepy and I'm sure the three of you will want a good night's sleep as well. Leeanah? Will you show Riley and Melanie to their rooms?"

Melanie blanched. *Rooms?* Were they being escorted to a suite or being separated for the night? Or for all time? She hadn't planned on this twist. Perhaps she could convince Leeanah to let them spend the night in the same bedroom. She'd try when the opportunity presented itself.

Synn excused himself, leaving Leeanah in charge of taking them upstairs. On the way, Riley kept up a one-sided conversation with Leeanah while Melanie wanted to kick him hard in the crotch to get his attention. When they stood at the top of the steps, she coughed, clearing her throat. They turned to her.

"Would it be all right if Riley and I bunked together?" She suddenly felt as if some of the liver paste she had eaten were spread on her chin.

Before Leeanah could speak, Riley did. "Come on Mel. You're a big girl. You've got your own room at home, haven't you?"

When she looked up, Melanie found Leeanah smiling confidently and quickly retorted, "Yes, but how many nights do I spend there?"

"That's not the point." Riley wouldn't leave it alone. "Leeanah already explained to me that she sleeps alone and so does Sebastian. When in Rome—"

Melanie wanted to curse. How could he? How could he be so stupid and thickheaded? It seemed more and more plausible that they were to be separated for some dark and evil reason.

"I can tell Melanie is upset." Leeanah placed a hand on Riley's when he opened his mouth to speak. "I hope you're not frightened of anything here in the house. You aren't, are you?"

Melanie decided Leeanah was being downright patronizing and hated her for it. "Where's my room?" she snapped. Fuck Riley. If he didn't use the good sense the Lord gave him, why should she worry about the dumb bastard?

"Right here." Leeanah opened a door. "The key is on the inside in the event you'd feel more secure with the door locked. You'll find gowns in the closet."

Melanie wanted to scream at her, *I'm not afraid of you, you high-class slut!* She felt sorry now, as if she'd fallen into a trap. The responsibility was hers for bringing Riley here. He alone might be the one in danger. Why not? Synn specifically wanted Riley for some reason. Some reason he would not share with her yesterday at the restaurant. Now, she wouldn't have a chance even to whisper in Riley's ear that he should be extra careful. Why hadn't she warned him? Because he wouldn't have come if she'd mentioned the fact. And if he hadn't, who knows what would've happened to the diamond and the promise of more wealth to come? He could take care of himself for one night. Perhaps tomorrow she'd have a chance to say something to him when Leeanah and Synn weren't around.

"Well, I guess I'll say good night, then," Melanie offered in a soft voice, doing her best to be nonchalant but knowing she was failing miserably. "See you in the morning, Riley. Leeanah."

After they said their good-nights, they turned and walked down the hallway. Melanie stood at the open entrance until Riley was shown to his room and Leeanah departed, too. Only then did she enter, closing the heavy oak panel behind her. A bitter smile crossed her full lips as she noted the key in the lock.

"Fuck you," she said, turning the key until the bolt flipped into place.

The room was large, done basically in white, with elements of color in the bed spread, the draped windows, and throw rugs scattered about on the white carpeting. She liked the room. It seemed almost Spartan in its decor, and at the same time flaunted the amount of money spent to gain such simplicity. She crossed to the double closet, sliding one of the doors open. Inside, she found a dozen gowns, thin, filmy, very feminine. Other articles of clothing hung to either side of the nightwear. Leeanah was a bit shorter than she. After selecting one of the gowns, she was astonished to find it the perfect length—as if everything in the closet were for her and her alone.

Dismissing the matter as trivial, she slipped out of her blouse and slacks, panty hose and bikini underwear. With the light blue gown from the closet draped over her arm, she went to the three-way mirror, admiring her nakedness from different angles before slipping the soft material over her head. It fell in place. Other than a bit of tightness across her breasts, it fit almost perfectly. She didn't buy clothes this well for herself. Who had purchased these? And had they been specifically bought for Melanie Brandt? If so, why? Just to spend one night here? Or did Synn and Leeanah have other ideas than those offered earlier downstairs?

Perhaps someone else owned these clothes. But who? Not Leeanah. The only other person she had seen in the house, except in the chapel, was Sebastian, and somehow she found the thought of him being a cross dresser a bit far-fetched. Now that she thought about it, she couldn't even be certain any women other than herself and Leeanah had been in the egg-shaped room. From what she could recall, most if not all of the hooded people had been men. Young men. She could not remember seeing any women.

But the amount of clothes in this closet, assuming they all fit as well as the nightgown, seemed to indicate the two of them might be spending a lot more time in the mansion than either anticipated.

She paled at the thought of being kept prisoner. Was that possible? Could these people hold her and Riley against their wills? She guessed anything might be possible, considering some of the strange events that had taken place in the last few weeks. An overwhelming urge to pray seized her and was just as quickly dismissed. Too late for that. She had already given herself over to Synn and whatever he represented for the promise of wealth. She still wanted it. But at the price of Riley Larson? She'd have to wait and make a more intelligent decision in the morning—in the light of day—when she and Riley might have a moment alone to talk. Then and only then could they make plans for the immediate future.

Immediate future? Did she and Riley have a future—a future of any kind while in this house?

She went to the bed, throwing the covers back. It looked inviting. Slipping between the sheets, she pulled up the blankets. It felt as good as it looked. She had to be certain of staying awake. She had to be the one on guard, so to speak, while hopefully everyone else slept and didn't go roaming about, looking for someone's head to chop off.

The Immortal

Grinning, she snuggled down further. That was silly. These people didn't do things like that. They were too refined, too dignified, too—too rich.

And she was too tired. Too exhausted to think any more. She'd close her eyes for just a minute. Then she'd sit up and keep her ears open for any out of place sound.

Her eyes closed. It felt so delicious. So warm. She wished Riley was with her in bed for a split second before she dropped off to sleep.

Riley lay on his back, a gentle snore grumbling from his throat. Leeanah hovered in his dreams, growing in size until she seemed gigantic. He grinned when he realized she was nude, and wanted to ask her how she controlled her vagina muscles. But her face looked at him in such a way that he didn't want to run the risk of losing her image by speaking, perhaps scaring her away.

His room, finished in dark mahogany paneling which reflected little of whatever light filtered in from outside, was filled with a blackness that seemed almost artificial.

He had fallen asleep almost immediately upon getting into the king-size bed. Sleep filled his every cavity. The sound of one of the wooden panels opening to reveal a Stygian figure did nothing to disturb him. The ghost-like shape flitted across the room to the side of the bed, where it stood for several minutes, drinking in the outline of Riley's body.

The instinct for survival, awakened by some unknown trigger, brought his sixth sense into play. His eyelids fluttered. When they opened, he saw the figure of a naked woman standing next to the bed.

"Who—who's there?" he asked sleepily, his voice thick.

PART FOUR

...and dust to dust.

CHAPTER 15

Friday morning, November 21, 8:15 A.M.

Sunlight blazing into the white room startled Melanie when she first opened her eyes. After several long seconds of orientation, she recalled where she was, the circumstances of her being at Sebastian Synn's mansion, and why she was alone. Was Riley all right? He'd spent the night alone as well. Rather peculiar when she thought about it. Synn knew that she and Riley cohabited, just as he and Leeanah did. Still, they'd been separated last evening when they retired. She remembered lying on her back before falling asleep, vowing to keep a vigilant eye open and listen for any sounds in the hallway, but she must have dropped off to sleep in seconds, wishing Riley were next to her. Then—she had opened her eyes to the bright sunlight flooding the room.

It all seemed so normal, so absolutely nonfrightening in the light of day. What was the reason they hadn't slept together last night?

Something about Leeanah and Sebastian not sleeping together and Riley agreeing wholeheartedly, like a dope. What had he said? *"When in Rome—"* or something equally inane.

She wondered what time it was and looked at the dresser. No clock. She didn't own a wristwatch, always relying on her built-in body clock to inform her of the approximate time. Not that she had ever been late for work. At home—at Worthless Acres—she and Riley relied on the alarm to wake them when they had obligations. Except for that, she had little if any use for clocks. But right now, she wanted to know the time.

Pulling herself from the warmth of the covers, she stretched before standing, slipped the blue gown over her head, dropping it to the floor and bent, touching her toes. It didn't hurt. As long as there was no strain in touching her feet or the floor with her fingertips, she didn't have to worry about doing that type of exercise. Her stomach was flat, hard and firm. Walking to and from work in town filled the bill when it came to maintaining her body's fitness.

When she passed in front of the three-way mirror, she stopped again to admire her figure. Then she showered in the private bath connected to the room and quickly dressed, wanting to find Riley and talk with him before they saw Synn and Leeanah.

The Immortal

What she really wanted to do was chew him out for being an ass last night. The memory still rankled. The idea! *"When in Rome—"*

Closing the door quietly behind her, she hurried down the hall on tiptoe. There were several things she wanted to talk over with him: his glassy-eyed look for a brief time while they were eating. What was wrong with him? He looked as if he were drunk. But within seconds he recovered and had to ask *her* to rejoin the party. Was she merely overreacting?

Then, too, the maintenance of this huge house, including preparation of the exquisite food they'd been served last night, bothered her more than a bit. Who cleaned? Who cooked? Who did laundry and sundry other things that needed doing on a grand scale for a mansion such as this? Certainly not Leeanah. Her hands were as soft as a baby's, and Melanie knew how her own hands reacted to the simple house work she did in the cottage. It could not be Leeanah. Synn? That would be something. Did they have outside help who came in during the day? Maybe. She and Riley had never been here in daylight. They'd have to check for signs of a staff.

She stopped in front of Riley's door and tapped gently. Nothing. She knocked again —harder this time. Still no answer. Was he already up? Downstairs? With Leeanah? Wondering if she might be the least bit jealous, Melanie reached out to touch the knob. Should she turn it? Without another thought, she gave it a twist and smiled, relieved that it opened.

Pushing the heavy door, she peered into night-like darkness. Her own room had been so bright, it seemed as if his belonged to a different house. On the opposite side of the hall, its draperies were still closed. She hadn't even thought of closing hers last night. Opting to open them instead of turning on the lights, she entered, tiptoeing to the tall windows. It was then she noticed Riley's form huddled under the covers.

Plunging the room into daylight, she walked to the side of the huge bed and kneed the mattress several times. "Time to get up, sleepyhead," she announced in a gruff voice.

Riley moaned but didn't open his eyes.

"Come on, Larson. Get your ass out of the sack. Hit the deck, rookie!" she growled in her best drill instructor voice.

He still didn't respond.

"Oh, for Chrissake!" She sat down on the bed, grabbing him by the shoulders and roughly shaking him. "Come on. Open them up, for crying out loud!"

He moaned again and struggled to sit up.

"What's the matter with you?" She looked intently at his sleepbloated face.

Shaking his head, he muttered something

unintelligible and coughed. "I feel lousy," finally emerged.

"Lousy? What's the matter? You're not hung over, are you? You only had one glass of wine last night. Jesus Christ, can't you hold your booze any better than that?"

He shook his head again. "I feel like I have the flu or something. Maybe it'll pass. What time is it?"

Melanie shrugged. "I don't know. I don't have a watch and there wasn't any clock in my room or in the hall." She turned, taking in his room with a glance. "You don't have one either."

"I'd better get up and see if I feel better after a shower." He got to his feet as she stood, clearing the way for him.

"Were you all right last night while we were eating?"

Screwing his face into concentration for a moment, he tried to think. "Yeah. I guess I might have had a wave of nausea sweep over me for a minute. Why?"

"You looked sorta peculiar for a while."

He sat down heavily on the bed, dropping his head into his hands.

"What's the matter? Are you really sick?"

He shook his head. "I—I just thought of something. I got laid last night."

"You what?"

"I got laid."

She frowned. Goddamn that Leeanah. No wonder she wanted to separate them.

Melanie concluded that Synn was as much in the dark as she, since he too slept alone. "How was it?" The inflection was bitter.

Riley looked up at her. "You're angry, aren't you?"

Shaking her head, she remonstrated, "It's just that Leeanah made such a big deal of everybody sleeping separately. Then you, you asshole, had to go along with it by saying 'When in Rome—!'"

He held his hand up. "It wasn't Leeanah."

Melanie's eyes flew open. "What? Then who was it?"

"At first, I thought you had come back after everyone was asleep. But it wasn't you either."

"Well, I know that much. Who was it?"

He shrugged again. "I don't know. She didn't have anywhere near the size breasts that you and Leeanah have."

"Tell me what happened, Riley. Come on. Confession's good for the soul. At least that's what everyone says."

"Well, I had gone to sleep and then—"

Riley struggled to sit up in bed, his sleep-befogged eyes straining to focus in the darkness. He could just make out the figure of a nude woman standing at the front of his bed.

"Who's—who's there?" His voice sounded loud in the blackness.

"Shhh-h-h," she admonished, stepping

The Immortal

around to the side of the bed. "Don't make a sound."

She slipped between the covers, reaching out to embrace Riley. Her body felt cool against his warmth and he pulled her to him in an effort to comfort her.

Slowly clearing, his mind raced. Who was she? What did she want? Where had she come from? A soft luminescence seemed to be emanating from somewhere but he couldn't see a lamp or nightlight of any type shining in the darkness. When he turned to his right, he saw a panel which seemed lighter, as if some source of indirect illumination were present. Yet when he reconstructed the bedroom in his mind's eye as he recalled it before dousing the lamp next to his pillow, the glow came from an area which was solid wall.

"Let me turn on the light," he suggested softly.

"No," the voice whispered. "I prefer the darkness. It's more intimate."

He acquiesced and clutched her body even closer to his own when she trembled for an instant. Once she began to warm up, he relaxed his hold and her hands began running along his shoulders, gently forcing him to the bed on his back. Barely touching his skin, the delicate fingertips flitted from side to side in an exhilarating, tantalizing massage. Down his arms to his hands, back to the shoulders, down to his pectoral muscles, playing with his nipples, sending minuscule charges of electricity into the hair follicles of his chest, her hands glided over him. Never had he experienced anything so arousing as the manner in which this woman —this stranger who simply materialized in his bedroom—touched him.

He felt her breath, hot, pulsating in tiny gasps as she brought her face close to his. Her tongue flicked out, not unlike a snake's, exploring his face, barely touching it, to duplicate the sensation that her fingers were producing elsewhere. Riley thought he'd go mad with the delirious pleasure building within him. And she hadn't even touched him that intimately yet.

The tips of her fingers traveled downward, toward his navel, where one savagely jabbed for several seconds. Radiating circles of feeling undulated outward in waves, not unlike the surface of a pond whose waters are disturbed. Toward his chest, throat and head in one direction, toward his lower belly, penis, thighs and legs in the other, the probing finger telegraphed its message to all extremities from the center of his being.

Then, dramatically, it stopped, only to begin again, tantalizing his abdomen. Lower, lower it moved, slowly, sensually, exploring the hair, emitting charges to the roots, which in turn sent out messages of pleasure never before experienced. Riley felt his head swimming. She was magnificent in the way she brought him to life, yet she suspected he hadn't begun to feel the joys and pleasure she could communicate before the night ended.

Sweeping around the base of his manhood, she moved down his left leg as far as she could reach without moving her head from his. While her hand felt every centimeter of his flesh, her tongue continued perusing his facial muscles and skin. Inexplicably wanting to scream in direct ratio to the way he felt inside, Riley turned his head, seeking the mouth she offered.

Their tongues engaged in a wet greeting before dueling for which would be master over the other. Riley, at the height of passion, allowed her to win, and she rammed her tongue into his mouth, claiming it as her property. When her dominance had been established, she withdrew, enticing him to follow. When he penetrated her mouth, she chewed lightly on his tongue, her hand moving delicately toward his crotch.

Without warning, she grabbed him, eliciting a scream of pleasure from somewhere deep inside Riley—a gutteral, animalistic cry that he hardly recognized as coming from within himself. Having proven her authority over him, she caressed his blood-gorged penis in the same manner as she had done to his body.

Now he felt a moan being born in his

depths, giving it full vent as it reached his throat and larynx. Then she was gone. He opened his eyes to find her over him, ready to straddle his body. When she lowered herself onto him, he brought both hands to his head at the indescribable sensation he experienced upon being enveloped. Her love muscles contracted, relaxed, contracted again and again in a gentle, yet demanding rhythm—and she wasn't moving any part of her body except her vaginal walls.

Leeanah? It had to be Leeanah. She could do exactly the same thing. Reaching out with both hands, he found her breasts and reassured himself immediately that it wasn't Leeanah. The mounds of flesh he enclosed in his hand were much smaller than hers, and soft, much softer than either Leeanah's or Melanie's. *Who had invaded his bed? Who was she?*

He felt the intensity in his groin grow to a pitch he had never before experienced. It seemed as if she were about to milk him of every drop of vital juice in his body. The sensation grew mightily until he thought his sanity would snap and he would be lost forever in a fit of pleasure and excitement.

She moaned as if enjoying the coupling as much as he, yet he was unable to comprehend how anyone could possibly feel the same pang of pure joy by creating the sensation in the first place.

When they climaxed, they did so together.

The Immortal

She remained rigid, statue-like astride him, though he jerked spasmodically emptying his seed into her. Riley tried to remember the last time he had ejaculated such copious amounts, but concluded as the flow continued that this was a new high for him.

Little by little the storm subsided. He felt himself wilting, withdrawing of his own accord as he shrank, seeking rest and relief from the erotic massage he had been given.

When she lifted him off, he felt her rise from the bed as if suspended from wires, seemingly not moving of her own accord. Standing at the side of the bed, she looked down.

"Thank you, Riley," she whispered huskily and turned, moving toward the patch of softly glowing wall, for an instant seeming to be framed by it. Then she was gone, and the strange light vanished. . . .

"I lay there for several minutes, Melanie," Riley concluded, "before I moved. At first I thought I'd dreamt the whole thing. I checked my crotch, expecting to find it wet—but it was dry. Just the least bit damp, as if I'd been sweating."

Melanie shook her head. "I'm bewildered, to say the least." She looked at him for a moment before continuing. "You say you have no idea who it was?"

He nodded.

"You're positive it wasn't Leeanah?"

Again he nodded. "I told you. Her boobs are almost identical to yours. I know yours. It wasn't Leeanah."

"And she just disappeared into the wall?"

"That was the odd part." He stood, slipped on a robe he said was hanging in the closet, and walked to the wall. Narrow panels, surrounded by delicate wooden beadwork, lined the partition. "You know, any one of these, or a combination, could open to a secret passage."

"The next thing you're going to tell me," she retorted sharply, "is that you saw ghosts, too."

"Hey, in this house, I wouldn't be the least bit surprised."

"Why don't you shower and we'll go downstairs and try to get the hell outta here. That is, if you agree."

He shrugged and went to the bathroom.

Melanie approached the wall where he indicated the woman had disappeared. Of course there could be a hidden panel opening onto a secret passage, but for some reason she found herself doubting such a possibility. If Riley had a bed partner last night, she found it much more intriguing to figure out who it was, rather than how she'd pulled a disappearing act.

Assured that if there were a secret panel, she hadn't found it, Melanie went to one of the occasional chairs and sat down. After twenty minutes passed, she decided he

The Immortal

needed a push and went to the bathroom door. Opening it, she called, "Come on, Riley. You're clean now. Let's go. What do you say?"

Her answer was a moan. Throwing the door open, she saw him lying on his back in the middle of the steam-filled room. She quickly turned off the shower and found the exhaust fan switch. Then, bending down she called, "Riley? Riley, what's the matter?"

Again he moaned, opening his eyes, weakly trying to speak. "I—I—" but could not get any further.

"What happened? Are you sick? What?"

"Weak," he managed in a hoarse whisper.

"Weak?"

"May—be the flu."

"But you were all right a few minutes ago."

Nodding, he whispered, "Get me back to bed—feel like I might go down—drain."

Slipping her hands beneath his armpits, she helped him stand. With one of his arms draped over her shoulders, she managed to get him into the room and to the bed. He fell heavily onto the mattress.

"Are you sure you have the flu?"

He shrugged. "Just feel—we—weak. That's—all. I'll—be—be—all—all right. Need sleep—rest."

"What will I tell Synn and Leeanah?"

Riley half smiled. "Tell—tell them—I'll—be—all—all right—after—I sleep—for—a—

a while." His eyes dropped shut and in seconds he was gently snoring.

"Well, I've seen it all now," she muttered under her breath and walked to the door. There was no reason to stay, with Riley sound asleep. Better to tell Synn and Leeanah he was sleeping in and not feeling too well. Briefly she wrestled with the idea of asking about his nighttime lover, but didn't want to make a fool of herself over what probably would turn out to be a dream and nothing more.

Descending the wide staircase at a light run, she slowed her pace when she saw Synn at the bottom, looking up at her.

"Good morning, Melanie," he said quietly. "How did you sleep?"

"I conked out right away," she began, waiting until she stood next to the man, peering directly into his eyes. "But Riley's not feeling well. I think he'll probably sleep late this morning, if that's all right with you."

"Of course. Why wouldn't it be?"

"I thought we were to start our training or whatever this morning."

"That can wait. The two of you are here and that's the important thing. When you begin your training is of small important next to the fact that we are all friends again."

She managed a weak smile but said

nothing, taking his arm when he offered it. They walked to the dining room.

The table was set for three and Melanie froze when she saw one place missing. Riley's? Had they already anticipated his illness? Did they plan it?

When she stopped, Synn turned, facing her. "Normally, I don't take breakfast. I'll have coffee while you eat."

She nodded, feeling her wave of fear wash away. She was becoming much too suspicious. Not everything would, could or should fit into her way of looking at whatever happened. For all she knew, Synn really was on the level with them both. But immediately she visualized the two murdered men Riley had described, which was quickly followed by the memory of Grendel—a white Grendel —crucified on the wall. Thanking her survival instincts for the reminder, she took the chair Synn held out for her.

No sooner had she sat, than Leeanah entered.

After saying their good mornings, Leeanah inquired, "And where's Riley this morning? Still sleeping?"

Melanie didn't reply, noting the lilt in Leeanah's voice, and wondered what explanation Synn would give.

"Riley is feeling rather weak this morning," he began. "Melanie told me he wishes to stay in bed. Is that not correct,

Melanie, my dear?"

She nodded, wondering how he knew about Riley being weak. She hadn't said anything more than the fact of his not feeling well. Had he listened? Was the room bugged? Had he done something to Riley last night to make him feel weak this morning? Maybe even cause him to have a colossal wet dream without ejaculating?

"So, what would you like to do this morning, Melanie, since we'll have to postpone your indoctrination?" Synn smiled over the rim of his cup as he drank.

She fiddled with the slice of toast on her plate, having no appetite. The coffee, though it was probably the best money could buy, tasted bitter. She wanted out. Out of the mansion. Out of Synn's and Leeanah's presence. Could she still be rich if she left now? She had delivered Riley. The poor son of a bitch wasn't up to par this morning, but once he recovered, he'd be able to take care of himself. Besides, if he really had fucked somebody last night—a stranger whose name he didn't know, why should she feel so goddamned loyal to him? Not that she was jealous. She'd watched him and Leeanah the last time they'd come here and it hadn't bothered her. Was it because this time he'd done it behind her back? She felt both betrayed and ashamed of herself. Betrayed because he'd made love to someone else—someone who had elicited raves from him about her style and technique, and ashamed because she felt jealous. It wasn't like her. If this was what Riley wanted, fine. She'd have no worries if Synn kept his end of the bargain. If she were rich, she'd be able to do whatever she wanted. Go wherever she wanted. Never have to worry about money again. That was Riley's one drawback. He didn't care about money and the stuff it could buy. She did. She'd take whatever Synn gave her and run with it. And be happy.

"I think I should go back to the house. I want to get some things and I'm sure Riley will want his razor and toilet articles. If he's going to stay in bed this morning, he'll want to shave when he gets up."

"I have a wonderful idea," Leeanah gurgled, her face brightening. "Why don't you and Riley move in until you are completely trained?"

"A capital idea! Capital, Leeanah. I should have thought of it," Synn gushed.

"But—" Melanie stammered. She didn't want to come back. Not ever. Whatever the diamond was worth would have to do. She definitely wanted to run. Let Riley take care of himself. If they were meant to be together, they'd manage somehow, sometime in the future. Right now, she felt he didn't want her around and she felt claustrophobic. She had to get away.

"It's all settled then," Leeanah stood.

"This morning, you can go home and get whatever clothing you both will need—let's say for a two- to three-week period. We should be able to have them thoroughly trained by then, shouldn't we, Sebastian?"

Synn furrowed his brow and nodded. "I think they should be finished by then."

Melanie didn't like the choice of words with which he answered Leeanah. Still, if they gave her the opportunity to leave, she should go—and the sooner the better.

"Well," she forced a smile, "if you two insist, I guess I'll do it now. I should be back around noon or one o'clock." She still had no idea what time it was and didn't care if what she said made sense or not. She watched Synn withdraw a gold watch from his jacket pocket.

"That will be excellent. Leeanah and I can watch Riley until then, and when you get back, you can take over. She and I must go into town on business matters this afternoon. Isn't it wonderful how these things tend to work themselves out?" He chuckled under his breath as he returned the timepiece to his pocket.

"I'd better be off then." Melanie rose. "I wouldn't want to keep you from your appointment. I'll hurry as much as possible."

"Hurry, yes. But do not take foolish chances," Synn admonished.

He walked with her to the foyer, leaving

Leeanah at the table in the dining room. When he opened the front door, he took her hand in his, placing something cool in it.

"Hurry back, Melanie," he cooed softly and closed the door behind her.

When it clicked shut, she looked down, opening her fingers, and gasped when she saw a blood-red ruby as big as her thumbnail nestling in her palm.

CHAPTER 16

Friday, November 21, 10:50 A.M.

Melanie turned off the Toyota's ignition, pressing the button in the same motion to release the key. After withdrawing it, she sat still, frozen in position, staring through the windshield. She hadn't even planned her next step. What should she do now? It had been easy just driving away from Synn's mansion. She tried hard not to think of Riley, lying in bed in the mahogany paneled room—weak as a newborn kitten, worn out and feeling as if he had the flu. But did he? Was he actually ill? He had told her about some woman who had come to his room, made love to him in a most exciting and erotic way before disappearing through a panel neither of them could locate. Was Riley slipping off the end of his mental table?

She had to think of herself or run the risk of being exposed to unknown danger. Riley had made his own decision. True, she helped lead him there and did it to achieve her own end. He hadn't been thinking of her when he fucked Leeanah during that weird ceremony —which foretold a double murder whose victims he just happened to have seen. Was that a coincidence, or had Synn manipulated everyone connected with the incident, covertly commanding the cop Hongisto to call Riley?

She had watched the news whenever she thought about the murders, hoping there would be some mention of the identities of the two men. Hongisto promised Riley an exclusive news release when the time was right. Apparently, the case was still in a state of flux and no one, other than the police involved, knew anything. When she thought about it, it seemed rather peculiar that Vicki's death had not shown up on the news programs either. Had Hongisto held back that information as well? If so, why? Did he suspect a possible connection between Vicki's death and those of the two homosexuals? That would be stretching things a bit, she felt. Riley was the only connecting link. Hongisto had told him he called that morning only because of his article about the burned-out church and the rite he had witnessed.

Melanie shook her head. She didn't know what to think any more. She felt she was having a hard time distinguishing reality from hallucination. How much of what Riley said he saw had he actually imagined? He was a writer. He was creative. How overly active had his imagination become in the last few weeks?

She pulled back on the door handle and got out. Half expecting Grendel to come charging around the corner, she fought a sob on remembering the dog was dead—buried behind the house.

Unlocking the front door, she walked inside. They had been gone only overnight, yet the house seemed starkly empty. Naked. As if they had been away for days or even weeks. The noiseless solitude ground on her nerves. Instinctively whistling to make some kind of sound, she went to the small stereo set and turned it to an FM station that broadcast classical music. Anything bouncy or modern didn't seem to be the right harmony for her mental state at the moment.

She reviewed her plan, which she felt to be vague at best. First she wanted to get her clothing together—packing whatever art supplies she might need wherever it was she wound up going. Then she'd call a cab. The Toyota would stay in the driveway. She wouldn't steal from Riley. Besides, she'd be able to buy a car once she converted the diamond into cash. *The ruby.* She had forgotten about it, and quickly withdrew it from her pocket.

Holding it between her thumb and forefinger, she held it up to the light streaming in through the window. Sanguineous darts of reflected light sparkled back at her wide eyes. It was a magnificent stone. Just like the diamond. She had no idea as to its worth but knew it would add to the sum of money she'd realize from the sale of the first gem. Opening her purse, she found the tissue-wrapped diamond and hid the ruby with it.

A sudden noise outside brought her attention to the front of the house. Running to the door, she peered through one of its small windows. The postman had just closed the mailbox and was pulling away. Without thinking, she went out to retrieve whatever had been left. She seldom got mail and didn't think it necessary to leave a forwarding address. Anyway, at the moment it would be impossible.

Pulling the metal door down, she looked at the small stack of envelopes and catalogs. Withdrawing them, she absently thumbed through the letters to see who wanted how much money this month. After skimming the first three, all of which had windows and return addresses telling her they were bills, she stared long and hard at the fourth. It was from the University of Chicago, the answer to the letter Riley had sent them. What should she do? Innate curiosity hammered at her, demanding she open it. Yet she feared what the contents might reveal, and had no idea as to the origin of her alarm. She only knew that something nagged at her,

The Immortal

overriding curiosity. *Don't open it.* The order came from deep within her.

Once in the house, she went to the small sideboard hugging one wall in the living room and found the silver letter opener. Maybe, just maybe, if she read it, she might learn that their fears—at least hers—would be erased. Knowledge was a tricky thing. If the contents of the envelope vindicated Synn, she would go back and claim the untold wealth he had promised her. On the other hand, if she found out that he was a madman —a killer of sorts who used black magical methods to gain his ends—she would flee, knowing that her every move, her every breath might well be her last. Then, too, the letter might be equivocal and Synn would remain a mystery forever.

Without giving the idea any more consideration, she slit the envelope, quickly withdrawing the pages of a letter written under a Patrick Gillespie Thomas's letterhead. She scanned it quickly before sitting down in the easy chair to read it in its entirety.

The antique schoolhouse clock in the kitchen ticked the minutes away, moving toward the hour of noon.

Melanie's eyes widened, disbelieving the words she found herself reading and rereading, to make certain she didn't misunderstand the weird tale they told.

When she finished, she sat back and muttered, "Jesus Christ! That's not possible! It's a fairy tale. This son of a bitch"—she looked at the letterhead when she found the signature a slanted row of parallel squiggles —"Thomas has got a few fucking screws loose someplace in his head."

Clutching the letter, she grabbed her purse, thrusting it inside. If Thomas was right, Riley could be in the worst sort of danger. He might be killed any minute. Or he might already be dead. If that were the case, returning to Synn's mansion would be mad folly on her part. Still, after reading the letter and going over several of the key passages, she concluded that she might be interpreting the information in too dramatic a way. No. She was wrong. It did not imply that Riley was in any kind of trouble. Nevertheless, her feelings for him and the absolutely intriguing message in her purse demanded that she return to Synn's mansion, to let Riley read it for himself.

The rusty Toyota lurched to a stop in Synn's driveway. Melanie inhaled deeply and waited several seconds—which in turn seemed like hours—before she got out. Synn and Leeanah were supposed to go into town, to the Loop or someplace on business. That meant she could talk to Riley, get him out of there and just start driving. Get away. Escape. That was the uppermost idea in

Melanie Brandt's mind as she ran up the steps toward the entrance.

The door opened and she stepped back when she saw Sebastian and Leeanah ready to leave, their coats on.

"I'm glad you got back, Melanie." Synn spoke graciously. "We'll just make our appointment if we hurry. Come Leeanah." Taking his companion's arm, he hurried her through the open door and closed it behind him.

"Yeah. 'Bye. Have fun." Melanie relished the sarcasm she added to the farewell. "See you around sometime, you fucking asshole weirdos."

Taking the steps to the second floor two at a time, she stopped in front of Riley's door, catching her breath before opening it. When she did, she found the room dark, gloomy, the draperies shut. Hurrying to the windows, she parted the curtains, brightening the room.

"Riley? Wake up, Riley. We've got to get the fuck outta here," she said loudly, throwing the covers back when she stood next to the bed.

He moaned in his sleep.

"Come on, goddamn it. We've got no time to piss around. Get your ass outta bed. Now! This instant!"

His lids struggled to open, and when they did, blinked at the unaccustomed brightness. "Melanie? That you? What time is it? Did I oversleep?"

"That's a fucking understatement. You've been snoring since last night, except for getting laid every now and then. How do you feel?"

"Wasted. Absolutely gone. Like I need about six or seven weeks solid sleep. No foolin'."

She turned, rushing to the bathroom where she dampened a washcloth and hurried back. Sitting on the bed, she swathed his face in the cold wetness of the terry cloth.

Sputtering, he sat up. "I feel so blasted weak. Like I've had the flu for a long time, or like I haven't eaten anything and I'm starving."

She picked up her purse which she had dropped on the nightstand before going to the bathroom. Withdrawing the envelope, she handed it to him. "This came in the mail. It's from the University of Chicago with information on that coat of arms."

His face brightened noticeably as he took the letter. "What's it say?" He noticed it was already open as he withdrew the sheets of paper.

"Read it. You'd never believe it if I told you. In fact, I've read the goddamn thing, and I'm still not certain I believe any of it. It sounds like so much bullshit."

He handed it back to her. "I can't focus

well enough to read. Read it to me."

She took the letter and cleared her throat.

"Dear Mr. Larson,

I received your letter and photographs, which I found to be most interesting. Every once in a while, a question such as that in your letter comes along, and we here in the department relish the opportunity to play detective. I must say, you certainly threw a challenge at us with this heraldic device.

"Firstly, I should like to say that this is like no other coat of arms I or any of my staff have ever seen. It is, we believe, of French origin. We make this assumption based on the shape of the shield, which is very definitely French. At first we felt we would merely be able to define several of the features, until one of my assistants came across a fascimilie of the shield in your photo, in an ancient book of heraldry. It lacks only the field of ermine fur, which is the white diamond-shaped area with black markings. We have concluded that this aspect of the device was added, more than likely, during the *Period of Decadence* in the eighteenth century, when armorial bearings were losing favor. That, of course, is neither here nor there, is it?

"At any rate, the coat of arms is that

of one Comte de Saint-Germain—a man of mystery. Most encyclopedias containing information on this person state almost without exception that the mystery surrounding him will probably never be resolved. He allegedly has lived for over two thousand years. You will note that I stated 'has lived.' There are reports on record of him being seen and talked with in 1929 in Rome, seen again in 1942 in England, and again in 1968 in New York City. That in itself is not strange, but when it is considered that he was a member of Louis XV's court and a good friend of Madame Pompadour, it is, to say the least, a bit on the extraordinary side. His death was reported to have taken place 27 February, 1784, when he appeared to be an octogenarian. He apparently had fallen out of favor with the French Royal Court, since he fled to Holland in 1760 where the Duc de Choiseul's men almost arrested him outside of The Hague, or *'S Gravenhage,* as it was then called.

"According to reports at that time, the Comte de Saint-Germain claimed to have known the Queen of Sheba and Jesus Christ, among other notable people of history. If you should want to read more about this man, I would suggest you look him up in various encyclopedias.

"It was the fact of the shield being that of Saint-Germain which made the

The Immortal

rest of the coat of arms readily decipherable. He was an alchemist, always with a ready supply of diamonds, rubies, emeralds and such valuable stones, which he used for money at the time. This made the figure of the mortar and pestle at the bottom of the oval-shaped shield on which the coat of arms is presented, rather easy to understand. These items were closely associated with alchemists. (They naturally became symbolic of apothecaries when the science of medicine grew out of alchemy, as did chemistry). The Latin inscription thereon seems to verify the fact that Saint-Germain was seeking eternal life. It means: 'Such is the way to immortality.'

"Perhaps our elusive Count, who used many different names, was in league with the devil, since the goat's head at the top of the French escutcheon seems to be 'Old Nick' himself. The Latin there translates to 'Without End.' Again, this could be a reference to his search for life everlasting, or to the fact that Satan or Lucifer is immortal.

"As I said earlier, the white patch is representative of ermine fur and was probably added in the eighteenth century. The parts I do not or cannot understand are the figures of what appear to be praying mantises on either side of this ermine field. Nor can I be of help in explaining what spiders, which are native to the Americas, might be doing on a European shield. (The two hourglasses on the lower sides of the ermine field are the undersides of black widow spiders.) We enhanced your photo and the outline within which the triangles appear, (in reality hourglass shapes) are very faint outlines of the female black widow spider. To add to your store of information, praying mantises and black widow spiders both consume the males of the species after breeding. I'm sure, though, this has nothing to do with understanding the rest of the heraldic symbols.

"We also examined the picture of the knife which you sent, and though a disagreement exists among members of my staff, the consensus indicated that the handle was probably a representation of a praying mantis with the legs missing. This may or may not be, since it is out of our realm of expertise.

"I believe you have one of two things —a most interesting coat of arms that is extremely rare, or a blatant forgery. In either case, I should be eager to see the original.

"If there is anything I can do to help you better understand what you have discovered, please feel free to call me. The pictures are being returned under separate cover.'

"Sincerely,
Patrick Gillespie Thomas"

"That's the most romantic piece of poppycock I've ever heard, Mel. I hope you don't accept it?" Riley struggled to maintain his sitting posture in the bed.

"What else have we got going for us? Synn has the coat of arms hanging big as life in his library. This guy Thomas seems to know what he's talking about, doesn't he?"

"Maybe. You know how some teachers are into smoking mushrooms and gaining insight into all the mysteries of the world. Maybe this turkey is like that. Got really high before sitting down at the typewriter and decided to lay a good one on us."

"I don't buy that, Riley. It sounds like something you'd expect to see on the Late Late Show on Friday night, but in a lot of ways it makes too much logical sense."

"Such as?" Riley snapped.

"Such as the diamond and ruby Synn gave me."

"What ruby?"

"This one." She fished in her purse for the tissue. When she found it, she threw it to Riley who unwrapped it.

"Wow!" he exclaimed, holding the blood-red stone up to the light. "Just like that, he gave it to you?"

Melanie hesitated. The last thing in the world she wanted to tell him about right now was the bargain she struck with Synn. Delivering Riley had been easy. Getting him out of there and away from Chicago was going to be the trick of the month. "I guess he likes me," she answered lamely.

Riley chuckled, then laughed as uproariously as he could. "This is crazy. Real insanity. You know, I really think you believe it. Right?"

She felt her face flush.

"The one thing I have to question is the guy who wrote this. If he wasn't on drugs, he must have gotten his job through a relative and is a moron with an I.Q. hovering around the Celsius freezing mark. Why would a serious-minded member of the intelligentsia take time to type a letter like this?" Derision rose in his voice as he threw the pages onto the nightstand.

Melanie bit her lip. He was accepting none of it. She had risked her life to come back here with the letter, hoping he would leave with her, and the poor fool was laughing at her and her belief in it. Turning, she stormed out of the room, slamming the door behind her.

There was something wrong with Riley—something wrong physically, and now she was sure his mental stability was shaky. Even if the letter were rubbish, even if Synn and Leeanah were completely honest, the fact that he became so exhausted from one glass of wine and getting laid, should make even the most cynical person a bit suspicious.

Turning, she went back to the room,

opening the door just wide enough to see Riley on the bed. He had thrown the covers back. Maybe he was going to get up and leave with her.

"Riley?" she called softly. "I'm sorry for slamming the door. Please get up and let's leave this place."

He looked at her standing in the doorway. "Okay, Mel. I'll get up and go away with you. What are you going to do?"

"I'm going down to the library and look at that thing you took a picture of. Hurry up. I'll be right back."

"Okay." He sat up as the door quietly clicked shut. Then he froze in position.

Melanie took her time walking downstairs, going directly to the library when she reached the first floor. After studying the coat of arms for several minutes, examining each detail mentioned in the letter, she turned, and before leaving the room, went to the bookshelves nearest the door to look at some of the titles. *The Proper Worshippe of Demons. Casting The Perfect Spelle, Malleus Mallificarum.*

She wrinkled her nose. What *nice* titles. Best sellers in their time, she was willing to bet. The selections on this shelf seemed to reflect some of the meaning of what had happened the last few weeks, and the coat of arms behind her. She circled the room in a slow, deliberate way, drinking in the strange titles, shaking her head in disbelief. How could anyone put so much emphasis on this sort of thing?

A wry smile crossed her lips. She herself had been willing to give it a try when Leeanah came to the house that night. Then, when they were taken to the egg-shaped chapel—

Coming around again to the coat of arms, she looked at the shape of the shield on which the design had been rendered. Egg-shaped. Coincidental? Maybe, but she doubted it.

Turning around where she stood, she took in the library one final time and went to the door.

Riley froze, staring at the panel as it slid back soundlessly to reveal the naked woman. She was coming to him again. He tried to move but found it impossible.

Gliding like a ghost to the window, she pulled the draperies shut and returned to the bed. Riley collapsed back on the pillows. He watched her pick up the letter lying on the nightstand, quickly perusing its contents. Finished, she threw it back before slipping between the covers.

She initiated the same ritual of running her hands over his body, licking his face, kissing him on the mouth.

He felt his erection jerk into being, amazed that he would again be able to give this insatiable bitch her satisfaction. In minutes she sat astride him, working her muscles without moving anything other than her vagina, drawing, taking, stealing Riley's sperm.

He closed his eyes, feeling the fit of exhaustion flooding through his limbs as he climaxed inside his ghostly lover.

CHAPTER 17

Friday, November 21, 1:55 P.M.

Melanie paused at the library door, her hand hovering over the knob. Maybe she should simply call Lieutenant Hongisto and have him come to their rescue. Turning, she started for the telephone on the desk at the far end of the room. Suddenly, she stopped. Wouldn't they be implicated in the murders of the decapitated homosexuals?

A wave of unsteadiness swept over her and she leaned against the wall. She could see it now: Riley arrested as an accessory before the fact or something. She thought that might be the charge since he participated in the rite before the men had actually been murdered. At least, that was her interpretation of such legal mumbo jumbo. If nothing else, they both could certainly be charged with withholding evidence in a murder investigation. Riley knew full well after seeing the headless bodies and the condition of the one face he had seen, that Synn was somehow responsible. He was in trouble from the instant he concealed his knowledge from Hongisto. And what about her? She became involved when Riley told her everything he had seen and *she* didn't call the cops.

Could she be charged along with the acolytes who stood by with doing nothing to stop the ritualistic slaying of two people? Was that a crime? She'd been just as fascinated by the strange procedures as anyone else in the room and— The thought of those others in the chapel bobbed around in her mind. Who were they? Members of Synn's "group?" She had no idea. How would the police react to that aspect of her story? *People seem to materialize whenever a ceremony is about to be performed.*

She shook her head, tousling her long hair. How could she possibly sort out reality from what the police would surely say were figments of her overwrought imagination? Had she truly seen the people? Yes. Definitely *yes.* One of the men had brushed up against her when they crowded around the altar just before Synn sliced off the wax dolls' heads. Was there even actually a chapel someplace underneath this mansion? There must be— one that could be shown to Hongisto or whoever showed up, in the event she decided to call.

Still, the whole thing seemed so fantastic, so delusory, that Melanie continued to find herself doubting her own senses. If the chapel existed, did the people? Had she and Riley simultaneously hallucinated them to assuage their own feelings of guilt for participating in a Satanic worship service? Then the hooded forms were only ghosts of sorts. But, she *had* felt one touch her. Or had she imagined that as well?

She stared at the telephone in the half-light of the library. At the other end of the line a giant of a policeman would probably agree to come to their aid. And then he would probably feel real bad about having to place the two of them under arrest, along with Synn and Leeanah. For the time being, contacting anyone seemed to be totally out of the question.

Inhaling deeply, Melanie turned and went out the library door toward the foyer and stairs.

As she walked up, she could feel her facial muscles tense. She had to get Riley out of here. He was the one in danger, not her. Synn had implied as much when he asked her to bring Riley back. But why? So some unnamed bitch could sneak into his room and fuck him clandestinely? That hardly made sense. She hated to admit it, but it seemed the little green-eyed monster had suddenly bitten her good. For the first time in years, she was jealous.

Hesitating for a moment at the top of the stairs, she looked down, admiring the foyer.

Why did Synn, an acknowledged devil worshipper, have to have all the luck in the world? A home like this. Untold wealth. Handing out diamonds and rubies like so many pebbles. It made no sense. Work your ass off, pay your bills, go to church and suffer through life. It seemed as though, on the surface of things, praying to Satan and keeping him happy paid off better than going in the other direction.

Melanie found herself questioning why she had stopped going to church. It had been the priest she talked to the last time she went to confession. Years before. When she was almost seventeen. She'd been fucked by three different boys in the course of the same night. Could she help it if she was very popular? She'd managed to handle three separate dates and gotten laid by each of them. For some reason the incident bothered her and when she confessed it to the priest, he'd asked questions about the boys, herself, and why she did it. Concluding that he was getting off on her failings, she'd gotten up, stormed out of the confessional, and left the Church—for good.

Somewhere deep inside her, she felt there was a God, and a good relationship with Him was vital to surviving in the life hereafter, if such a life indeed existed. But she'd never had her mortality challenged before now. She'd made the decision several years before, to return to the Church once she was forty or fifty, when that mortality could suddenly prove to be as fragile as a breath. At present, she felt the chances of seeing her next birthday might be nonexistent if she and Riley couldn't get out of Synn's clutches. He didn't yet know they knew all about him, and because he didn't, he would still put on the gracious act the next time he confronted them. But soon he would learn. Then the two of them would be found, faces punched in with the point of a gigantic knife, heads cut off.

Shuddering, she turned, running the few steps to Riley's door. Throwing it open, she stopped, her horror-filled eyes widening. Everything she saw in the bedroom seemed to be moving in slow motion. She tried to scream but only a slight gurgle came out. She watched, bug-eyed, as the naked form climbed off Riley's inert body. For an instant the two women faced each other, the one in the doorway trying to speak but unable. The nude smiled in such a way that Melanie felt a chill flow down her own body. Paralyzed, she watched as the form glided toward the open panel in the far wall. Stepping inside, one arm reached out and the panel soundlessly slid closed.

For a full minute, Melanie stood rigid, fixed to the spot. When Riley moaned quietly, she snapped out of the spell and ran to him, fumbling in the semidark with the nightstand lamp. When she knocked it over, she stood, racing to the windows, tearing back the heavy draperies. Returning to him, she gasped when she saw how weak he appeared.

"Oh, God! Riley!" she called, shaking him roughly by the shoulder.

His eyes flew open from the sudden movement but stared sightlessly upward.

"Jesus Christ! Are you dead, Riley? Come on, get outta that fucking bed. If you don't, I don't know what will happen. Come on, haul-ass outta here!"

She continued shaking him, then stopped when she realized he wasn't about to awaken.

His breathing came in labored gasps, his complexion as bleached as the pillows on the bed. She had to do something. But what? She needed help to get him up, dressed, down the stairs to the Toyota and away from this madhouse. Hongisto?

Her brow knitted and she bit her lip. She had to try. She had to call him. Even if he were late and they were both dead when he arrived, she would at least die feeling that help was on its way.

Die? Did she actually think they were going to die? She looked at Riley lying on the bed, his breath coming in raspy rushes. The possibility of *his* dying certainly existed if she didn't get help. What could be wrong with him? Could someone fuck a person to death? She shuddered. Anything in too huge a quantity could probably do anyone in. Even something as pleasurable as sex.

"Riley? Can you hear me? I'm going to call Lieutenant Hongisto to come and help us get away. Do you hear me, Riley? Come on, you poor son of a bitch! Nod your fucking head. Give me some sign that you can hear me." She shook him again. Nothing. Without another word, knowing every second counted, she turned, running to the door, not seeing his head move up and down in a superslow nod of agreement.

The only phone she knew of in the house was the one in the library. Racing down the steps, she stopped halfway. Sebastian was entering the library.

At the sound of her steps, he turned, looking up. "Don't run, Melanie." He spoke kindly. "I wouldn't want you to fall and hurt yourself."

"Sebastian!" Her voice cracked weakly as she continued down to the first floor. "Riley needs help."

"Help? I don't understand."

"I—I think he might be dying."

"Wh—what? Dying? From what?" His complexion drained of all color and he stepped closer to her.

Melanie bit her lip hard for fear she would say or do something wrong from this point on. He seemed so natural, so properly concerned, so kind. How could she think this patriarchal type could harbor malice in his heart for anyone? Then the beheading ritual exploded in her memory and just as quickly she recalled how angry he had been that night as she and Riley arrived. She'd have to be careful not to arouse his anger or say the wrong thing. "How many women are in the house, Sebastian?"

"I'm afraid I don't understand." He moved closer and she retreated a step back, trying to keep the same distance between them. "What does the number of women in the house have to do with what you just said about Riley?"

"Some woman came to him last night after everyone had gone to bed. She got into bed with him and they—they—well, they made love for a long, long time. That was the reason he felt he couldn't get up this morning."

Synn laughed. "That seems to be a very good, a very natural reason for wanting to stay in bed. Don't you think it is?"

"Normally, yes. But Riley said he'd never had anyone like her before. Mr. Synn—Sebastian—I'm good in bed. I think I could keep up with just about anybody when it comes to endurance. Riley and I have had some marathon nights of our own. But he was always fresh in the morning and ready to take on the world."

"Well, who is this phantasm who visits him?"

"Why did you say phantasm?"

"No reason. Just my choice of words. I'm sorry if it upset you. Who is this woman?"

"At first, Riley thought it was me, then Leeanah. But once she was in bed with him, he knew it was neither of us."

"How did he know that?"

"Her breasts and mine are apparently considerably bigger than this mystery woman's. I just saw her a few minutes ago. Now that I've seen her, I agree with his appraisal. She's much smaller in the chest."

"What does she look like?" He cocked one eyebrow and took another step toward her.

She backed away again only to find herself against the wall next to the library door. His eyes flashed brightly and she wondered if he actually suspected that she and Riley knew everything. How could anyone live to be two thousand years old? That was the tough part. She looked at him more intently than before. Something was different. But what? She couldn't put her finger on it but something had definitely changed about him. "She's taller than Leeanah. I'd say maybe about as tall as I am."

Synn smiled again, his even teeth sparkling when he spoke. "It's not you, is it, Melanie?"

"Goddamn it, it's not funny. You're poking fun at me. Riley's ill and I think he might be dying. I've got to get him away, to a hospital. If you don't want to help, get the fuck outta my way, mister." Stepping forward, she tried to go around Synn, but he held her in check with a hand on her arm. She felt the strength in his fingers. At the same time her own strength seemed to flow from her like water through a sieve.

"Calm down, Melanie," he said soothingly.

"Where's Leeanah? Maybe she can help if you won't."

"Leeanah's not here. Nor is there anyone else in the house, I assure you."

"You can't convince me that easily."

"What would you have me do? I'm sure Riley is in no immediate danger."

"If he's in no danger, then help me search the house. There's a woman running loose who keeps attacking him. My God, that sounds so stupid." Melanie shook her head.

He smiled. "See, even you're beginning to think the idea is a little preposterous."

"Like hell I am. Will you help me?"

"I can't. I'm sorry. I've a meeting to attend and if I don't get going immediately, I'll be late. What are you going to do?"

"If you don't mind, I'm going to search the house."

Synn puckered his lips but said nothing for a moment. Then, "Very well. Do be careful. I hope you find whatever it is you're looking for."

"A woman."

"I know. I know. You've said it enough. Don't look behind closed and locked doors, though. Please?"

She wanted to scream. The bastard was so nonchalant, as if there were no reason whatsoever for her to suspect him of anything. Maybe he had no idea of the information she and Riley had put together in such a way as to point an accusing finger at him. She felt reasonably certain that Sebastian had committed two murders, possibly three, if Vicki's death were included. Then there was Grendel. Naturally she couldn't count that a murder, but certainly the dog had been killed and Riley's office wrecked for some vengeful purpose.

"How long will you be, Sebastian?"

"Quite some time, I'm sure, although I can't give you an accurate estimate. Good luck with your search."

"Yeah, thanks." She hoped agreeing with him would allay any suspicions he might have about her.

He turned, freeing the path to the library, and went to the front door. She watched him slip into a topcoat. After donning a homburg, he opened the door and left.

For several minutes she stood there, suddenly realizing that droplets of sweat were on her forehead, building sufficient weight to drip down her face. Slowly, she made her way to the staircase.

What had been different about him? She tried, unable to think of anything specific. Still, some alteration in his appearance nagged at her. But what?

Should she call Hongisto? It might prove an escape, yet possibly out of the frying pan into the fire. She decided it was more important to check on Riley and then search the house, starting with that panel. If she could find the way to open it, she would be on the trail of the strange woman that much faster.

When she stood over him, Riley appeared to be sleeping soundly as if nothing were wrong. Dropping to the bed, she placed an ear on his chest. His heart beat steadily, strongly. He seemed extra pale, but otherwise none the worse for wear, tear and too much sex. A sly smile crossed her lips as she wondered for just an instant if she would ever be able to render a man as weak and spent as he appeared. It wasn't funny and she sobered immediately, covering him, going to the far wall to search for some way of opening the secret panel.

After twenty minutes she had run her fingers over every piece of decorative beadwork, pressing each with no results. Returning to the bed, she prodded him, "Riley, can you hear me? Wake up. Just for a fucking minute. Please?"

A soft moan, a tiny flutter of eyelids, proved to be his only response.

"Shit," she muttered. Could she go off to search the house and leave him unprotected? She looked closely. Unless the woman could perform miracles, he was finished with the

The Immortal

sensual side of life for the time being. Briefly, she wondered if he'd ever be able to perform again. Turning on her heel, she went to the door, stopped, checked him once more from there, then stepped into the hall.

Where should she begin? How many rooms were in this place? What had he said? Something about not looking behind closed and locked doors. What did he have hidden? If he were two thousand years old he probably had a warehouse full of skeletons, not a mere closetful or two. If she did look, what would she find? A sex-starved woman? Leeanah? The people who showed up on cue when needed?

She brightened. Of course. She'd start in the chapel, behind the door through which the hooded members had entered. Crossing her fingers, she relaxed when the doorknob turned and she stepped onto the stairway leading to the lower level. At least that door wasn't locked.

The chapel was empty, dimly lit by soft, indirect illumination around the ceiling perimeter. No one. The chapel was empty. For a long moment she stared at the closed door at the small end of the room. Would *it* be locked? Only one way to find out. Tiptoing across the inlaid pentagram on the floor, she stopped in front of the door.

Slowly reaching out, she grasped the ornate knob and turned it. Locked. Now what would she do? The memory flashed in her mind of Synn reaching up alongside the doorjamb to take down a key. Stretching, she ran her fingertips along the wood until they encountered a latchkey hanging on a small nail. Lifting if free, she brought it down, quietly slipped it into the lock, and gave it a twist. The mechanism turned over. Holding her breath for fear of making a noise, she opened the door and peered inside. Complete darkness masked her view. Wondering if she should go farther without some sort of light, she noticed a switch on the inside of the entrance and flipped it.

Light filled the area, spilling into every corner. Melanie caught her breath at sight of a line of cells along the narrow hallway. Barred doors stood shut or ajar as far back as she could see. It looked like an old jail of some sort. Hanging from pegs beside each entrance were dark cloths, which, when stepping closer, she recognized as the acolytes' robes.

Approaching the first door, she peered through the barred window. A young, handsome man hunched in one corner, looking up at her dumbly. He wore nothing other than a collar with three-inch spikes extending from it.

"Who—who are you?" she asked quietly.

He opened his mouth to speak, but nothing intelligible came out and he stood, mumbling gibberish.

Melanie fell back, not sure if the door was

locked. Then she saw the chain attached from his collar to a ring in the wall behind him. As his hands reached out toward her, he came up short when the chain's length went taut, holding him in check.

What was going on? Who was this man? She went to the next door and found the same situation: a handsome nude youth tethered by a spiked collar. This one, on a slightly longer chain, stood and came to the window. She looked at his eyes. The pupils, completely dilated, remained so even in the brighter light near the opening in the door. In every cell into which she looked, she found a young man drugged into a stupor, unable to communicate, chained like an animal to the wall.

At the end of the row, she turned to check the opposite wall of doors. The first was empty, as was the next, and the next. When only two remained in which to look, she stopped. Why only men? For Leeanah? For the nymphomaniac who practically wasted Riley? Probably the latter. Leeanah had gone with Synn after she arrived with the letter. The letter? It had been left on the nightstand next to Riley. Was it there when she found the woman in bed with him? Concentrating, she decided it was, but had it been read?

Melanie moved closer to the penultimate door and stretched to look inside. A new thought slammed into her memory as she saw the wide-eyed beauty secured to the back wall, a chain fastened to the spiked collar around her neck: neither the Rolls-Royce nor any other car had been in sight when she arrived. Nor had she heard anything like a car door opening and closing as she took off her coat before going up to Riley with the letter. Had Synn actually left?

Now she knew Leeanah had not as she blurted, "Leeanah? What—what are you doing in there?"

Leeanah made no reply, reaching out as if to claw Melanie's face through the bars.

"Leeanah, what's wrong with you? Do you want my help? Did Synn do this?"

"Sebastian Synn is the harbinger of evil and lust, power and riches. I am his. I am Satan's. *You* will die. Your Riley Larson will die. Sebastian lives—for all time."

"Leeanah! Leeanah! Stop talking so crazy. Jesus Christ, the next thing you'll tell me is that you like being tied up like a dog."

"I'll do anything—ANYTHING—my master asks of me. I am loyal to him. I am Satan's to do with as he chooses."

"You don't *mind* this?"

Leeanah fell back toward the wall where the chain was held in place. Leaning against it, she intoned, "Sebastian can do with me as Satan commands. I desire it. I wish it. I want it."

Melanie watched as the willing prisoner caressed her bare breasts with one hand and masturbated vigorously with the other. Leeanah's breath came in short panting gasps as she neared her climax, continuing long after she achieved numerous orgasms.

Melanie stared, transfixed by the sight. Everyone was crazy in this place. She and Riley had to get out of here. She might even call Hongisto now, with something pretty concrete to complain about. Naked men held prisoner in the basement of a mansion might seem a bit irregular nowadays—even to a detective who claimed to have seen so much.

She'd help Riley dress; they'd get out of the house and away in the Toyota before Synn returned.

Whirling to run from the dungeon, she screamed and fainted, falling into Sebastian Synn's outstretched arms.

CHAPTER 18

Friday, November 21, 4:15 P.M.

Melanie floated between wakefulness and unconsciousness—between reality and hallucination—desperately trying to determine where she was. A floating sensation rippled through her body and she felt as if she might be in someone's arms. Whose? Had her knight in shining armor arrived to save her? Save her? From what? From whom? Where—

Synn!

Rocketing to the surface of her mind, came the thought of Sebastian confronting her in the cellblock. The dreadful impact of that tore her eyes open. He was nowhere in sight. Only the surface of a wall loomed inches from her eyes.

Cold. She felt miserably cold—chilled—as if she had no clothing on. When she moved, it was instantly clear that in fact her slacks and blouse—her underwear—all were gone. What the hell was going on? She sat up to the accompaniment of clinking chains and saw she was in the egg-shaped chapel. The icy links of the chain hung down to her backside, suspended from the collar—the spiked collar—now around her neck. Where was—

The muffled sound of people descending the carpeted stairs brought her attention to the portal through which they had to pass in order to enter the room. She waited, her breasts rigid as she held her breath. Who would it be? Had she managed to call Hongisto? No. It had been her intention but when she turned to run, she'd fallen into Synn's arms. The shock of him being there must have made her faint. She descended into what seemed like a bottomless pit, its blackness and terror closing in on her. Now she had awakened to find herself chained to the wall of the chapel, naked.

Her eyes were riveted on the large end of the room. She waited. Then the procession of robed acolytes moved in. Each carried a black candle except for four who bore the nude body of Riley Larson on their shoulders. Behind them came Leeanah, a brilliant cape over her shoulders, her nudity exposed in front, eyes fixed on the cowled head in front of her. Bringing up the rear, Sebastian entered, head erect, shoulders thrown back.

For an instant, Melanie blinked, not quite certain if it really was he. The walk was that of a much younger person. Then her concern for Riley drove all else from her mind. What were they going to do with him? Chain him like an animal next to her?

Animal! While she floated in that warm cocoon of semiconsciousness, she had heard slobbering, grunting and what she interpreted as growling. Until a voice, Synn's if she remembered correctly, shouted, *"Silence, you animals!"* Had he been referring to the captive young men? Who were they? Where had they come from? Had Synn conned them, as he did with Melanie and Riley, into coming here, only to wind up chained in a human zoo? What was their purpose? Studs for the sex-crazed woman who had ravished Riley into his present weakened state? But where was she? Her part in this was crucial or nothing made sense.

She watched the coterie approach the altar, on the flat surface of which Riley was carefully deposited. No reaction when his skin touched what had to be cold marble. Had they already killed him? Was he dead?

A sob fought its way through her larynx up to her mouth, emerging in a gasp. "Riley? Get up, Riley," she half sobbed, half screamed. "Get off that fucking altar, right now! Do you hear me? Get up! For the love of God, get up!"

The mention of God brought a chorus of derisive laughter from those gathered around his motionless form. Then, their hilarity over, the robed men encircled the altar, backing down the steps until they reached the floor, where they prostrated themselves.

Synn stood perfectly immobile, barely breathing, his cold eyes scanning Riley's form. Leeanah, her bare breasts thrust out, stood opposite, an evil smile twisting her full lips into an ugly scimitar.

"Riley! Move!" Melanie screamed. "Get up. These assholes are going to slice you up. Come on. Get your ass off there. NOW!" This time she avoided using the name of God for fear of upsetting the mad people surrounding the dais and the two standing on it. Besides, by now she felt God had abandoned her, that any cries or pleas of help would go unheeded.

If she were to help Riley—and herself— she would have to rely on her own wits to effect an escape. Half turning, she covertly examined the hook to which the chain holding her was attached. She wiggled it slowly, surprised to find it moved. The fixture was not that secure. Maybe she could— She grabbed her chain with both hands after turning her back to it, then moved it back and forth ever so slowly, doing her best not to make a sound.

Horror creeping through every fiber of her body, she watched Sebastian turn suddenly and move toward her. Had he seen what she was doing? Dropping both hands to her side, she squatted on her haunches, making certain that her head was in his line of vision to the anchor in the wall.

"I must ask you to remain quiet, Melanie," Synn commanded. "What you are about to witness has never been seen by anyone living on the face of the earth with the exception of myself. I have seen it many times."

She looked up at him, desperately trying to determine what had changed about her captor. Slowly standing, she rose to his level, eyes boring straight into his. Then she knew. The lines in his complexion were gone. The skin was that of a young man—or boy. It could even be the soft, yielding skin of a woman. The eyebrows were now dark, contrasting sharply with the white hair. Sebastian looked years younger than he did two days before when she sat across from him at the restaurant.

He spun about, returning to the altar, but not before kicking one of the prone men. "If she makes another sound—kill her! Instantly!"

Striding up the steps to stand next to Leeanah, he bowed deeply and intoned, "Master —see fit to give me the essence of life once more. Make it possible for me to live forever and I shall worship you for all eternity. Those who fight you will pay with their lives. I shall continue to bring souls to you as in the eons that have passed since I became yours."

While he continued, Melanie mouthed the words, "essence of life," wondering what the phrase meant. Confident that she could return to freeing her chain, she reached behind her and continued moving the iron loop back and forth.

Biting her tongue to keep from screaming at Riley to get up, she watched, fascinated by the strange rite unfolding on the altar. Leeanah had moved to eclipse Melanie's view of Sebastian. From the motions she made, Melanie guessed she was undressing him. Perhaps they were going to fuck right there on the altar the way she did with Riley.

Melanie watched the pile of clothing grow. The suit jacket, the tie, the shirt, a T-shirt, *a long winding bandage* which Leeanah took from around the upper and middle part of his body. Then the trousers fell on the heap, followed by a pair of shorts. When the socks and shoes had been removed, one more item, a white wig, topped the pile. He turned again to the altar, backside toward her. Leeanah stepped to the far side, and Melanie's eyes widened even further when Synn, long flowing black hair hanging to either side, bent to kiss Riley on the mouth.

"He'd shit if he knew," Melanie mumbled to herself, working more diligently, more carelessly on the iron ring.

Then Sebastian turned and she could see the breasts, the triangle of hair with nothing protruding from it. Sebastian Synn was *a woman.*

It had been Synn who invaded Riley's room, whom Melanie had seen, who had rendered him weak to the point of senselessness.

Melanie watched, her eyes bulging, as Leeanah helped Synn onto the altar where she straddled Riley's lower body. Aroused to the fullest by the machinations of the two women, he still slept. Slowly, ever so slowly, she lowered herself until his erection penetrated her.

Melanie waited for the pumping to begin, but Synn did not move. Instead, her eyes closed, she seemed to be concentrating on something other than what appeared. After ten minutes had passed, Synn released Riley's limp member and rejoined Leeanah, standing.

"Get them," Synn pronounced softly to her. Then, turning to Melanie, who stopped prying the chain, she smiled. "I suppose you are full of questions? Am I not correct?"

Melanie did not respond, too dumbfounded by the revelation of Synn's gender and the lackluster orgy she witnessed.

"Let me introduce myself. You may have heard of the Comte de Saint-Germain. The man of mystery? He who could turn rocks into precious gems, lead into gold, cure the dying, who has lived since the dawn of time.

Since— As you can see, the count is not a man at all." Synn held both arms out to the side, bringing in her hands to cup her breasts. "I thought it would be easier to pass through life existing as a man and adopted the guise of one Comte de Saint-Germain."

"If—if you're not a man, and not the Count, who or what are you?" Melanie recalled some of the contents of the letter.

"It was rumored in the eighteenth century that I had lived over two thousand years. That hardly touches the number. It was rumored that I was supposed to have known the family of Jesus Christ—to have been familiar with King Solomon and the Queen of Sheba. Most of that is true except for one thing: I *am* the Queen of Sheba. She disappeared from history after her memorable trip to visit Solomon, because it was then I first donned male garb. I wanted to see the rest of the world, but not as a woman, subject to the manner in which I had been treated by Solomon and his court."

Leeanah returned with a leather case which Synn took from her, opened, withdrew some tubes and a small pump. Standing two bottles upright, she bent over Riley for an instant and began moving the handle of the pump back and forth.

Melanie continued prying the ring behind her whenever Synn became involved with him. She had to escape. Had to stop this madwoman from harming him. Momentarily

The Immortal

she stopped struggling as she looked at the bottles. A feeling of nausea swept over her. Then her attack on the masonry and iron behind her was redoubled, while blood flowed into the clear glass tubes next to the pump.

"What are you, lady?" Melanie asked in a quiet voice, fearful of raising Synn's ire, but compelled to speak. "Are you a fucking vampire or what?"

Synn laughed, throatily. "No, my dear. It is just one of the things I need from your Riley Larson to continue my trek through life, the world, and time."

"Why him? Why not one of these other wimps who don't give a shit about anything? Christ, they're all walking around in a daze, without brains. Why not—"

"That's just it. They have been fine for the purpose to which I have put them, but have nothing beyond their penises that can help me. Riley has everything: brains, vitality, strength, the very essence of life itself. I will take it all."

"You're fucking crazy," Melanie whispered and continued working at the stubborn bond between iron and concrete, raising her voice to cover any noise. "Will Riley have to die?"

"If I take everything he has which is vital to life, it would hardly seem fair to leave him in such a sorry state. He'd be worse than these poor animals." One arm made a sweeping gesture as she continued working the pump with the other.

Melanie watched the bottles slowly fill. She fought a sob when Riley moaned as the needles were pulled from him. Synn was definitely like a praying mantis or black widow spider. She had fucked him and now she was killing him—not devouring him literally, but in a way that was just as effective, just as nourishing to her, sustaining her life.

Melanie's soul in torture, she forced her voice to be calm. "What—what about me? What happens to me? Are you going to do the same thing to me, too?"

"Hardly," Synn replied, a hint of a chuckle in the word. "You and the others will simply remain here. You're already secured in your place of death. The rest will be returned to their cells when I finish." She picked up a syringe filled with an amber liquid, and, bending over Riley's head, sent the point of the needle into his ear, pushing the plunger in a slow, even way until the cylinder was empty.

Melanie turned away, vicariously experiencing the pain he must have felt but to which he couldn't respond. So, she was to die as well. But in a crueler way. Without water, food or the possibility of help arriving, she would slowly go mad with hunger and thirst as the hours and days crept by. How long would it take? She recalled reading

The Immortal

someplace, or hearing someone say, that the human body can survive approximately seventy-two hours of water deprivation. By that time, Synn and Leeanah would be long gone.

What about Leeanah? Why had she been chained up like the men? Was she only a servant—a lackey? Remembering some of her responses, Melanie figured that was exactly what the beautiful Leeanah Thorndyke allowed herself to become—a slave—a chattel of this female pervert, Sebast— What name did she go by when not posing as a man? Hardly the Comte de Saint-Germain.. Or the Queen of Sheba, for that matter. Why bother worrying about her name? Anyone who could survive for centuries, as she claimed to have done, would have had a million names.

Synn bent down again, this time on Riley's opposite side. In her hand was the empty syringe, whose needle she plunged into his other ear.

Melanie winced again, holding her breath when she saw the cylinder being filled with a clear liquid. What the fluid withdrawn from Riley's head might be, she had no idea. But the words, "essence of life," and "brains, vitality, strength," zipped through her mind. "Please," Melanie sobbed. "Don't kill him. We'll never tell anyone. Just don't harm him. Please?"

Synn did not look up from her work,

merely laying down the full cylinder next to an empty one, before picking up a third—filled with a black substance.

Raising it over Riley's midsection, she said in a clear voice, "Lord of evil. Master of lies. Ruler of the world, I offer this husk of humanity to you. His soul you already have. Take those of the animals cowering before your altar. Take the red-haired bitch for your own when she is ready."

Without another word, Synn drove the long needle into Riley's navel, emptying the blackness into his body. Withdrawing it, she picked up the syringe with the clear liquid and emptied it into another flask. When everything was capped securely, the bottles containing the essence of Riley Larson's life were placed in the leather case and the lid fastened shut.

He jerked on the altar, strange bubbly sounds spilling from his mouth as his head lolled back and forth.

Melanie stared. Maybe, just maybe, he wasn't going to die. Maybe, just maybe, Synn didn't know what she was talking about. Maybe, just maybe, she was nothing more than a madwoman who thought she was the Queen of Sheba and had merely injured him without doing any great harm.

Oh, God, Melanie prayed. *If You can see fit to help me, let Riley be all right. Let me break away from here and get the two of us out of this madhouse. Please, God. I'll come*

The Immortal

back to You, body and spirit, if You'll only help me.

She felt the chain ready to give way behind her.

"Leeanah," Synn barked, "put these animals into their cells and chain them."

Without a sound, Leeanah turned, motioning for the men to follow her. They entered the cellblock single file, slipping out of their robes as they did, displaying the spiked collars around their necks.

Melanie reached up to touch her own. A shudder ran through her and she returned her attention to its chain and anchor behind her.

Synn left the dais, going to the door through which the others had disappeared. Once she was out of sight, Melanie focused on Riley's inert form. Why didn't he move any more? Just a little jerk of some sort would fuel her desire to finish pulling the chain free. Why didn't he move?

When Synn reentered the chapel, she called over her shoulder, "Good-bye, Leeanah. You've been most faithful."

"Then take me with you! Don't leave me chained here like these other beasts!" Leeanah's voice from inside was desperate, hysterical.

"I'm sorry. You agreed. Our Master will treat you well." Synn continued toward the entryway, stopped when she reached it, and turned to look at Melanie.

Before Synn could speak again, Leeanah began cursing her from the cell wherein she had been chained. Her cries brought responses from her fellow inmates, and some, as though the effects of the drugs that held them in check were dissipating, joined her in a mad cacophony of yelling, chanting, and cursing.

"I'm finished with your Riley Larson," Synn called above the racket and took a step toward Melanie. "You can have him for all eternity when you and he are together before the Master." She laughed, lending her own degree of madness to the cries of anguish and hatred being hurled at her from the cellblock. Then she turned, hurrying up the steps.

Melanie pulled with all her power. "Come —on—you—bastard," she grunted through her teeth. "You rotten son of a bitch— give. Give, you worthless, no-good, dirty, rotten mother—" The ring gave a little. She thew all caution to the winds now that, with the exception of the mad people in the next room screaming at the top of their lungs, she was alone. She had to get to Riley. If he were still alive, he needed her help.

Turning, she sat down on the cold floor, braced her feet against the wall, grabbed the chain close to the ring and pulled with all her might. It gave—just a bit more. Then more and more, until the ring and its long shaft fell to the floor, clanging hollowly. Her sound of victory.

Scrambling to her feet, dragging her chains behind her, she ran the few yards to the dais and mounted it. He lay motionless. "Oh, Riley," she cried, throwing herself onto him.

Pulling away just as quickly, she stared unbelieving as his body crumbled into dust. Then her own screams joined the others, filling the room, filtering up the deserted stairway to the empty mansion above.

EPILOGUE

Caracas, Venezuela, Monday, November 24

"Here is your passport, Senorita Saint-Synn."

Charmaine Saint-Synn picked up the wallet containing her passport, gesturing for the porter with her luggage to follow.

Outside the airport she got into the limousine, which waited for her suitcases to be loaded into the trunk, then drove away toward the mountains of Venezuela.

EERIE NOVELS OF HORROR AND THE OCCULT BY J. N. WILLIAMSON, THE MASTER OF DARK FANTASY

1168-9	**THE RITUAL**	$3.25
2074-2	**GHOST**	$2.95
2133-1	**THE OFFSPRING**	$3.25
2176-5	**PROFITS**	$3.25
2228-1	**THE TULPA**	$2.95

MORE BLOOD-CHILLERS FROM LEISURE BOOKS

2039-4	**LOVE'S UNEARTHLY POWER** Blair Foster	$3.50
2112-9	**SPAWN OF HELL** William Schoell	$3.75 US, $4.50 Can.
2121-8	**UNDERTOW** Drake Douglas	$3.75 US, $4.50 Can.
2152-8	**SISTER SATAN** Dana Reed	$3.75 US, $4.50 Can.
2185-4	**BLOOD OFFERINGS** Robert San Souci	$3.75 US, $4.50 Can.
2195-1	**BRAIN WATCH** Robert W. Walker	$3.50 US, $4.25 Can.
2215-x	**MADONNA** Ed Kelleher and Harriette Vidal	$3.75 US, $4.50 Can.
2220-6	**THE RIVARD HOUSE** Edwin Lambirth	$3.25
2225-7	**UNTO THE ALTAR** John Tigges	$3.75 US, $4.50 Can.
2235-4	**SHIVERS** William Schoell	$3.75 US, $4.50 Can.
2246-X	**DEATHBRINGER** Dana Reed	$3.75 US, $4.50 Can.
2256-7	**CREATURE** Drake Douglas	$3.75 US, $4.50 Can.

Make the Most of Your Leisure Time with
LEISURE BOOKS

Please send me the following titles:

Quantity	Book Number	Price

If out of stock on any of the above titles, please send me the alternate title(s) listed below:

Postage & Handling
Total Enclosed $

☐ Please send me a free catalog.

NAME

(please print)

ADDRESS

CITY   STATE   ZIP

Please include $1.00 shipping and handling for the first book ordered and 25¢ for each book thereafter in the same order. All orders are shipped within approximately 4 weeks via postal service book rate. PAYMENT MUST ACCOMPANY ALL ORDERS.*

*Canadian orders must be paid in US dollars payable through a New York banking facility.

Mail coupon to: **Dorchester Publishing Co., Inc.
6 East 39 Street, Suite 900
New York, NY 10016
Att: ORDER DEPT.**